If You Love Me, I'm Yours

Lizzie Chantree

Lizzie
Chantree

CROOKED
CAT

Discover us online:
www.crookedcatbooks.com

Join us on facebook:
www.facebook.com/crookedcat

Tweet a photo of yourself holding
this book to **@crookedcatbooks**
and something nice will happen.

With love to Martin.
I'm yours.

About the Author

Award-winning inventor and author, Lizzie Chantree, started her own business at the age of 18 and became one of Fair Play London and The Patent Office's British Female Inventors of the Year in 2000. She discovered her love of writing fiction when her children were little and now runs networking hours on social media, where creative businesses, writers, photographers and designers can offer advice and support to each other. She lives with her family on the coast in Essex. Visit her website at **www.lizziechantree.com** or follow her on Twitter **www.twitter.com/Lizzie_Chantree**

Acknowledgements

Thank you to all of my wonderful readers for buying my books, telling your friends, taking time to post reviews and for sharing them on social media. Your support is what keeps me writing.

A big thank you to my publisher Crooked Cat, my amazing editor Alice Cullerne-Bown and to my Crooked Angels for making me smile every day.

This book is about an eccentric family, and I do have one of those! Each and every one of them is incredible and I feel very proud to call them my own. If I began to write every name, the list would go on forever, but they know who they are, and how much they mean to me. Thank you all for being the people that you are. To my mum and dad… I love you. Thank you for your years of encouragement and for being such inspirational parents.

Also from author Lizzie Chantree

NINJA SCHOOL MUM

Obsessive-compulsive school mum, Skye, is a lonely elite spy, who is running from her past whilst trying to protect the future of her child. She tries hard to fit in with the other parents at her son's new school, but the only person who accepts her unconventional way of life is new mother Thea.

Thea is feeling harassed by her sister and bored with her life, but she suspects that there is something strange about the new school mum, Skye. Thea has secrets of her own and, although the two become unlikely friends, she hesitates to tell Skye about the father of her own child.

Zack's new business is growing faster than he could have dreamed but, suddenly, he finds himself the owner of a crumbling estate on the edge of a pretty village, and a single parent to a very demanding child. Can he make a go of things and give his daughter the life she deserves?

When three lives collide, it appears that only one of them is who they seem to be, and you never know who the person next to you in the school playground really is.

If You Love Me, I'm Yours

Chapter One

Maud closed her eyes and prepared to jump off the emotional cliff she was teetering on the edge of. She shuffled forward until she felt sick with nerves, took a deep calming breath and waited.

'Oh, Maud...' her mother sighed. 'Not again.'

Maud cringed at the familiarity of those words, and in her mind, she stepped off into the void and plunged into the icy darkness without a whimper. In reality, she was still in her lounge, but being around her mother made her feel like an abject failure and the words she uttered sliced through Maud and filled her with doom. Her mum pushed her to the edge of reason on a regular basis. She wished that for once her mother could try harder to be nice. Surely it couldn't be that difficult to be grateful for the anniversary gift she had been given and to offer a smile, even a fake one, for the sake of her child? It was the same every year and Maud was finally ready to surrender and stop trying so hard to make them understand her and compliment one of her paintings. It was never going to happen, she realised with a heavy heart.

Maud didn't mind being boring, not really. She had a sensible job, sensible clothes, a sensible love life... if you counted two overbearing exes and a one night stand who had thanked her, rolled over and was snoring before she even realised he had started! She was ok with not fulfilling her dreams or being outrageous and carefree, she just wanted her parents to pay her a compliment, just once, after years of disapproval and disappointment.

Maud knew that as far as her mum was concerned, she was the most amazing parent who encouraged her daughter to have a responsible career until she settled down and found a 'suitable' husband. Granted, Maud was a very good, well-liked and adept teacher's assistant in the local primary school, but every time she pushed against the boundaries set by her parents for their perfect daughter... 'Oh, Maud!'

It was ridiculous, she was twenty-four, thought Maud. She wished she had a big glass of wine to slug back, but her mother would disapprove of that too, suggest in horror that she was a 'wino,' and hand her the number for AA, which she would have readily available in the little brown Filofax she carried everywhere in her patent handbag. The woman was a menace.

'You don't like the painting, then?' she asked. Her mother tilted her head to one side without a word, her lip between her teeth as she concentrated and her brow furrowing as she looked at the artwork in confusion. It wasn't the reaction Maud had hoped for. She had spent hours delicately drawing the lines of the little landscape painting of her parents' house and she felt salty tears scratch her eyes. She refused to let them spill out in front of her mother, though, and bit her own lip until she tasted blood. The painting wasn't Maud's preferred style, spidery black lines depicting beautiful animals, filled in with splashes of vibrant colourwork to bring them to life. She had hoped that by toning down her eclectic style and drawing such a personal space as her parents' home, her mother would finally see the little girl who desperately wanted to paint.

Her father coughed into his hand and looked at his daughter. 'Well...' Maud's heart almost stopped beating in her chest as she waited to hear his response to her work. She turned towards him with unshed tears in eyes shining with hope. He had seen this look so many times and she knew that he hated to disappoint her, but her mum would make his life a living hell if he encouraged her. Her mum saw anything creative as frivolous and a waste of time, and generally her dad agreed with her. He said quietly to her sometimes that he appreciated that Maud enjoyed painting, but her art wasn't exactly going to set the world ablaze with awe at her talents, now was it? The words had cut into her heart and she'd cringed in pain. She knew he felt that it certainly wasn't appropriate for a serious young lady who wanted to teach children and catch a husband. The thought of her attracting a layabout artist and spending her days smoking spliffs must horrify him, as he often left articles about wild artists who were living outrageous lives around the house when she visited. He must have gone out to buy the magazines especially, as her mother would never leave anything out on the table otherwise, she was such a neat freak. Maud sometimes wondered how many hours he must spend sifting through the shelves at the newsagents, as how many articles about wild and out of control artists could there be? Maybe he stored them in the garage in a cardboard box? She had never actually picked one up, as that would fuel their obsession. Perhaps he just recycled the same article? She'd have to pay more attention next time.

He moved to the edge of his seat to scrutinise the little work of art and scratched his head in obvious confusion. She hoped he could see it was quite pretty and that Maud had obviously spent much of her free time on it. She could imagine the thoughts in his head, like where would they put such a colourful picture on their mostly beige walls? He looked across at her and must have noticed the unshed tears in her eyes. 'I wish with all my heart that I could see what you do, but art is a complete mystery to me,' he sighed. 'I'm not one for artsy stuff. We have racks of your paintings in the spare room from when you were younger. I've put up shelves in there,' he paused and she could almost hear him add to hide them away, 'but we do appreciate the effort you put in and are grateful for this year's anniversary present, darling.'

Maud was sure he couldn't help but notice that she was almost hopping from foot to foot in agitation and her eyes were bright with questions. He looked pained, as if his guts had just turned over. She knew her mum would hide this little painting in the spare room as soon as possible after she had stepped through the front door at home, but hopefully he could see how much it meant to Maud. He gritted his teeth and her heart melted as his shoulders straightened and he stood a bit taller. She could see that he'd decided that for once he was going to stand his ground. 'It's pretty, love.' Maud let out the breath she'd been holding and rushed over to squeeze the life out of her dad in her excitement, until he was laughing and gasping for air.

'But...' interrupted Rosemary, getting up. Maud wondered if she had told her dad not to react when Maud gave them another painting and finally to talk her out of this most unsuitable habit. 'For goodness sake, Maud! You're a teacher with lots of other ways to fill your days. Why are you mucking about with paints when you should be trying to find a husband?' Maud's smile dropped from her face and her dad looked upset. She could feel the gloom returning.

'It's pretty,' he repeated firmly, making Rosemary sit back down in confusion at his forceful tone. 'We can put it by the window in the kitchen so that we can look at it every day.'

Rosemary's face went white with shock and she looked like she might faint at the thought of that monstrosity in her pristine cream kitchen, but one glance at her husband silenced her protest. She lifted her face and saw Maud's slightly unkempt hair and wild eyes and her face softened slightly.

'I don't know why it means so much to you for us to have some of your pictures, but maybe we can find a corner for this one if it's that important. I'm not a monster. I don't know where you get this painting thing from, Maud,' she added, getting up and running her hands down Maud's soft blond hair to straighten out the kinks.

Maud dressed impeccably in neutral tones and her hair didn't usually have a strand out of place, as she tamed the unruly curls at the ends with hot hair straighteners every day. Even her bungalow, with its stark white walls and modern but functional furniture, was always immaculately clean, even if it was a strange choice of home for such a young woman. Maud's mum didn't really have anything to complain about, as Maud did everything in her power to please her parents, other than this one small thing. For some reason her mum had a deep rooted fear that Maud needed to be kept under control in case she started running around naked or dying her hair pink, orange and blue again, like she had as a child.

Rosemary often recalled the memory to Maud. She blamed

her own older sister, Maud's aunt – whom she too often referred to as 'the annoying one' – for starting this mess by buying her then five-year-old niece a set of colourful finger paints. For the next few years it had been chaos. Rosemary said her stomach often turned over at the recollection. The beautifully clean walls of their three-bedroom terraced home were spattered with every colour of the rainbow, as Maud decided that they should be 'smiley colours.' Her clothes, which her mum spent hours laundering and ironing, began to be covered with pen and ink blobs and smears, which were the faces of their pedigree, non-shedding cat and his rather less salubrious neighbourhood friends. Every surface Maud could find followed suit.

Her mum had initially thought that it was a phase that Maud would grow out of, and yelled at her sister for being so bloody inconsiderate. She got haughty distain in return, and it explained why they still couldn't stand being in the same room together. As Maud grew up, she learnt not to paint on the surfaces of her home lest she invoke the wrath of her parents, but she began doing odd jobs for extra pocket money and bought paper, pens and an art folder to hide under her bed. Within weeks it had been full to bursting and her mum had wrung her hands in despair at the clutter and nearly kicked the poor cat as she constantly tripped over tubes of paint, which had escaped from the desk drawer. Admittedly, Maud's room was mostly tidy, but her homework desk overflowed with art supplies and the smell of fresh paint now made her mum feel faint.

Over the years, Maud had realised that her art was a frivolity and she had gradually dwindled to painting only occasionally, until she had stopped altogether. Now she had her own private space, the 'phase' had begun again, and her mum was distraught. At least the mess was at Maud's own house and she didn't have much time to paint now she had a full-time job.

'You do seem to be happy here,' Rosemary sighed, looking around at Maud's home and mentioning that the kitchen cupboards needed rubbing down and repainting. She watched

Maud as she leaned forward and hugged her dad again, dodging away from her mum's hands, as Rosemary tried to brush a speck of dust from her soft blue jumper and then tugged at the hem of her skirt to straighten it.

'Thanks, dad,' Maud beamed at him, generously turning and enveloping her mother in the hug too, making her blush furiously and shoosh her away.

Chapter Two

Dot straightened one of the five pigtails on top of her head and made sure they were sticking out at the right angle. She moved the chunky jewellery she was wearing to the correct spot on one side of her neck and patted down her checked skirt and sparkly blue tights.

She glanced around to assure herself that everything was in place and the paintings were lit properly. The drinks were all set out along the temporary bar, which was actually her receptionist's desk; glasses sparkled and surfaces shone with the elbow grease that had gone into making this evening perfect. Tonight was a big deal for her and the largest art show she had personally organised. Working as creative director for her parents and big brother was lively and interesting, but her soul cried out to be part of the inner circle of artists, rather than on the outside echelons as their manager. She knew she was brilliant at her job, but her family was a dynasty of talented artists and she was the oddity, the black sheep with colourful hair.

Dot adored painting, but unfortunately she was completely atrocious at it. It was hopeless. She didn't just stink at painting; she was abysmal; a word she'd heard whispered about her work by a visiting uncle en route to his latest exhibition. The look of pity on her parents' faces when they scrutinised her painterly offerings, and the confusion in her brother's eyes when he tried to find a meaning in the splotches and swirls, were enough to make her hang her head in shame. As a consolation, and to make her feel involved when she was old enough, they had kindly offered her the chance to manage their work, as she had the advantage of understanding them all so well. She had taken on the role after much persuasion and a little emotional blackmail over their hurt feelings and she was determined to make everyone see she was one of them.

She dressed accordingly for someone who was part of the art community, with zany and outrageous clothes, and worked determinedly to ensure her family's art was seen all over the world and reached markets and customers they had never considered before. They had been suitably astounded as, satisfyingly, she was surprisingly good at her job. She handled their work with flair and was a real asset to them, but as a failed artist and family member, Dotty still felt that she had something to prove, however much they told her she was irreplaceable.

Anyone could sell art this good, surely? thought Dot.

Out of the corner of her eye she spotted a light above her brother's second piece of work flicker and die. All of his creativity was dark and stormy and the public went mad over his brooding good looks and grumpy demeanour. She loved him dearly... but what the hell was all that about?

She could see the appeal of his art; it was sublime, but her brother was not the best advertisement for relationships. Women flocked to his feet, but he could barely remember their names and left her fielding calls from the moment she arrived at the gallery each morning. The fact that he only gave them his work number should have alerted them to his intentions, but they all thought he was worth mooning by the phone for. Yuck. It was almost enough to put her off dating for life... almost.

Chapter Three

Maud reverently stroked the embossed surface of the invitation she was holding to a private gallery viewing later that evening. She'd visited many galleries over the years, but none so glamorous or exciting as this one. The Ridgemoors were world famous artists, and attaining a ticket to the preview show was like getting back stage passes to an Ed Sheeran concert and being allowed to snog his face off afterwards.

Maud's best friend Daisy had forced her to go alone tonight, which wasn't very kind of her. Maud had claimed one of the prizes in an art competition, which she hadn't even known she'd entered, as her friend was a common thief and had stolen one of her little paintings and entered it without Maud's knowledge.

When it had won, Daisy had plied Maud with alcohol at the local pub, which Maud should have instantly found suspicious as Daisy hardly ever bought a round of drinks, and then confessed to stealing her work. Maud was slightly mollified by the fact that it had won a prize and even she couldn't turn down the opportunity of getting so close to one of Nate Ridgemoor's paintings.

The prize for her winning entry was one precious ticket to the private view. She grudgingly accepted that Daisy thought she was helping her to get out and meet new people. Then her best friend had called her that evening and put on what Maud could only describe as the worst acting she had ever heard, coughing and spluttering that she couldn't drive her to the viewing, which was Maud's stipulation for accepting the invitation, even though Daisy had been perfectly fine earlier in the day at work. Daisy thought Maud's knickers were made of concrete as they were so tough to get into, and she was desperate for Maud to meet a man. She used every excuse to dump her alone somewhere, even if it meant her getting the train on her own at night.

Daisy was one of the few people that Maud had confided in about her own love of painting, although even she hadn't seen Maud's latest work. The art she had submitted on Maud's behalf was pretty enough, but it wasn't her usual style at all. Nonetheless, the turbulent seascape had won a prize and the expensive invitation in her hand had arrived with a letter saying her work had shown promise and that she had been one of five entries selected to win tickets to the private view.

Maud remembered how Daisy had danced around the simple room when they had arrived back at her bungalow and she'd realised that Maud wasn't about to dive over the table to strangle her for being so deceitful. She'd tried in vain to entice Maud to bring some of the vibrant cushions she had strewn across her hand-sewn bedspread into the lounge, to brighten the place up, but Maud had remained resolute that it was unnecessary and would give her mother a heart attack when she visited.

Luckily, Rosemary had never ventured into Maud's bedroom or seen the serene forest mural on the wall. Daisy said she thought this was strange, but Maud just shrugged, as if the fact didn't hurt, and mumbled that they didn't have that kind of girly relationship. Daisy often wondered aloud if Maud actually wanted her mum to poke her nose around the house and take an interest in the way her daughter expressed her true personality, with the vibrant colours and fabrics she had hidden away. Daisy thought she wanted to shock Rosemary, but anyway, the moment had never materialised, as her mum was too focussed on how neat the kitchen was or if Maud's clothes were ironed to perfection while she was wearing them.

Maud kept her bedroom door firmly shut and her mum never expressed an interest in staying too long, before busily pronouncing she had somewhere else to be. Rosemary enjoyed Maud visiting her own house, but only at the most convenient times, preferably when there was someone else there for her to brag to about Maud's teaching career, which made Maud cringe in embarrassment as she'd had the same job for ages now and hadn't bothered to apply for anything else. Maud wished she had a brother or sister to confide in, but that was her fault too. She had been so messy and inconsiderate as a child that her mother had told her that she couldn't cope with more children like her.

Maud slid open the door to her wardrobe and ran her hand along her collection of rich, textural fabrics hidden inside. Sighing heavily, she slid the door further along and grimaced at the rows of bland tops, skirts and dresses. Her fingers itched to grab something frivolous, but the vision of her mother's angry face and bugged-out eyes always stopped her.

Maud hated her magpie tendencies to buy beautiful, sparkly clothes, as she'd never wear any of them. She just couldn't walk past a shop window and not bring them home; she had to have them, even if it was just to look at. Reaching out and selecting a simple black dress, she stuck her tongue out at her reflection in the mirror in the en-suite bathroom and hung the offending dress up on the back of the door, before turning on the shower to warm the water up a little.

Towelling her hair dry after an invigorating shower, she plugged in her hair straighteners and watched the tiny light on the side turn green. She had to get up half an hour early every morning to tame her hair and tonight she needed to get a move on if she was going to arrive on time. She was the only person she knew with straight, curly hair. Her hair was completely poker straight until it reached just below her ears, then it sprung into unruly curls. What the hell was all that about? She was sure her hair was rebelling and wished she had the courage to do the same.

She couldn't have a perm as her hair wanted to be straight and it didn't take hold. The bottom section could be straightened, but as her hair was thick and golden-blonde, this took forever to get right. She grabbed the irons, narrowly missing scorching her hand, and began the laborious process of taming the curls into submission.

Chapter Four

Nate growled at his friend, who laughed with good humour then ignored him. He knew that Elliot was well used to his best mate being annoying and impossible before a gallery showing. To be honest, Nate admitted to himself that these days he was pretty much always that way. He'd been told that he had one of those auras that told everyone within a ten-foot radius to bugger off, but for some unknown reason, women lapped it up. They clamoured for his attention as if he was a rock star, and it would drive a less amiable friend than Elliott completely nuts. Luckily, Elliott had grown up around Nate and his madcap family and he knew that, although Nate looked mean and moody and could be a complete ogre, the rest of the time, he was daft, friendly and fiercely loyal. Elliott understood all too well that Nate had withstood some tough breaks in life. He'd witnessed it first hand.

Elliot glanced at his watch and called out good-naturedly, 'come on, you oaf, we need to get a move on.'

When Nate didn't budge, Elliott cuffed him on the shoulder. 'Look, I know you hate all this publicity for your work and your crazy sister barrages you with appointments and adoration from your public, but really… we are now running late and you know how aggravated Dotty gets when she can't tick every planned item on her itinerary.'

Nate wanted to sulk some more, but it was practically impossible when faced with the eternal sunshine that was Elliott. You couldn't keep the bastard down, however hard Nate tried. Sighing theatrically and wishing he could be anywhere else but at his own gallery opening, he knew he couldn't disappoint Dot after all her hard work. He'd watched her try to paint her own art and it made him mad that she couldn't, when he found it so easy. He would do anything for his slightly bonkers sister, even when she was prancing around with her hair standing on end and wearing tights the colour of mustard flowers.

He noticed Elliott do that impatient jiggle thing he did when he was anxious or needed to pee and smiled in sympathy. El had been in love with Nate's impossible sister for as long as he could remember, but Dotty was completely clueless and adored him 'like another brother,' making Elliott turn puce whenever she said it, which was often, the poor bastard.

Kicking Elliott's shin as he passed to wake him out of his daydream, and hearing him yelp with a sense of satisfaction, Nate decided he might as well enjoy himself, for his sister's sake if nothing else. She had worked on this project for months, even though he knew it broke her heart each time he produced another artwork, while her own studio remained untouched. He had heard her lug loads of boxes up there last month, and then refuse to let anyone in, so he assumed that she was trying a new medium and he didn't intrude. He understood what it was like when an artist was working and he respected her enough to leave her alone with her muse.

Elliott was rubbing his sore leg and looked up. 'Ok, tiger, let's go!' He aimed a swift kick at Nate, who deftly darted out of the way. 'Your sister will hang my guts up as a sculpture if I don't get you down there soon.'

Nate chuckled as he descended the stairs, before Elliott realised he had been left behind as usual and swiftly kicked the door shut behind them. Nate heard him yelp in pain as his foot connected with the door and smiled in satisfaction, as it was Elliott's fault that he hadn't been allowed to stay in his studio and immerse himself in his latest painting, until everyone in the gallery beneath the studio had got bored and gone home.

Chapter Five

Maud wiggled uncomfortably in her black dress. She knew it flattered her curves and skimmed her ample bust and hips, but it was just plain boring. She wished she could be glamorous and sophisticated but, with her small waist and big boobs and bum, she couldn't pull off the current androgynous waif look. She had found the courage to wear her favourite black high heels, which she had delicately painted with tiny red roses creeping up from the base of the heel up to her ankles. It was her little act of rebellion, but she hadn't quite managed to wear the siren red lipstick she'd added to her evening bag. She wished she could listen to her inner butterfly and don something seductive and beautiful, but it was firmly caged and fluttering against the bars. The little black dress said nothing about her except that she was dull and unexciting.

The only occasion that she felt truly alive was when she closed the door on the summerhouse at the bottom of her garden. This was the reason she had bought her bungalow, as it was squirreled away at the bottom of the ample garden, behind a wall of hedges and through a little gate.

Nancy, the lady who had sold Maud the bungalow, had been steadfastly refusing offers for her home, until she met Maud and agreed to the sale on the spot. Maybe she had seen the wistful way that Maud had drooled over the detailed artworks that were hung on the stark white walls and proudly displayed everywhere.

Nancy had been relocating to live closer to her family, but confided in Maud that she was loath to leave her haven. Maud had immediately understood why when she had been shown through the gate at the bottom of the garden. It seemed, at first, as though this belonged to the house backing onto the bungalow, because of the hedges. The house specification from the estate agents had said that the bungalow had a 200-foot lawn. Surely that would mean thousands of hours walking up and down with a lawnmower? The only reason she had entertained viewing the property was because it was so close to Daisy's flat and she would be able to walk home after a night at the pub. Maud's social life was so non-existent that she wanted to hold onto the bit she did have. Unfortunately, there were no smaller properties in the vicinity that weren't sold within minutes to a local building firm. Maud was sure they would have snapped up Nancy's pretty bungalow if she had agreed to the sale. The garden was ripe for development, if you couldn't see the beauty in the varied plants and trees. The thought of several flats sitting in this relaxing space made Maud cringe.

On stepping through the front door when she was viewing the place, Maud had immediately been enchanted by the paintings and discovered that Nancy was a local artist. They spent an hour chatting over tea and prettily iced biscuits that had magically appeared on the table on a dainty porcelain plate, before Nancy had taken her hand, led her to the bottom of the garden and disappeared through the little gate.

Maud had fleetingly wondered if Nancy was one of those tree huggers her mum was always complaining about, who wandered round patting plants and talking to them. Maud was partial to the odd chat with a pretty ivy plant she had on her desk at the school, so she couldn't say much about it. It hadn't seemed like the old lady was coming back, so she'd reached out and pushed the door with some trepidation, hoping an irate neighbour wouldn't emerge from the foliage and bash her over the head with a branch, or that there wasn't some sort of weird swingers' convention going on and the little old lady would jump out of the hedge half-naked with a strange man. You just never knew these days.

Maud found Nancy on the other side of the hedge, beaming at her. She stood on a porch, in front of a wooden building that filled the whole width of the garden. The front was made of glass with double doors that were open and hinting at the treasures held within. Maud's feet carried her forward as she gasped in awe at the artist's studio before her. Her mouth hung agape in shock, before she realised she was probably dribbling. She snapped it shut and wiped it with the back of her hand. Reverently, she moved towards the door. 'Is this part of the house sale?'

Nancy beckoned her inside as a warm smile touched her lips. 'I get the feeling you're an artist?'

Maud almost jumped out of her skin as if she'd been stung. 'Me? No. Not at all!'

Nancy's eyes twinkled with mischief and she rubbed her chin and kept looking at Maud's bright red face. 'Hmm. My art is coming with me when I move, but I'm happy to leave the furniture as part of the sale. I pretty much use the house as gallery space, so everything is white and simply designed. It helps the art to stand out.'

Maud stumbled and grabbed the handle of the double doors to steady herself. 'But I'm not an artist. Though I love art... I do paint...' she admitted gloomily.

'I thought so,' said Nancy, eyes sparkling, as if that sorted everything out to her satisfaction.

'My little paintings are nothing. They're useless...' stammered Maud, cheeks flushing that this vivacious woman would offer this gem of a property to someone who could most certainly never do it justice.

Nancy took her hand and rubbed some warmth into it. 'Even if they are, if you enjoy painting, then you will put this space to good use. The previous four people who wanted to buy this place planned to rip it apart. The most recent one said he would add a hot tub and a secret sexy area!' Nancy made a gagging sound and Maud burst out laughing, the tension ebbing away as wonder filled her bones. Could she really own a place like this?

'You never thought of making this into a sexy area, then? Maud giggled, blushing at her own audacity.

Nancy gave her a mischievous wink, until they were both snickering again and Maud walked over to run her hands over the beautiful wooden easel, which was set up to catch the afternoon sunlight across the neighbour's garden.

Watching Maud reverently stroke the easel, with its chipped wood and years of splattered acrylic paint, as if it was priceless, Nancy had a look of determination on her face. 'If you buy the bungalow today, I'll drop £3,000 off the asking price. I told the agent it was overpriced anyway.' She held up a hand to halt Maud's protestations.

'I don't want to have to pay for storage for this lot and my son has kindly set me up with a full studio at my new house. He says all of this is ancient junk. I was reluctant to move on, but now I can see he has a point.'

Maud was aghast. 'But…' The equipment looked expensive to her and there must be hundreds of pounds' worth of paint tubes and furniture. The little writing desk in the corner and comfy couch in the other looked well-used but expensive too.

Nancy smiled and ignored her protest. 'Like I said, I haven't sold to the other buyers as they would rip the heart out of this place and the offers were way too low. I know I'm getting doddery and I have to move, but it doesn't mean I will just abandon this place to its fate without finding someone special for it.'

Maud blushed. No one had called her special before. Obviously satisfied at the young woman's response, Nancy clapped her hands together, then patted Maud's arm affectionately. 'I can see the passion burning in your eyes, but there is something holding you back. Maybe you're a frustrated artist or maybe you can't paint for toffee, but my gut is telling me that you will love the place and that's enough for me.' She sighed as if she was becoming tired and Maud began to worry that, although the woman before her was sprightly, perhaps this beautiful bungalow was too much for her now? 'My son has been ringing me daily and telling me off for not accepting the first offers, so today I will be able to shut him up gently,' said Nancy, sounding pleased with the outcome. 'All of the traipsing around after estate agents and people viewing the house is starting to drag me down, and I can finally start the next chapter of my life. It might even be inspiring for my work.'

Nancy explained how she had been selling her work in galleries across the world for many years and she cherished her easel and little studio, but finally she could see that her son was right. She had made her own decision, though, and she'd found a new guardian for this haven she had created.

'Will you take it?' she asked as if it was a simple decision that Maud could make just like that.

Maud mumbled and stared at her feet, totally embarrassed by this woman's generosity, or insanity, she wasn't sure which. 'I was looking for a flat, really.' Maud didn't want to look up into the eyes that seemed to be able to see into her soul, while her own parents couldn't. She hesitated for a moment before defiance set in. 'I'll take it,' she said resolutely, feeling a ball of fire light up in her stomach at her bravado, loving this new emotion.

Nancy's eyes twinkled merrily and Maud was pleased to see her satisfaction at the way her day had turned out. She waited patiently as Nancy leaned down to open the delicate little cupboard under the desk and revealed a row of jars, housing an array of paint brushes, and row upon row of acrylic paints, next to beautifully sharp drawing pencils.

'Show me what you can draw.'

Maud thought back to the day she had met Nancy and how, although she had moved away, they had become unlikely friends. Maud's own grandmother was much like her mother, uptight and prissy, so it was a revelation to have someone who didn't think she was unable to make a decent decision about her own life, and she had blossomed under Nancy's watchful eye. They had both discovered video chatting on the computer and spent hours talking about their latest work from their screens. Maud's little studio was her secret and an act of rebellion against her parents. They didn't know anything about it and she hadn't found the courage to bring her work into the house. She did spend every spare moment in the studio, though. Her studio. She still felt astounded that she had her very own artist's studio.

Maud gazed at the opulent dark grey facia of the gallery she was visiting and thought how much Nancy would have loved it there. Maud didn't mind attending functions alone, she'd got used to it over the years. She didn't have the confidence to talk to men very often and was more comfortable in the company of the children at the school – she didn't get tongue-tied and go bright red in conversation with them, and they didn't judge her or find her lacking. None of her friends appreciated art, except for Daisy, and Maud was pretty sure that she was with her boyfriend, Ryan, tonight. Holding her invite out to the smart doorman, who ticked her name off a list on his clipboard, she stepped inside. Her eyes lit up at the sight of the dark and expressive art that hung on every wall. The lighting in the gallery was just right to draw your eye subtly to each sultry work of art. The colours depicted tempestuous city views, but Maud almost felt embarrassed to be looking at them, there was something deeply sensual and tempting in each stroke of the artist's brush. Her skin grew warm and flushed, so she self-consciously pulled her hair across her face to cover her reaction.

She'd read about the famous artist who painted these pictures. He was from a big creative dynasty. She thought she'd heard that the love of his life had died tragically when they were teenagers, but this could so easily be celebrity gossip. Rumour said that she had died in an accident on a lake. Maud felt desperately sorry for him if that were true.

She stopped in front of the second piece and tilted her head before blushing again. How could a painting make her flush like a schoolgirl? It was so embarrassing. She glanced around to see if anyone had noticed, but they were ignoring her, as people usually did, and were crowded round a large installation further into the gallery. Shrugging and smoothing her hands along the sides of her dress to calm her nerves, she wished she'd worn some jewellery so that she had something to fiddle with other than her hair, as she drank in every nuance of the painting mounted on the wall. She began to fidget and crossed one leg behind the other whilst she tilted her head from side to side to take in every detail and etch it onto her brain, so that she could tell Daisy all about it at work the next day. She leaned her nose nearer to the canvas, then realised her mistake and valiantly tried to untangle her feet. She stumbled and gasped in horror as she tipped over and began to fall.

A hand reached out and she fleetingly glimpsed scarred arms as they folded around her and set her none-too-gently back onto her feet. Her saviour noticed her staring at his hands on her arms and he glowered slightly before snatching them away. 'I'm so sorry...' she blustered, mortified to be caught gawping at him. 'Thank you for helping me.'

He paused, taking his time, perusing every detail of her appearance, and she cringed, knowing he would find her lacking. 'You're welcome. What was so interesting that it required you to study it in such close detail?' He cocked his head to one side and examined her as if she was a strange flower.

Maud blushed furiously again for being caught making a fool of herself, as usual. Why on earth couldn't she go for one day without causing herself some sort of embarrassment? She chanced a peek in his direction and was immediately drawn to his thick jet-black hair, dark brooding eyes, and amused expression. He appeared as if he was really interested in the answer. She put her head down and looked at her feet, feeling tongue-tied in front of such a gorgeous man. There was no way on earth he would have stopped to talk to her if she hadn't practically fallen into his lap. Daisy had wanted Maud's knickers to thaw, but this man could set them alight!

He was still waiting patiently for an answer and she glanced about her in panic. People had begun to notice that he'd moved away from his group and was talking to her, and some were blatantly curious.

Oh, well, she thought, I may as well be honest. 'I was immersing myself in the detail of the painting. It's so full of turmoil and passion. I have to keep looking in case I've missed anything,' she explained. 'I feel like there are people in there hiding somewhere, but every time I look they're gone again.' She wished she could stop sounding like a prissy schoolteacher and prayed even more that she hadn't said the word passion out loud.

Hearing him roar with laughter at her candour, Maud smiled shyly and Dotty looked round the shoulder of the businessman she was talking to, raising her eyebrows in surprise. 'I haven't heard Nate laugh like that in public for years,' she hissed into Elliott's ear, making him wince as he was standing close to her side and Dot's whispers were quite loud. 'He usually hates these kind of events, he's such a grump.' Dot stared at the blushing girl by his side, before grinning. 'The woman next to him looks awkward. Maybe Nate's charms have failed him for once?' she smiled, her eyes alight with mirth. 'It had to happen sometime, and it looks like today's the day.'

Maud tried to muffle a giggle into her hand at how funny the stranger seemed to find her. She had gone and said exactly what she was thinking again. It didn't usually matter in her job as a school teaching assistant, as the children were far too busy to notice her mutterings, but she really wished she could stop blurting stuff out when she was nervous. Luckily, it seemed to have amused her saviour and she darted a look around to see who else had noticed her faux pas.

Unfortunately, it seemed that everyone had, especially the funny-looking girl with pigtails sticking out of her head at all angles. She saw Maud look at her, smiling and waving before turning back to the conversation she was having with a group of expensive-looking men and women. From the size of the diamond around the one of lady's necks, Maud guessed that they were all regulars at places like this and didn't have to win a ticket in a competition.

Nate was waiting patiently for Maud to stop gawking at everyone else and look at him. 'I've been watching you study the paintings, from the moment you stopped in front of the first one. The inquisitive way you moved around it and turned your head from side to side as if it held a secret for you, intrigued me.' Maud knew she looked normal enough in her simple black dress, with her glossy straight blond hair falling just past her shoulders, so maybe it was the delicate flowers creeping around her heels and towards her ankles that had caught his eye. She wondered in horror if she had something stuck to her shoe. He certainly kept staring at her legs. She looked at him pointedly and he had the grace to look a bit abashed to be caught out.

'Sorry,' he apologised, seeming to find it difficult to drag his gaze away from her silky skin. 'The tiny flowers on your shoes look hand-painted, they're exquisite.' Luckily, after a quick peek at the floor, she knew she didn't have anything like toilet paper trailing from them, which was a relief, as this had happened before. Maud should have known it wouldn't have been her legs he was looking at. He just liked the design on her shoes. Maybe he wore ones like them at home? Just because she'd thought he looked so manly, like he wanted to eat her alive, didn't mean he didn't have his own shoe collection, she sighed. Why did she always lust after men who weren't interested in her? It was the first time someone had wanted to swap clothes with her, though. Maybe he had a foot fetish?

'Ahem...'

Maud tried to look him in the eye, but he was just too good looking and it would get even more embarrassing soon, as she was sure she would start salivating all over him or trying to lick his face. It seemed like he wanted to talk to her, but maybe it was for a bet or something? Either way, she was momentarily lost for words which, to be honest, stopped her from saying something inappropriate for at least three seconds.

'Did you come here alone?' the low timbre of his voice swirled around her like velvet and made her nostrils flare.

'Ah no... of course not!' She didn't want to look like even more of a sad loser, frantically glancing round and seeing the girl with the pigtails looking at her again. 'I came with her,' she said, pointing to the girl briefly, then turning back to him. She grabbed a brochure about the evening from a nearby pedestal for something to do with her hands and then nearly threw it at him as if it had scorched her skin after seeing his photograph under the name Nate Ridgemoor. Oh bloody hell. Could this get any worse?

Nate frowned at the group of chattering people. 'Do you

mean Dotty?'

Yes, it could apparently. Maud cringed as he obviously knew everyone here, it being his private viewing. 'Ah, yes, Dotty,' she hedged, crossing her fingers behind her back and crossing her legs over in nerves, before remembering how that turned out last time and quickly straightening them out again.

Nate smiled down at her and she felt her knees buckle at the smell of his aftershave, it was pure sex on legs. 'I haven't heard her mention you, but then I don't know your name.' He left the question hanging in the air and Maud all but swooned, before shaking herself and trying to think of a way out of her blatant lie. She had guessed that the crazy girl would be the least likely to know him well. Now what was she supposed to do? Keep as much to the truth as possible, she quickly decided. She cleared her throat and tried to stand up a bit straighter, which only managed to thrust her chest out and she saw his eyes go wide in surprise. She held her hand out towards him and tried to recapture his attention. 'I'm Maud.'

He took her hand and studied her legs again, a smile touching his lips. 'Are those shoes artisan?' He was rudely staring now, but seemed like he was rather enjoying himself.

Maud frowned and lifted her foot in confusion. She'd momentarily forgotten about his interest in her footwear. 'My shoes?'

'They're beautiful, as is the woman wearing them,' he said simply, staring at her thigh as she examined her shoe.

Maud was taken aback by the compliment and begun blushing furiously before dropping her foot with a clunk. She noticed that people were breaking away from their groups and heading their way now. 'I painted them,' she said simply as if he was a bit slow and he sent her a wolfish grin. If he was surprised to see such an ordinary girl in great shoes, then he didn't show it, he just gazed into her eyes as if they shared a delicious secret. Her toes curled up and her pulse began to race. She felt like she was standing before him naked, in just her towering shoes.

She was about to explain about the shoes when the pigtail girl, Dotty, joined them in a flurry of sparkles and layered skirts. She gave Maud a strange look before sweeping Nate away, with what felt like pretty insincere apologies. Maud tried to catch her breath before she collapsed into a gushing heap, but Nate sent her an apologetic smile before letting himself be drawn into a discussion about a different piece of art, with a lively group of people standing nearby.

She drooped against the wall to catch her breath and, when she found the courage to glance his way, he didn't look up and was engrossed in whatever dazzling repartee the diamond necklace woman was saying as he gazed into her eyes, the same way he'd gazed into Maud's a moment before. Maud sighed as the bubble of elation burst. Maybe it was a party trick, picking up women and telling them they were beautiful, to make sales? Choose something about them to make them blush and remember him, then move on to a brighter conquest. It would take Maud years to save up and be able to afford a small painting, so he was wasting his time with her.

It had been delicious to bask in his attention for a short while, but he'd already moved on and she felt like a complete idiot for coming to an upmarket event like this on her own. Taking a deep calming breath and a chilled flute of champagne from a passing waiter, she gulped some down and silently moved away to view each painting quickly. They were too good to miss. Then she would go and bury her head under the covers at home, and try to forget the whole debacle.

She did fleetingly think of trying to pick up a dishy man so that she had something other than art to tell Daisy about, but looking around and finding everyone paired up or in small groups, she felt isolated and stupid. These guys were way out of her league. What had she been thinking?

Chapter Six

Nate wandered over to Dotty and gently touched her back, which made her jump and scold him. 'Who was the girl with the amazing shoes?'

'Huh?' Dotty was busy working out delivery schedules for the paintings they had sold the previous evening, her smile reaching from ear to ear. The preview show had been so successful that she felt like she was floating around on a cloud while hot men massaged her shoulders. Nate had actually been charming, for once, and not bitten the head off everyone who approached him. She didn't know why that was, but she wasn't going to worry about it.

She had enough going on with keeping the gallery diary up to date and managing the events calendar. She looked down at the little glittery unicorns on her tights and despaired. Her stomach clenched suddenly and all of the earlier satisfaction faded away. Everyone expected her to look this way now, but it made her skin itch and her back hurt.

She'd begun being a bit more outrageous in her choice of clothes to copy her nan, who was bonkers, and to make her parents annoyed, but being arty weirdos themselves, they absolutely loved that she was 'finally able to express herself creatively' or some such bollocks. She knew she should tone it down, but the more outrageously she dressed, the more they applauded. It was getting to the stage where she would have to start putting antennae in her hair to up her game, then she remembered her nan had already done that last month. The whole process was exhausting.

Dot scrolled back through her memories of the previous night to see whom her brother might be talking about, then struck on the awkward girl in the amazing shoes. She shrugged and went back to her paperwork. 'No idea.'

Nate frowned and she could see his mood darken. 'The girl interested me for some reason. The way she gazed into my work as if it held a secret made me notice her.' Dot silently added that he'd then spotted those sexy shoes and long legs and his groin had taken a hit. Dot thought back and there was nothing about the girl he'd been standing with that had suggested she'd wanted anyone to notice her, but the shoes were a subtle indication of her personality. Girls understood these things. Dot glanced at her brother, who was looking grumpier by the second. Men often missed the signals completely. While the dress the woman was wearing was chosen to blend into the wall, the shoes dripped with seduction. It was a contradiction. In fact, her clothes and lack of make-up or jewellery positively screamed leave me alone, while her shoes hinted at creativity and passion. Dot could see why her brother's interest had been piqued. The woman had played her game well.

Nate coughed into his hand and straightened his back, trying to regain his sister's attention, as she seemed to have wandered off into one of her dream worlds again. 'She said she was a friend of yours? I think her name was Maisy, May or something.'

Dot turned and frowned. She was sure she hadn't spoken to the girl before, but to be honest she met so many people at parties and openings that they might know each other vaguely and Dot could have forgotten about it. Dot was quite prolific as a top art agent, even though she was only twenty-four. Pretty much everywhere she went someone knew her, even if she didn't know them. She shrugged and was tempted to ignore him. It would just be another woman he would ask Dot to send flowers to, and then get her to dump on his behalf. Dot was a serious artistic agent and not his slave. If he needed someone to run his personal life, he should hire an assistant. 'I can't remember where we met,' she said honestly, much to his disgust.

'Can you find her?'

'Why?'

Nate gave her a hard stare, but she was his sister and had seen him pee his pants when he was five, so he didn't intimidate her with his, 'I'm a famous artist' game. 'She was wearing a fitted black dress, and those shoes with roses painted all over them.'

Dotty was used to her brother's odd behaviour, and he'd been living in his own hell since Lena died. He'd been so sweet and adorable when he was a teenager, but the accident had changed everything. Dot knew he blamed himself, but Lena was a head case and it would have happened sooner or later. She had killed herself and tried to take him with her and it had left lasting scars, not just the ones that snaked their way up his arms.

Dot waggled her eyebrows theatrically at him, trying to decide how nice she wanted to be to her big brother today. 'Oh, well.' Nate's forehead creased and he looked like he was about to growl at her, so no change there. She did love him even though he drove her nuts with his perfectionist demands and mind-boggling artistic abilities. She sighed at how unkempt he looked today, his thick black hair all messed up and his t-shirt full of holes and threads as if it had seen better days, although this could be an enormously expensive designer T-shirt that was supposed to look like it had been stolen from a tramp, for all she knew. 'Ok. You look like crap and I feel sorry for you, so I suppose I could check the guest list for last night's event and find her for you.' She went up on her tiptoes and dropped a feather light kiss on his nose. 'How much do you love me?'

Nate looked at her silky shoulder-length hair, freshly dyed bright pink to match her slouchy top and the manes of the sparkly unicorns that danced around on her tights, and smiled. 'A lot. You are so much like Nan,' he said affectionately. 'When you get older, you'll drive an electric scooter covered in graffiti too and terrify the neighbours. God help the universe.'

The first answer seemed to satisfy Dot, although the second was mightily rude. She gently smacked his backside and then looped her hands around his waist and squeezed him into her slight frame for a big warm hug. He was a hulking wall of man, even to her lanky five foot ten frame, but she had hugged him like this from childhood, with her head fitting snugly into his shoulder. His arm came round to scoop her into his chest as he rested his chin on her vibrant head for a moment. He wouldn't tolerate all of the love she lavished on him, but he usually gave in eventually and let her hug him like this. It was a beautiful habit and she gave him a squeeze before letting him go and walking over to make them both a strong coffee, whistling out of tune as she went and making him wince at the high pitch. All of their family could hold a tune, and parties involved raucous dancing and singing, but Dot was a complete anomaly, who could make birds drop in fright mid-air with the noise she made, so they had stopped the group sessions. It was a bit of a family joke, but Dot just thought they'd all grown out of that phase, and she still loved to whistle and sing at work. Only Elliott found it charming. She didn't know why Nate wound him up so much, saying that he felt his friend's pain when Dot treated him like another brother, i.e., a pain in the arse. She secretly thought Nate was jealous of Elliott's relationship with her, but he should be used to that by now, and the things Elliott had been through with them all had earned him the title of honorary family member anyway. And, in this case, two brothers were better than a single moody one.

Chapter Seven

Maud glanced up as Daisy leaned across the coffee table in the staffroom, sliding a newspaper in front of her. Everyone else was standing around the decrepit coffee machine, waiting for it to splutter out another cup of watery sludge. It was almost like a sideshow of sorts and, although no one liked drinking the coffee from the machine, it held a grisly fascination each time someone new tried to make it behave and supply a drinkable beverage. The teachers were enjoying a few moments of peace before stepping back into their respective classrooms. Maud's forehead wrinkled and she turned her nose up at the sight of the paper. She was fed up with reading bad news and had given up buying the local paper in the last few days in disgust. She glanced at the page and wondered what Daisy had been looking at. Then she straightened it out with her palm and shuddered.

It was an article with a full colour photo of a piece of art. The journalist explained there was a mystery artist in the region who was leaving valuable paintings in public areas. The photograph displayed a delicate canvas of a badger, with lots of interlinking spidery lines submerged in a wash of beautiful colour. The detail was exquisite, but the story was based around the fact that these little artworks came with a hand-written tag, saying, 'please take me home and cherish me. If you love me, I'm yours.'

Maud gasped as if she'd been slapped, and a couple of her colleagues turned round before she smiled and waved them away. She grabbed the paper and hid it on her lap so that nobody else could see it. The colour drained from her face and her hands started to sweat.

Daisy waggled a finger at her and sat down next to her. 'It's no good hiding it. There are thousands of copies in people's houses by now. It's all everyone's talking about. What the hell were you thinking?'

Maud's stomach hurt. She rubbed it with her hands. Daisy must be embarrassed to know her. Maud had been so fed up with her parents' derision of her work, whilst Nancy applauded her delicate style and intricate drawings. She'd decided to let the public decide. Originally she had left one or two very small paintings on park benches, and then she'd hidden in a nearby bush to gauge the reaction of the first person who came along. The problem was that, upon seeing the little brown tag that accompanied the paintings, the recipients' faces had lit up with joy. One lady had clutched the frame to her chest and had tears in her eyes. She'd rummaged around in her handbag for her mobile phone and called someone. Maud hadn't been able to hear the whole conversation from her hiding place, but the gist of it was that, after the awful time she'd been having, she must have a guardian angel after all and maybe things weren't so bad.

Maud now felt it was that lady's fault that her secret had become a bit of an addiction. She didn't stalk the people who found her art, but she did hang around for a while, then pop back the next day to see if her paintings were still where she had placed them. They never were. It was like a drug and it gave her an adrenaline buzz to think that someone appreciated her work enough to take it home, even if it had been thrust on them for free. Just to be double sure, she had taken up pretend-jogging, and had checked out all of the rubbish bins in each vicinity. She was getting fitter as a bonus, as she usually hated any kind of exercise, although she did need to invest in a good sports bra if she kept this up or she'd end up covered in stretch marks or knock herself out with her bazookas. She counted in her head and realised she had given away eight paintings so far.

Daisy's face was so angry and red, and she was giving Maud one of her death stares that could bring small children – and some adults – to their knees, and make them behave in seconds. Maud cringed. Perhaps she would be found out now.

Her parents would be embarrassed again, and her mum would disown her. She considered whether this would be such a bad outcome, and decided reluctantly that it would.

Daisy threw her hands up in exasperation and bent down to hiss in Maud's ear. 'Why would you give your work away to strangers? Give them all to me, and I will proudly hang them on every wall, but don't sell yourself short, if you are finally showing people your work.'

Maud felt momentarily ashamed that she had doubted her friend. Daisy was her biggest supporter and already had several of Maud's older-style paintings proudly presented in her home. Maud had been too embarrassed to sign them in the normal way, but she had created a logo out of the letters of her name, looking like a little fox's face, which she hid in the corner.

'I'm always telling you that you should sell your stuff,' Daisy's voice was rising as she got angrier, and she was now attracting more attention from the coffee machine crew. 'You could make a fortune if you didn't listen to your mum and dad for once in your life. It says here they are valuable artworks.' Daisy's jabbed her finger at the article, and her nose was almost touching Maud's now.

Maud moved back in the seat, her palms slick with sweat as she chanced a quick smile at the teachers grabbing their things to return to class. Daisy gave Maud some room, but then held her palm in her face to stop her protestations. 'Your parents are completely short-sighted and ignorant about art… or fashion… or design… or anything that you enjoy as a talented creative!' Daisy sucked in some air and slumped back into her seat, anger abating as she looked up and realised almost everyone else had left the room. She sighed heavily and rubbed her temples, as Maud looked on miserably. 'Why do you listen to them when they clearly have no taste?'

Maud's eyes shone at last and she hid a giggle with her hand. This was a regular argument from Daisy, but it did seem, after reading the article, that perhaps she might have a point? The thought rocked Maud. She hadn't questioned her parents' authority since she'd discovered how angry her actions made

33

them as a small child. Her mum had become unwell and had spent weeks in bed. Maud had been terrified that she was going to die of stress, as she'd been deathly pale, and her dad had tried his best to keep the house running smoothly, but it had been a disaster. Maud had been so young and cried herself to sleep at night and had never forgiven herself for making her mum ill. She frowned and tried to recall a time when she didn't try and please her parents or listen to their every word. She'd never asked her mum, as she didn't want to upset her, but maybe she'd just been ill? Could her parents be wrong about her?

Daisy nudged her on the shin to get her attention and Maud yelped in pain, as it was a spot she'd banged on the shower door the night before. Her friend looked like she meant business this time, and wouldn't be fobbed off with excuses. 'You've been leaving your paintings on park benches?' she accused. She was so mad at Maud, her hair was starting to stand on end and her eyes were bugging out of her head. Maud understood that Daisy had tried for years to get her to be herself, and show her art to others. She'd also implored Maud to wear the divine outfits she stored away in her wardrobe at home. Daisy couldn't understand why she wasted good money on them if they were only going to hang morosely behind a closed door.

Maud noticed that there were still one or two people chatting in a corner and felt a bit sick again. She implored Daisy with her eyes, then added, 'people can hear you, Daisy. They're looking at us, wondering why we're hissing at each other.' She saw the head of PE turn their way and offered her a bright smile, and nodded to her friend Laura, another teaching assistant, as she passed. Both smiled back and resumed their conversation as they left the room.

Daisy was in her stride now. Maud could see she'd pushed her friend too far from the bright spots of colour on her cheeks and the way her fists were holding the seat cushions as if she wanted to throw them at someone. 'I don't care who hears me! Why don't you spend all day in that studio you hide from the world, or do a job you would actually enjoy, if you're going to waste your time on anything? You know you've never really liked this job. You could be an art teacher, but you didn't put yourself forward for that job. You like the kids, but it's not your vocation.'

Maud sat back in shock. Daisy always supported her, never scolded her. She was too sweet-natured for that. Being a receptionist at the school, she had helped Maud hear about the teaching assistant job before anyone else, and listened to Maud moaning about her parents without too much judgement. They had gone to school together and fallen into the same career path. The difference was that Daisy adored her job. Maud enjoyed working with children, it was so rewarding, but Daisy knew she was a frustrated artist and bored senseless. Maud would happily spend her days immersed in her art, if only she didn't think it was indulgent and a waste of time. She felt a big salty tear form in the corner of her eye and she brushed it away with the back of her hand. 'I have a mortgage to pay.'

Daisy sighed at the sight of Maud's tears, took her hand in her own and patted it affectionately, pulling her in for a hug. 'I understand that... well, I don't really. Why didn't you just buy a little flat like mine?'

'I got a massive reduction and a studio,' Maud leaned backwards and grabbed her hand away indignantly.

Daisy spoke slowly, as if she was talking to one of the children that turned up at the school reception window and stood on tiptoes to peek over the counter. 'I do know that... but your mortgage is a huge responsibility, and you don't show anyone your art.'

'You have a mortgage!' This all seemed so unfair to Maud, who was getting fidgety as she'd just heard the five-minute warning bell that classes were about to start.

Daisy was speaking slowly again and Maud wanted to ram a cushion in her smug face. 'Yes, but I have a small flat. You have a two-bedroom bungalow, and you never invite anyone round in case they ask to see your etchings, which they never would, by the way, as they're hidden behind a gate and a twenty-foot hedge.'

Maud felt angry hot tears burn the back of her eyelids at her

35

gentle friend's outburst, so she squeezed her eyes tighter shut. 'I didn't know you felt that way,' she said, ashamed that her stupid hobby had taken over so much of her life. She'd let her best friend down and made a complete fool of herself yet again.

Daisy held up her hand to stop Maud. 'Before you think it,' she said, gulping in some calming air after her outburst. 'I feel relieved that you have finally plucked up courage to strike out on your own, but this isn't the way to do it. Your confidence is so fragile and I hate seeing tears in your eyes, but it's time to speak some home truths.' Daisy waited a second and Maud could see her courage growing. 'I want to slap your parents for the way they treat you, and to he honest I'm just as bad, for always simpering in their company and not standing up for my friend. They are just so intimidating. I'm going to be stronger with them – and so must you, Maud.'

She grabbed Maud's hand again and squeezed it in solidarity. 'I'm not trying to upset you.' She reached out and gently wiped away a stray tear on Maud's rosy cheek. They heard the children race in from playtime and start to file into their classrooms, so Daisy picked up the newspaper and put it on the table in front of Maud. 'Read it again. Listen to what the journalist is saying, then decide what you are going to change.' Daisy looked around the staffroom at the worn-out furniture and the functional design. 'You might feel comfortable here, but it's just not for you.'

'That's the problem...' Maud regarded her friend sadly. 'I don't know what is for me or who I am.'

'Well, isn't it about time you found out?' asked Daisy, resolutely getting up and leaving Maud on her own.

Chapter Eight

Dotty pored over the article in front of her and she started tapping her long blue nails on her desk in excitement. She was sure that thousands of people had read it by now and found it interesting, fascinating even, but Dot was determined that she would be the one to find the artist everyone was now searching for. She knew she could make a great success of their work.

It was about time that she began branching out on her own and having clients outside the family. The distinctive style of this particular artist was sublime and the character in the line work, together with the way the artist had added colour and tone with such reverence, almost bought the faces of the animals they portrayed to life. Their eyes looked like they could see into your soul and were eerily realistic.

Dot knew the area the artist was working in, it was a suburb just out of town. The paintings had been mainly delivered to parks across a five-mile radius. Some of the people interviewed in the article were named too, so she could start her amateur sleuthing there. If there was a pattern to where the art had been left, she would find it. She scratched her hair as it was itchy and a twig fell out. She sighed and picked it up, throwing it into the bin nearest to her sculpted desk. The new nest hairpiece she was wearing from a very exclusive designer was literally digging into her skull and twigs kept getting tangled in her hair. Her shoulders ached and she tried to knead them, but just succeeded in knocking off another bit of tree. Being artistic was so exhausting.

She grabbed a pencil from the steel pot on her desk and drew a line between all of the art drops. She squinted before remembering that she was wearing new coloured contact lenses that were supposed to make your eyes an exquisite blue, but in reality were so uncomfortable that they made her feel a bit sea sick. She muttered to herself and scraped them out of her eyes, aiming for the bin and shaking her hands in annoyance as they stuck to her fingers. Flicking them away, she picked up her tortoiseshell glasses and rammed them onto her nose. The lines she had drawn came into focus and she saw that they crossed over at a little village called Twigleston, of all the names in the world. She grabbed the bird's nest from her head and threw it unceremoniously towards the poor overflowing bin, where it bounced and settled onto the nearest chair as if a bird had flown in and nested there.

Dot looked up distractedly as her parents knocked on her door, and then walked into her office without waiting for her to invite them in. Her mother, Camille, rushed over and held Dot's face in her hands, looking deeply into her eyes while her daughter squirmed in embarrassment. Why did her mother feel the need to look into her soul every time they met? She always cupped Dot's face and stared into her eyes and said they were a window to her psyche, or some such rubbish. It freaked Dot out and never worked, as her mum thought she was a tortured artist, when in reality she was just tortured by not being a 'real' part of her family's legacy.

She straightened up, making her mum drop her hands, and then leaned in to hug her warmly. Looking over her mum's shoulder she studied her dad, Cosmo, who wore a jaunty trilby hat and was holding a long lightweight coat over his arm. He looked like an English gent who was just about to burst into song and splash in puddles, and she'd just noticed his 60's-style shoes and tailored trousers, which he had tucked in at the ankle. Why, oh why, were her parents so odd? She was sure everyone else had a perfectly normal mum and dad who burnt the sausages and spent hours in the potting shed. Her parents thought Wednesdays were a good day to dance around the house naked and the weekends were best spent in bed! The rest of the week was for frivolity and the serious business of art. They were incorrigible. She couldn't even turn to Nate to understand, as he seemed to find everything they did highly amusing.

'Daaaarling!' trilled her mother when she finally released Dot. She looked like she was about to say something else, but then she noticed the bird's nest hat on the chair by the bin. She bent down to retrieve it, and was soon studying the craftsmanship from every angle.

'Dad?'

Her dad was watching his wife with an amused smile and he turned to Dot to give her a hug. 'Hi, darling. We thought we'd pop in on our way to the Swansons' to say well done on Nate's preview show. He's sold ten pieces already.' The corners of Dot's mouth turned up at the compliment. It was hard to be mad at her parents for long, because they were... well... mad. However much she despaired at their antics, she secretly wished that she could comfortably throw seven colours together and still look dreamy like her mother, or quietly create exacting works of art like her father. She just didn't fit in.

Her dad began inspecting a new painting she had hung on her wall and he linked his hands behind his back and begun humming under his breath, which was a sure sign he was up to something. Her stomach plummeted and her shoulders sagged in exhaustion. The previous evening's hosting was starting to catch up on her. Her dad always started humming to himself when he wanted to distract you from something ugly. 'What have you done?'

She turned to her mother who was standing in front of the floor length, intricately-carved silver mirror near Dot's desk and angling the bird's nest hat on her tawny hair. Annoyingly, it looked like it had been crafted by angels just for her. Her mother's voice rose a pitch, which meant Dot would hate what she was going to say. 'It's nothing,' she flushed slightly and waved her hands around theatrically before realising that the movement had dislodged the hat and sent it flying back onto the chair. 'The teeniest inconsequential thing is that we have invited a few more people to your birthday party, as we were so sure you wouldn't mind.'

Dot rolled her eyes. 'Not again.' She hadn't wanted the blasted party for her twenty-fifth birthday, but had acquiesced to a very small gathering at her parents' house. She knew how much they adored entertaining, as they used the excuse of their goldfish's birthday to throw another bash. Dot cringed at the thought of how big this event had become. Considering she arranged glittering events for completely bonkers artists, she actually hated her own parties. Ever since she was five, her parents had made her stand up in front of family and friends and give a birthday speech. These days she mostly got drunk and swore a lot during her speech, which they all found hilarious, but more people witnessing her embarrassment was just too much.

'Who have you invited now?'

Her mother clapped her hands with glee as if she had the most delicious secret to impart. 'He's a delightful man.'

'Mum! Not again...'

Her mother looked up and batted her eyelashes at her daughter. 'What? Can't I introduce my beautiful daughter to a few eligible bachelors now?' She had the audacity to look wounded and Dot felt her blood start to bubble and heat up.

'A few?' Dot wanted to stamp her feet and then throw herself on the floor in a tantrum, but her shoes had towering heels with fake sharks' teeth protruding from every angle and she was worried she could do herself some serious damage, so she tried to grab her emotions and squelch them back down again before they erupted in fury.

Her father started to put on his coat and signalled to his wife that it was time to make a run for it before Dotty threw something. 'I did advise Camille against telling you about the extra party guests, as it's such a bothersome and trivial matter, and you are so busy these days. We have just over 200 guests so far and a few extra bodies will just blend in, surely?' he looked round in a panic for inspiration or distraction, as Dot was turning puce. 'Mum wanted to congratulate you on your good work at the art preview show, Dotty, and I have to agree you've done a stellar job.' Dropping a kiss onto his daughter's hair, and spitting out a twig that had lodged itself at the side of his mouth, he laughed at her eccentricity and practically ran to the door and waved goodbye, dragging his wife behind him.

Dot slumped in her seat and spread her arms out across her desk, in a complete huff. As she leaned forward to plug in and recharge the iPad next to her computer, she recalled she'd promised Nate that she would look up her guest list and find out who the mystery girl was. Maybe she was an art critic, or from the media?

Scrolling through the main guest list, she recognised every single name, so she clicked on the page of people who had won invites through social media or competitions. The prospect of attending a preview of the work of a famous artist like Nate had created quite a buzz and Dot felt a swell of pride on seeing all the names of people who entered the competitions listed in black and white. The results had been satisfyingly wide-reaching, hopefully creating a plethora of new Nate fans.

Five gilt tickets had been given to painting competition winners. She peered closer to the screen as she took in the name and address of one of them. Excitement rising in her chest, she glanced over to the map she had been studying earlier. The lines had crossed at Twigleston, and that was the same hometown as this mystery girl. Dot felt adrenaline rush through her veins. What were the chances of that? Maybe she could pay… Maud Silverton, she noted the name on a piece of paper, a visit? If she lived near the main areas where the artwork in the newspaper was being deposited, she might be able to point Dot in a direction that outsiders couldn't. If Maud helped Dot to find the incredible new artist, Dot might feel generous enough to introduce her to Nate properly. She opened her carpet-covered handbag and scooped everything off her desk into it. She had no time to waste now. This must be a sign from the heavens above, and she wasn't about to let anyone else steal her prize.

Chapter Nine

Little Robbie Whitman was doing it again. He was ramming his finger up his nose and then about to wipe his hands down the back of poor unsuspecting Becky Loper, who was studiously writing her alphabet into her exercise book and trying hard to ignore the disgusting boy next to her.

Maud danced between the chairs and grabbed the offending hand mid-swipe, being careful not to get her own clothes covered in the gloopy detritus from his nostrils. 'Robbie. Perhaps you should go and wash your hands?'

The boy looked confused at first and then grinned at her and she felt all resistance melt. It was outrageous that such a small child could bend an adult to his will, but although Robbie could be a pickle, he was a real character and Becky was whiney and annoying, if she was honest.

Maud glanced up to where Tom was sitting at his desk at the head of the class, golden head bent as he concentrated on deciphering the handwriting in their homework books. Maud's stomach growled embarrassingly. She'd forgotten to eat breakfast, she had been in such a rush that morning, and all the children looked up and laughed. Tom looked, too, and smiled those big blue eyes at her. She almost forgot her embarrassment and swooned until she realised everyone was staring at her. She covered her hair over her face and hunched down next to one of the children to begin to explain the next class task.

Although she loved her job, it didn't really inspire her, or it hadn't until Tasty Tom had arrived as the new temporary teacher in her class for a few months, while Zoe was on maternity leave. After she returned, he was going to be a roving teacher and help in any class he was needed in and run lunchtime and after school clubs until a full teaching job came up, as the school was often short staffed, but didn't have room for another full time employee. Although everyone liked Zoe, Maud thought that they were secretly hoping she took a year off to be with her baby and they got to keep Tom for a little longer. Zoe could be a bit of a taskmaster and often reported the teaching assistants if they spent ten minutes too long on their coffee breaks. Maud liked her anyway, but Daisy called her a snitch.

Daisy's eyes had popped out when she'd seen Tom, and the rest of the predominantly female staff were now behaving as if they were permanently on heat. Most of them were loved-up in a relationship, or married, but as Lila, the other receptionist who was sixty-eight and engaged to a hot Italian, said... a girl could look.

Tom wasn't poster-boy good looking but he oozed confidence, had amazing hair and eyes and, to be honest, men were in such short supply in the school that someone even half as nice to look at would have been news.

When Maud got up from helping Susan with her work, she realised the children were mostly still snickering at her and even boring Becky had raised a smile. 'Sorry about that,' she said.

'Someone miss breakfast?' asked Tom, his eyes crinkling at the corners as he smiled and ran a hand through his hair. He set the pile of homework books to one side of his desk as he gave an admiring glance to Maud's immaculate silky blond hair and simple skirt and white blouse, which was buttoned up to her chin.

Maud laughed and leaned over the table, collecting the books to start handing back to the children. 'I had a friend round last night and we ate so much that I didn't think I needed breakfast.' Maud thought back to the two giant pizzas that she and Daisy had demolished the night before while they watched a soppy film together, huddled up on the sofa.

Tom tutted good-naturedly, but had a slight gleam in his eye that piqued her interest. 'Male friend?'

Maud was surprised by the question and heat rose to her

cheeks. Tom actually sounded a bit jealous. She knew that this was the part where she should coquettishly simper and dance away whilst looking back over her shoulder and saying, wouldn't you like to know, or some such rubbish, but she had never been good at flirting and a classroom full of seven-year-olds wasn't really conducive to seducing their teacher, however blue his eyes were.

Instead she laughed and balanced the pile of books under one arm. 'No, it was Daisy, although she did once have a moustache,' she winked, then nearly walked into a desk as she wondered what the hell she was thinking, actually winking at a man? Tom looked highly amused, but probably thought she had something in her eye or had a nervous tick. He turned his attention back to the lesson plan he was about to start, as humiliation burned in her stomach.

Daisy stuck her head round the classroom door some time later, as she did every afternoon, to see if Maud had finished for the day and waved jauntily at Tom, who grinned at her and waved back. 'Have you cracked him yet?' she nodded towards Tom, who had his head bent over the rucksack by his feet as he prepared to head home.

'Not yet,' sighed Maud. 'I'm working on it.'

'Work faster,' hissed her friend, which made Tom look their way. Maud dug Daisy in the ribs to shut her up for a second. She was so embarrassing. Daisy didn't know how to be subtle and stomped into any situation with her petite size four feet. She usually wore black high heels, which were so unsuitable for a school environment, but made her look slightly taller than her five foot four inch frame and assisted everyone else with knowing when she was in the vicinity, as they could hear the clickety-clack of the heels on the stone floors of the school and make a sharp exit before she discovered them doing anything they shouldn't be.

Maud grabbed Daisy's arm and waved jauntily to Tom before shoving her out of the door and into the corridor. 'What do you want me to do? Wait for the children to leave and then drape myself naked over his desk?' she asked in exasperation.

'It would be a start!' joked Daisy, heading towards the

school reception to collect her bag, which was the latest trend of soft blue canvas with an oversize clasp, which Maud thought was ridiculous as it kept snagging on everyone that walked past. Daisy loved it, though, so Maud just made sure she walked a step behind her when she was carrying it.

Maud rubbed her temples to give herself strength and to stop the pounding headache that was starting to seep into her brain from the stress and excitement of the day. 'Come on. I'll walk home your way and we can discuss tactics for Tasty Tom.' Daisy seemed appeased by this and swung her bag over her shoulder, narrowly missing garrotting Maud, who ducked out of the way just in time.

'Lead on. I can't wait to hear how we are going to bring your libido out of retirement,' she joked.

Maud hoisted her small handbag further up her shoulder as she walked home and felt glad that it was Friday today, so that she could hide in her studio and paint for a couple of days. Daisy was going on a dirty weekend away with her boyfriend where she would 'ravage his body,' which sounded suitably disgusting. Maud did have other friends and occasionally went out with staff at the school, but many of them had families of their own and preferred to spend evenings and weekends with them. Plus, Maud's painting hobby kept her isolated a lot of the time. Maud thought back to the moment just before Daisy had come into the classroom, when she had discovered a yellow sticky-backed note from Tom inside her daily school classroom planner, and a broad smile spread across her face while her cheeks went pink. All it said was, 'dinner?' Her pulse had started racing and she'd felt sick when she'd first seen it. She was also a bit terrified, as she hadn't been out with anyone for quite a while. Her last boyfriend had pretty much dominated her and borrowed money from her, which made her feel like a sad loser. Her mum had been so happy to see her coupled up with someone in a suit, but the man inside the clothes was far from perfect, she realised now. For some reason an image of Nate came to mind, with his brooding good looks and watchful eyes. Maud dashed that thought away, as

Tom was the one she should be thinking about, not the famous artist. She'd made such a fool of herself in front of Nate, it was a good job she'd never set eyes on him again. She hadn't told Daisy about Tom's note on the walk home today as she wanted to keep it to herself for a moment first, and Daisy would start telling her what to do about it if she did. For now, it was her secret. She would tell her on Monday, when she'd decided for herself.

Chapter Ten

Dot leaned forward in her little blue sports car and squinted at the iron number next to the door of the bungalow, deciding that this must be the address she was looking for. She'd expected an elegant apartment block or a bohemian residence, not a little bungalow in a leafy suburban street, which sat alongside a row of similar properties.

This particular bungalow stood out from its neighbours as the garden had been cleverly designed to entice you to the front door, with lush green plants and a winding path that led to a whitewashed wooden door. It was really quite beautiful, so Dot got out of her car and ambled over to admire the handiwork of the garden designer, before reaching out to ring the bell.

The sound was melodious and Dot really wanted to sit in the pretty wicker chair against the front wall of the house. It had been a hard slog to organise Nate's art show and, although his work pretty much sold itself, to keep up the momentum of his celebrity took a lot of hard graft. She hadn't realised how draining it would be until she had stood on this doorstep, waiting for someone to answer when they were obviously out. She paused and was drawn into the view of the inviting garden again. It almost looked like a painting, with complementary shades of flowers and shrubs. Even though everything was manicured to perfection, the garden was visually striking without appearing over-designed; a bit like Monet's garden in Giverny. Clever stuff, thought Dot. It didn't seem like anyone was in, so she decided to plonk herself down and take a five-minute rest while she resolved what to do next.

As she approached her front garden, Maud stopped short. A very colourful vagrant was slumped in her chair and appeared to be fast asleep, if the loud snoring was anything to go by. The vagrant had big clothes, big hair and clompy boots. Their huge coat had birds sewn all over it, and was quite beautiful. Maud shuffled closer to take a better look and whispered reverently under her breath, 'You're one fancy tramp.' She coughed slightly and Dot opened one eye and groaned as she realised she'd fallen asleep. A young, smartly-dressed woman was peering at her with concern and Dot quickly straightened up, which was quite difficult as she was wearing the latest trend of a spring coat, which was bloody suffocating.

'Sorry,' said Maud. 'I was tempted to nudge your boot with my foot, but was afraid to startle someone sleeping as I've read all about people's fight or flight instinct where they lash out when backed into a corner,' she tried a feeble joke, eyes darting behind her and across to her neighbour's lawn. 'I didn't want to startle you, but my garden isn't the ideal place to take a nap.'

Dot felt frustration burn in her chest. The woman looked ready to run off at a moment's notice and she was scoping the area, which didn't suit Dot, as she really needed to talk to her. She was definitely the woman from the gallery show and Dot was a very determined lady when she wanted something.

Dot stretched out her hand in greeting to the woman, trying to help her relax. 'Is this bird's nest hat too much? My mother talked me into giving it another go as I'd chucked it into the bin,' she said as if this explained everything. 'I'm Dot. I'm here to meet Maud,' she explained.

Maud looked into Dot's brown eyes, surrounded by sooty black lashes and freckles that dotted their way prettily across her nose. 'Are those where your name comes from?' she asked, then slapped her hand over her mouth, seeming horrified at her lack of tact. Dot just smiled and ignored the question, as she'd been asked it so many times. Her parents had actually named her after Dorothy from The Wizard of Oz as they liked her sparkly red shoes. Dot would cringe in embarrassment whenever they told this story, to the hilarity of others. She was just thankful that she now had a nose full of freckles as she would much rather people thought that instead. Most children hated freckles, but she'd adored hers.

Maud tentatively took Dot's hand and shook it. 'You look familiar but...' Suddenly Maud flushed to the tip of her nose, as she seemed to recall their last meeting. Dot wasn't sure why she would be so embarrassed about it, unless her brother had said something inappropriate to her in some way, which was entirely possible given how he was used to women drooling all over him. The man had a huge ego.

Maud hesitated, 'um... I'm Maud.'

Dot tried to straighten her shoulders, but the coat was set on weighing her down and it took some effort to shake it off onto the floor, where it puddled into a big dollop of fabric. She gave it a victorious glare and then turned back to the woman in front of her. 'Great! Thank goodness I fell asleep or I might have missed you.'

'Missed me?'

'Yes. I was only stopping by to say well done for winning a preview ticket. I run the gallery you visited.'

Maud frowned and started wringing her hands in confusion. 'Do you go to the homes of all of your competition winners?'

Dot thought about the idea for a moment before her face creased up in laughter and she let out a snort of mirth that was so loud it almost made Maud take a step back in surprise. Dot smiled up at her from where she had bent to retrieve her coat. 'It does sound a bit odd, doesn't it? No, I don't usually stalk my competition winners, but my brother Nate mentioned that we had met and I felt so rude, as I couldn't recollect where. I thought visiting you might jog my memory, I usually remember people I meet. I felt awful I didn't say hello at the preview. I left it to my promotional boys to show the winners around, as I was with clients. I was in the area today and thought I'd pop in and say hello.'

Dot stood there expectantly, still smiling at Maud who was gaping and staring at her hair, as if a bird had just flown in and nested in it. She hesitated, then said, 'would you like to come in?'

Dot, delighted at this outcome, glanced quickly at her watch with its huge dial, and then nodded. 'Great idea. Have you got any camomile tea?'

'Uh... sorry.'

'Oh, that's good! My mum said I have to drink it to stop me being quite so hyperactive, but I hate the stuff. Honestly, if I wasn't so energetic, I'd collapse in a heap of exhaustion, the amount of shepherding my family take.' Seeing Maud's shocked expression, Dot pulled a face and giggled while Maud reached for her keys, opened the front door and finally began to join in with the laughter. Dot knew she made people smile, but wasn't completely certain it was always for the right reason.

Maud turned to face her as they stepped into the corridor that led to her kitchen and open plan lounge. 'I lied,' she blurted out.

Dot was confused, then horrified. 'You didn't paint the picture?'

'Oh no... of course I painted my competition entry,' said Maud, frowning as Dot's shoulders sagged with relief. 'Although I'm working on a different style now, and I was surprised to win if I'm honest. I assumed you hadn't had many entries?'

'We had thousands,' said Dot drily.

'Oh...'

'What did you lie about, then?'

'We've never met before. Nate... your brother... asked me who I was with and I felt like a sad loser for admitting that I'd arrived on my own.'

'So you pointed out the most obvious person in the room?' Although this was said without malice, Dot knew Maud would be able to hear the sadness behind the words. She wanted to stand out, but the feeling that this was a good thing was starting to wear thin. She wasn't sure others took her seriously, especially her family. She worked really hard, with visible results, so why did they view her as a joke?

'Not obvious, no,' Maud said slowly as if carefully choosing her words now, but her eyes began to sparkle and her lips formed a cheeky smile. 'I looked your way and thought you looked interesting. Having interesting friends is very glamorous, I'm told.'

Dot's lips rose at the corners too. 'Who told you that?'

'Not my mother,' Maud burst out laughing.

Dot had no idea what was so funny, but seeing the merriment made her laugh too. 'How's that?'

Maud walked towards the little island unit that nestled in the open space between the kitchen and living room. She dumped her bag on one of the stools tucked underneath and reached for two glasses from a cupboard by the sink. She waved one at Dot who nodded her assent, while Maud poured some chilled lemonade from the fridge and topped it up with a splash of orange juice. 'My mother thinks that normal people dress like this,' she gave herself a disgusted look and held out the hem of her A-line skirt. 'She wouldn't know individuality if it was curled up in her lap and snoring loudly. If I as much as wear a colourful belt she freezes me with one of her death stares, or tells me she's feeling faint.'

Dot sipped her drink but her eyebrows shot up. She started to splutter and giggle as Maud spoke so vehemently. An ungainly snort erupted from her nose, and she almost choked on her drink as she visualised Maud's mum with big bulging eyes and flaming nostrils. Maud started giggling again too and they both moved to the cool tones of the living room and collapsed onto the soft white cotton couches with a sigh of pleasure.

'Nice to meet you, Maud,' Dot said finally, when she had caught her breath and could talk again.

Maud seemed shocked that she'd dumped all her personal baggage onto a complete stranger. 'Maybe my friend Daisy is right and the anger I've had simmering for years is bubbling to the surface and ready to explode. Perhaps I should confront my parents, and stop being such a pathetic wimp?'

Dot sat herself up and looked earnestly at Maud. She made a swift decision and took a deep breath before sighing and rolling her shoulders to try and ease some tension. 'My parents are completely insane. I have to wear a bird's nest in my hair to impress them, and my brother hates women.'

Maud was aghast. 'What?'

'Well… not me obviously,' said Dot conversationally. 'His ex… my ex-best friend,' Dot's face filled with pain at the memory and then started to go a bit red as her jaw set in anger, but she kept her tone neutral to try and mask the hate she felt. 'She burnt herself alive and tried to take Nate with her.'

Maud's face paled. 'How awful!'

Dot slapped her forehead with her hand, then jumped up and threw her arms wide in exasperation 'Not you as well? What is it about the moody git that makes women want to literally lay naked on the floor before him and surrender all wit and will?'

Maud blushed furiously. 'Of course not me as well! Anyway… I have a sort of boyfriend.'

'Sort of?' scoffed Dot.

'He asked me out today.'

'Hey! Congrats.' This made Dot feel so much better. She breezily grabbed her drink and took a cooling sip as she sat back down. 'What's he like?'

Maud hesitated. 'He's dreamy…' she said finally, giving a brief description of Tasty Tom.

Dot sighed in relief that this poor girl had escaped the dastardly clutches of her big brother, and she decided she quite liked her. For all of her protestations of normality, she seemed pretty quirky to Dot, who had lived around these types of people all her life and could spot one a mile off, even dressed like a nun. Dot was well known for making swift decisions and, given that half the people who lived in her family home had been collected along the way over the last twenty-five years by her parents, a gleam of excitement lit her eyes.

'I'd like to invite you to a party.' Why on earth she would feel an urge to invite this stranger, Dot didn't know. She wished her big mouth would stop running away with itself sometimes. They were of similar age, both around their mid-twenties, but other than their mutual respect for art, and nutty parents, they surely couldn't have anything in common.

Maud looked up sharply. 'A party? Whose?'

Dot looked at her strangely, as if she was the dimmest human on the planet. 'Mine, of course,' she said, as if that explained everything. She decided she quite liked Maud, as she hadn't thrown her out yet and looked like she was bored and up for a challenge. Dot thought that inviting someone to her own party that her parents hadn't met yet was hilarious. Why hadn't she thought of this before? The fact that Maud had a boyfriend and Nate obviously had the hots for her made it even funnier. Finally, she could make them all pay, Dot plotted happily. She would never intentionally hurt Nate, as he was already living in his own kind of hell, but it was about time that he was taught a lesson on how to treat women. She saw Maud's hesitation as she frantically glanced round the room for inspiration for an excuse as to why she couldn't make it, which made Dot even more determined to get her there.

She put on her best I'm going to make you do what I want voice. It was friendly, but persuasive. 'I'd really love you to come. It's not for a while yet, but it's at my parents' house and they've already been planning it for months. They begin as soon as the last birthday party finishes and make it even more extravagant than the one before. There will be free booze and food, and their house is full of art for you to gawp at. Surely that's enough to tempt someone who paints?'

Dot could see the cogs of Maud's brain go round as she thought for a moment, before excitement lit her eyes. She'd obviously chosen to live a little. Dot had decided that they were going to be best friends anyway. She assumed Maud's daily existence was humdrum – and Dot always got what she wanted in the end. Looking at the boring interior of Maud's house, and seeing no smiling photos of gorgeous men or raucous friends, Dot decided she had a new project to keep her busy until she found her artist. She loved a challenge. Dot could sense that Maud wasn't quite ready to let go of the excitement that ebbed and flowed around her, and found her slightly exotic.

Maud's eyes sparkled suddenly. 'I'd love to come.'

Chapter Eleven

Maud felt relieved that Dot hadn't discovered what she was talking about earlier. She'd started to panic that someone had found out she was leaving paintings around the vicinity. For the first time, she wondered if she could get into any trouble, for fly tipping or something. She'd only been trying to be nice and finally find people who liked her pictures. Then she felt the panic reduce slightly as Dot jumped up, clapped her hands in glee and turned round to start opening doors and peering through them. Maud wondered what the hell she was up to, as within minutes she had found the second bedroom and the bathroom. 'Uh, hold on. What are you doing?'

Dot just laughed as if Maud had lost the plot. 'Looking for your bedroom, so we can find you something to wear to my party. It will be…' she paused and seemed to make a quick decision. 'I don't want to frighten a new friend away, but it's a fairly big party…' she hedged, smiling apologetically, but not looking in the least bit sincere at Maud's suddenly ashen face. 'I think it's best to be honest and I may as well get all the details out of the way now. There may be a few crazies coming, but you will still need to look knockout.'

'I do? Crazies?' Maud felt her stomach form a tight knot. Who were these crazies and how on earth was she going to look a knockout? Dot obviously didn't know about straight curly hair. Before she could make a grab for Dot's hands to pull her away, she had thrown open Maud's bedroom door with a big, 'aha!' Maud groaned and surrendered to her fate.

'Don't worry. The crazies are what I affectionately call my family. They all drive me mad.' She stood in the centre of Maud's bedroom and hitched her hands onto her hips with a frown as she took in every detail. She craned her neck to look back out to the lounge and frowned again. 'Spill?'

'Spill?'

'Yes. Spill. What's going on here? I know we just met, but surely your mum must know this is the real you? You can't tell me that a boring bungalow hides this lush interior…' she paused as she gazed at the huge double bed with soft grey padded headboard, which was covered with a delicately-sewn throw and an array of colourful and textural cushions. The walls were painted with slim trees that leaned into each other, with endless green leaves that seemed to be reaching out. 'It's magical and even I'm almost lost for words, which is rare,' Dot joked. She looked stunned, and seemed to remember something she should have thought of saying earlier, but then gazing at the detail of the art made her go quiet again, as if she'd decided it wasn't that important. 'Sorry, I can't think when I'm looking at this. It's so perfect and all I want to do is to immerse myself in the feeling of being surrounded by a beautifully painted and gorgeously lush forest. I want to jump onto the bed, put my arms behind my head and lie there gazing at the walls forever. It's breathtaking. Who painted this?' she asked in awe. Maud got the impression Dot was going to ask if it would be ok to rip out the walls of the bungalow to steal the artwork for her gallery, as she was reverently running her hands across the murals. Surely she couldn't like it that much?

Maud hesitated. No one but Daisy came into her bedroom, and she felt her privacy had been violated. Dot didn't seem to notice the polite formalities of being a houseguest. Perhaps she was more like her 'crazy' family than she realised? 'It was here when I arrived,' she lied quickly, crossing her fingers behind her back and hoping that lightning wouldn't strike her for two lies in one week.

Dot screwed up her face and moved even closer to the walls for a better look, running her palms reverently over the surface again. 'People would pay an artist a fortune for a design like this.'

It was Maud's turn to frown now. 'Surely not?' She peered closely at her own work as if seeing it with fresh eyes.

'Really. The artist is very talented. It reminds me of

something, though. It has similarities to your competition entry. Is this where you got your inspiration?'

'Um… yes,' Maud admitted, as it was true. She had wanted to create the same feeling of serenity that engulfed her when she went to bed at night, in the little seascape Daisy had entered. She had saved a spot for it on her bathroom wall, but the gallery hadn't returned the artwork yet.

'I don't blame you,' said Dot candidly. 'I would probably do the same. Such a shame you don't know that artist. I would love to represent them.'

'You would?'

Dot looked at Maud as if she was thick and then plonked herself, without invitation, onto Maud's bed and turned onto her side to stare at the walls with a big sigh. Make yourself at home, why don't you? Maud huffed silently, but the buzzy feeling in her stomach was back. This girl meant change, somehow, and Maud was scared that she wasn't brave enough to cope with it.

Chapter Twelve

'So how did it go?'

Daisy looked at Maud in confusion, then a wicked grin spread all over her face. 'Are you referring to the dirty weekend away I've just enjoyed with my boyfriend, where we only surfaced for sex and food?' She gave Maud a lascivious wink and a smug look that said it all.

Maud smothered a grin and then stuck out her tongue at her friend's glowing face. 'One of us needs to be getting some action and it certainly isn't me.'

Daisy rolled her eyes heavenward. 'If you loosened up a little and let up from ironing your knickers every once in a while, maybe you would attract a man too.'

Maud pictured Daisy's perfectly nice boyfriend, who looked as though he was part of a grunge metal band. He had messy hair, a long beard, and was dynamite in bed, apparently. Daisy had never been happier. He was about two inches shorter than Daisy too, but she had started to babble on about how this made the 'downstairs' sex so much better, before Maud stuck her fingers in her ears and started singing, 'la la la la,' so that she didn't have to hear the gory details. Ryan treated Daisy like a princess and Maud had never seen her friend so happy; she just wished she could find a man to adore her, the way Ryan adored Daisy. Maud thought Daisy was beautiful inside and out, with her curvy figure, abundance of blonde curls and round cherub face. Daisy looked angelic, but could drink more than most and had a filthy laugh, which was so loud when she was drunk, that Maud often vacated the building.

Maud suddenly remembered what she had come to see Daisy for in the first place and started hopping from foot to foot and clapping her hands with excitement, which was not a good idea while she was standing in the school reception area, as various children and their parents who were arriving at the school stopped to watch with interest.

Daisy quickly shepherded her to the back of the little reception room, full of row upon row of brightly-coloured files and walls covered in A4 daily rota sheets. She sat Maud down in the little blue school chair that was used for the sick bay. It was in the furthest corner and a square cabinet was hung on the wall nearby with a big red cross on the front, full of various Mr Men plasters and a thermometer.

Maud tried to wriggle around to get comfortable and realised how massive her bottom seemed in the child's chair so she sprang back up. She was about to hop about again, but saw Daisy standing expectantly with her hands on her hips, making Maud panic that she would have to get a move on to her own class. She leaned forward conspiratorially. 'I almost forgot to tell you. I spent the weekend with a madwoman and Tom asked me out!'

If Maud had wanted to shock her friend, then it worked. Daisy looked dumbfounded and confused about the first part of the statement, then registered the last bit and started hopping around and clapping her hands in glee too.

Maud realised that they must look like a couple of demented penguins, but then coughed as Daisy squeezed her so hard she felt she might crack a rib. She broke the contact with a smile and a wince.

'You got asked out by Tasty Tom? When, why and how did I miss this?'

Maud blushed and hid behind her hair, but Daisy flicked it aside. 'He asked me out on a little yellow note last Friday.' Maud reverently straightened out the small square of paper and handed it over.

Daisy took it carefully and read the scribbled text, noting the kiss after his initials, and her eyebrows shot up into her hairline in surprise. 'Well?'

'Well, what?'

'When's the big date?'

Maud's face started to grow hot and pink and she looked at her feet. 'I don't know. I guess we'll talk about it today.' Her stomach plummeted and she suddenly felt her breakfast of porridge and a rather old banana come back to haunt her. 'What do I do? Do I just saunter over and say... hey sexy pants... about that note?'

Daisy seemed to be enjoying seeing her friend blush as she was grinning from ear to ear. 'You might want to find a different opening line. It's been far too long since you've even mentioned a man by name, other than 'bastard'. You'll be a dried up old prune and your lady parts will shrivel from under-use, if you're not careful!'

Maud tried to ignore Daisy's unfair remarks as she walked to her class and pushed open the door, which creaked a little, making Tom look up from where he was seated at his utilitarian wooden desk. He winked at her, making her blush, and he grinned before turning back to his work. The children filed into the room and chatted noisily before Tom cleared his throat and raised a hand to quiet them. How did he do that? Maud wondered in awe. The kids usually talked over her when she asked them to pipe down. One look from Tom and they all hushed immediately. It must be a skill he'd learnt before he came here as it had worked from the moment he arrived. Maybe that was why Maud was a little bit intimidated by him, and perhaps the kids felt that way too? Although a frisson of heat tinged her skin when he looked at her – and that was all adult.

She was on edge all day, expecting him to approach her about meeting up, but he left her in a state of anxiety and excited bliss until the very last child had left the room for the day and she was bending over her own desk, collecting her belongings and shoving them into her bag in readiness to go home. Just as she was despondently pushing the shoulder strap of her smart leather bag over her shoulder, preparing to face the fact that he'd obviously changed his mind, he came up behind her and ran his hand along her hip, making her spin round and smack her side on the desk at the contact, her skin prickling with goose bumps where he'd touched her, then stinging where she'd collided with the desk. This was getting so embarrassing. She'd burst into flames next if she wasn't careful. If this was how she responded every time he came near her, she really needed to get out more – or get laid.

'Are you free this Friday?' he asked, eyes sparkling.

Maud could see he was enjoying himself, the sure smile on his lips told her he already knew her answer. She really should play hard to get, and say she was busy or shaving her legs or something, but her stomach was churning and her knees felt like jelly, as he invaded her personal space and started sniffing her neck.

'You smell heavenly,' he murmured while she stood stock still in shock. This was not the Tom she had come to know in the staffroom, and the full-on flirting was filling her senses and making her take a step back to clear her head. 'Um, thank you... and yes, that would be great.'

Tom seemed pleased with this response and gave her room to breathe, and she gratefully sucked in some air. He pecked her briefly on her lips and then headed for the door. 'That's great. I already have your number, from the staff list,' he winked, and gave her one of those smouldering smiles that made her heart start to pound. 'I'll text you the time and you send me the address where you'd like to go.' It was a statement, not a question, and Maud nodded dumbly as he smiled at her mute state and left her standing there like a fool. She grabbed her hand to her chest to try and ease her pulse rate in case she had a cardiac arrest. She'd thought it would be nice to date a teacher like Tom, as he'd be dependable, and steady. Who knew he could be so sexy and commanding? She fanned herself with her hands and rested back onto the desk for support. Wait till she told Daisy.

Walking home after she had spent ten minutes splashing cold water on her face in the cloakroom and calming herself down, Maud decided that it was a good thing that Tom was such a confident man otherwise she certainly wouldn't have approached him, however much she fancied him. She was worried about making a complete idiot of herself, which seemed to happen far too often.

Her phone trilled and she fished in her bag to grab it before the caller got bored and rang off. Considering Maud was so neat and tidy, the inside of her bag was more like her true self, a complete and utter mess. Grabbing the phone, which luckily lit up when it rang, she plastered it to her ear and was thrilled to hear Dot's voice, which was as excitable as Maud remembered.

'Maud, I'm having a dinner party in an absurdly creative restaurant this Friday. I desperately want you to come as I think you'd love it there. It's dark, mysterious and dripping in sculpture and photography.' Maud smiled at Dot's persuasive tone and wondered if the place really was full of art, or if Dot had added that to entice her out of her cave. Did everyone think she was some kind of reclusive hermit? Maud cringed and set her bag at her feet, while she tried to picture an exotic place where interesting people met to eat and talk about art. She would really love to find out for herself and thought about accepting Dot's kind invitation, then she sighed heavily as, for the first time in years, she was double-booked.

'Oh Dot, I would have loved to have joined you,' Maud meant it, too, she was so flattered that Dot had thought of her. They had spoken twice over the weekend already and Maud was enjoying the fledgling friendship. 'But Tom has just asked me out on a date on Friday.'

Maud could hear the excitement in Dot's voice. 'Bring him.'

Maud grinned suddenly. She had two offers on the table and it felt good to be in demand. 'Bring him?' Maud stared at the phone quizzically, as if it was an alien object, before pressing it back to her ear.

Dot laughed. 'Why not? First dates can be excruciatingly embarrassing. Wouldn't it be better to have a few friendly faces there?' she wheedled.

'But I won't know anyone else, other than you.'

Dot paused for a moment in thought. 'Oh yes. You may have a point, but we're all very friendly.'

'Who will be there?' Maud's brow furrowed and she tried to decide if Dot getting her own way was a good idea, as she seemed quite bossy. Maud was terrified of dating Tom on her own and having other people there did seem inviting. She also wanted to see for herself what the restaurant was like, as it sounded divine. And how often did she get invited somewhere that would probably top up her creative juices for months and months to come?

Dot hesitated. 'I'm wondering how truthful to be,' she said frankly, 'as Nate could either scare you away or encourage you to join us. He's going to be there, with Elliott, and my parents and a few other friends,' she said quickly, not pausing for breath.

Maud stomach started somersaulting again. 'Um… Nate…'

'Yes. He's bringing his new squeeze apparently. I've met her once and she bored me half to death. Please, Maud. It will be excruciating without you. I need someone normal there.'

'You just said everyone was friendly. You're not selling them that well.'

Dot laughed before becoming deadly serious again. 'It will be good for you to meet everyone from the madhouse before my birthday party. Then you'll feel much more comfortable, because you'll know them all.'

Maud pictured a friendly and warm group of artists, then the picture changed to one of green-eyed monsters, who would trample each other for fame. The way Dot described her family was with a mix of love and anger.

'Please…' pleaded Dot desperately. 'I promise you can get drunk really quickly.'

Maud's mouth widened into a grin and she pictured Dot's earnest face at the other end of the phone. She liked Dot and her life had been far duller before she burst into her home and decided they would become friends. Maud had never known anyone quite like her. The hidden part of her cherished finding someone she could be herself with. She had a feeling that Dot felt the same. 'Tom might not like the idea…' She knew she didn't sound convincing.

'Well, put the invite to him and let him decide.' Dot

sounded like she was dancing round her office in glee, 'I'm hoping this means an almost certain yes, and that you can use your womanly charms to persuade your new man to join us.'

Chapter Thirteen

Maud ducked back down and into the bush she was hiding beside. She noticed a small child looking at her strangely, and put her finger to her lips to signal they should be quiet, getting a mutinous look in return. Maud sat back on her haunches and wondered what the hell her life had come to.

So far, she had left ten paintings around, and the press had taken an avid interest in her story. She had been sure that Daisy had tipped them off, but then remembered her puce face when she'd heard that the art was being left out for strangers to pick up and walk away with.

Maud still didn't believe her work was good enough to cause all this fuss, but it had become a bit of an addiction now, she got a buzz when someone liked her work enough to take it home. The papers were saying that her art was daring and unique. Maud had never experienced anyone except Daisy and Nancy appreciating her work before, and now she found she couldn't stop wanting more.

All this cloak and dagger espionage was going to give her a heart attack if she wasn't careful, though. If anyone from the school caught her hiding in bushes and scaring children, she could lose her job and her reputation, plus her mum would kill her for bringing shame on their upstanding family name.

The little girl who had spotted her earlier was now grabbing at her mum's arm and pointing to the bush Maud was hiding under. Her stomach grumbled noisily and she started to panic. The mum was talking to another woman and seemed to be telling her daughter off for interrupting her. Maud quickly backed out of the hedge, brushing a stray twig out of her hair and fleetingly thinking of Dot's bird's nest hat. She reached into her pocket and thanked the heavens that she had confiscated a big bouncy ball from Robbie during registration in class that day and she turned to show the girl that she had found the ball she had lost, which made the girl stop pulling at her mother and just stare her way. She straightened her back, which was aching from hiding in a small shrub, and nonchalantly strolled away as if she had not a care in the world. Her heart was beating so fast she thought she might pass out, but she made her feet move one in front of the other and in minutes, but what felt like an age, she was safely seated back behind the steering wheel of her car.

She sat with her hands grasping the sides of her seat and tried to steady her breathing. This had become so ridiculous. Maybe she needed art AA or something? Surely this wasn't normal behaviour? She craned her neck to see if her little painting was still on the bench, but she was too far away now and she felt crushing disappointment that she'd gone to so much effort with the artwork for nothing. She had spent many nights with this particular painting, and she craved seeing the person's face when they saw the little tag attached to it. She needed her art fix. Despondently, she turned the key in the ignition and headed towards home.

She tried to clear her mind and thought back to the pathetically timid way she had tentatively asked Tom about coming with her to Dot's pre-party party. He had looked a bit perplexed at first, but as she'd babbled that Dot was a new friend and that Nate would be there, she'd discovered that Tom loved trying new restaurants and meeting people. He'd heard of Nate and thought it would be a complete blast. Maud had very unattractively stood there gawping at him for being so happy. Her life was getting stranger by the minute. She'd assumed he'd hate the idea. Instead, Tom had jumped up and grabbed her hand, then began going on about how much he admired Nate's work, as he'd read about him in the Sunday supplements the previous weekend. Surprisingly, and a little annoyingly, Tom hadn't stopped talking about it since.

Maud was grudgingly happy that he seemed so excited about their date, though, and felt proud that she sort of knew Dot and had met Nate once. She was nervous about going to a family dinner with her new boyfriend but appreciated that it would be even stranger for Tom.

The phone rang as she pulled into her driveway and she turned off the engine to reach into her bag, seeing Dot's now-familiar name on the screen. Answering the call, she could barely hear anything, as Dot seemed to be having some sort of fit. She held the phone to her ear in panic. 'Dot? Are you ok?'

'Huh? Oh yes. It's an experimental art piece that someone sent me. It has an audio file that seems to set itself off every time I move. It's doing my head in and I'm ready to chuck it off the top of the building. I'm not sure it's right for my customers,' she said sarcastically.

Maud stifled a giggle. 'Don't they like the sound of a whale's mating call?'

'Not this month,' said Dot drily. 'Awful, isn't it? I had to give it a chance as I'm trying to build my own client base, and it was made by one of my old school friends. She asked me for a favour.' Dot paused and Maud could picture her cringing as she tried to blank out the gut-wrenching screeches. 'I thought my art was atrocious, but hers is even worse. I've finally found someone with less artistic talent than me!'

Maud could sense an undercurrent to her words. 'Have you been painting again?'

Dot stopped for a second before replying. 'I've been experimenting, I suppose,' she sighed. 'I've been working a full day for my family and then spending the evenings in my studio until dawn, which is taking its toll on my sanity. It's why I've called you. I'd like to have your honest opinion on my new work.'

Maud realised how hard it must have been for Dot to ask someone outside of her family to view her work, and felt incredibly flattered that she had chosen her, of all people. 'I'd love to. When can I see it? And where?' she asked, trying to conceal the anticipation she felt brimming inside, not wanting to scare Dot off or change her mind.

Maud heard Dot slump back in her chair. 'My eyes are red from staring at the detailing on my new work. I need someone else's point of view. Maybe we can meet up at the weekend after the dinner party?'

Maud could imagine Dot trying to steady her nerves. It was the first time she'd heard uncertainty in her voice.

'I feel a bit nauseous at the thought of another person seeing my art, even if it is someone who paints for a hobby and is far from being an expert,' Dot said candidly, not listening or bothering to notice Maud splutter in disbelief at the other end of the line. 'I feel you're the right person to show first, for some reason. You're so calm and rational, unlike my parents, who would find it difficult to mask their confusion and distaste, however hard they tried.'

Maud wondered if Dot could sense her jiggling up and down on the other end of the line, but wouldn't realise it was with both fury and excitement over what she was hearing. A reluctant smile crept onto her face, regardless, as she really did want to see Dot's new work. 'My place or yours?' Maud asked through gritted teeth, after she'd had a moment to stop fuming.

She couldn't believe that she'd only known Dot for such a short while, as they had spoken on the phone every day since meeting outside her house. She wondered if Dot was this insulting and full-on with all her friends, and a spark of jealousy seared through her, making her frown. Dot was so vivacious and exciting that Maud didn't want anyone else to have a friendship like the one they had. She hadn't seen Dot's place and she wondered whether it represented the real Dot, or the façade she presented to the world, like Maud's own bungalow. The thought made Maud confused for the first time about how her life must seem to Daisy and Dot. She'd been so sure she was right, before, but picturing Dot's strong and colourful outfits, and getting the occasional glimpse of the delicate and complicated personality living inside them, made her think that maybe she had been wrong the whole time. She supposed Dot's place would have huge picture windows, sparkly fabric that was painful to sit on everywhere, and clashing walls. She'd probably have an exotic pet too, like a llama that spat at you as you walked in.

Dot looked at the phone in exasperation. 'Maud, have you fallen asleep, or wandered off somewhere? You've gone quiet… Maud?'

'Still here.'

'Oh good. I've got a studio. It's above Nate's painting lair, and so much more refined,' she joked. 'I don't bed restless women there and I don't work in the dark, unlike some,' she said pointedly.

Maud's gasped in shock. Dot giggled and swung her feet up onto her desk with a clunking sound. 'I'm only joking. He doesn't let anyone in there, except me, or our parents if they happen to be behaving that day. That's why I call it his lair. He's like a big black bear, guarding his territory. All grumpy and hairy,' she giggled again, as if picturing Maud's surprised face.

'I don't know why I tease you about my brother, Maud. I would never do this with anyone else, but the words just tumble out of my mouth. Obviously you know I'm joking…' She reeled off the address of her studio before she let her tongue run away with more insults. 'The thought of being a bit braver and letting someone else see the few precious pieces of art that have poured from my soul and driven me to near madness over the last few weeks is terrifying, but necessary,' she said with finality.

Maud felt glum and put the phone back into her bag with the decision to start being a bit more courageous, too, and to make Dot and Daisy proud of her.

Chapter Fourteen

Maud bit her lip and fiddled with the button of her shirt before Tom took her hand and squeezed it in support. It felt strange to be out with him and not surrounded by thirty small, questioning children. He was looking gorgeous tonight and had obviously made an effort, with smart dark blue trousers and a pristine white shirt that was open at the collar to reveal a glimpse of firm chest. He looked preppy but hot, with tortoiseshell glasses perched on his nose and floppy blond hair swept to one side of his forehead.

Tom had been remarkably chirpy about the weird first date idea from the moment it had been arranged. In fact, it had been a bit like he was going on a date with Nate, the amount of times he had begun a conversation about him and said how thrilled he was to be meeting such a famous artist. Maud had tried not to be too grumpy about it, but she would have preferred her first date with a new man to be focussed on her.

They walked towards the restaurant Dot had directed them to in a text earlier in the day and Maud almost swooned at the creativeness of the surroundings. As soon as she approached the main entrance, she could feel her heart ramp up a notch, and begin to beat faster in excitement. The door was a majestic carved artwork with ironwork sensuously weaving its way from the ground and reaching to the stars. It was imposing but beautiful and they stopped and stared at the detailing in awe.

As they stepped closer to peer at the masterly sculpture, the doors whooshed open and a smartly-dressed doorman smiled warmly and beckoned them inside. They had to sidestep quickly out of the way as a very glamorous woman brushed past them and disappeared into the restaurant without a backward glance. Maud and Tom grinned at each other in delight at the drama of it all, as they were led inside to an enormous room that looked like an opulent palace, with grand tables covered in layers of delicate fabrics, set into alcoves. The tables, which stretched as far as the eye could see, were surrounded by softly padded armchairs and benches, covered with rich vibrant materials that seemed to scoop up the people smiling over expressive conversations in secluded corners. The walls were covered with hand-drawn illustrations depicting people entwined in lust, and the tables were overflowing with fresh flowers in crystal bowls, their deep-coloured blooms dipping towards the tablecloths, where candles were lit to create a breathtaking ambience, filling the room with an enticing scent. Sparkling glasses and silverware adorned the tables. The illustrations seemed to be set with gold leaf that shimmered as they passed, making the whole place glow. It was the most sensual room Maud had ever seen, and it wasn't until Tom gave her a friendly dig in the ribs that she realised she had been standing still and gawping. She was embarrassingly near a full table, and she quickly rearranged her features to appear as if she frequented establishments like this often and did not have a powerful urge to steal a few things and stash them. She could add a small shelf and sit them in her sparkly hidden wardrobe collection at home, she mused delightedly.

She shook her head to clear it and peered into the restaurant, before spotting what looked like a brightly-coloured parrot hopping up and down. She squinted, then realised that Dot was wearing a bejewelled bird attached to a headband and was jumping and waving to get her attention. She looked like a very glamorous pirate with her red striped dress and blue underskirt. Only Dot could manage to make an outfit like that look remotely sexy. Maud would have to ask her for tips later.

She clasped Tom's hand again and pulled him towards the heaving table. Maud realised that, far from the intimate gathering Dot her had told her about, with a quick calculation, it seemed that about twenty people were now staring their way. Nate was halfway down the table and was in conversation with his Amazonian companion, but he turned and saw her. A wide smile broke on his face before he noticed her fingers enclosed in Tom's and his hand at her waist as he guided her towards the table. Fire burned in Nate's eyes as he cocked his head and once again began to listen to his date's words.

Maud's stomach clenched and she tried not to yank her hand away and break Tom's fingers. Her step faltered and she felt confusion cloud her mind. Why was Nate angry? He had seemed so pleased, a fraction of a second before. Maybe he hadn't realised it was her and when he did, he was displeased she was hanging around his family like a bad smell? Embarrassment made her stand still before Dot bounded over and hugged them both, dragging them towards the table and making introductions to expectant faces.

Maud blushed profusely when she was introduced to Dot's famous parents, although Tom seemed in his element and was ecstatically shaking their hands. Maud couldn't look Nate in the eye for some reason, but he was pointedly staring at her now and ignoring his date, who was gently touching his arm. Maud noticed the spidery silver burns running along his arm again, as the woman pulled at his shirt, and she wondered what had happened. She felt shocked to see the imperfections marring his skin and appalled that something had hurt him, before realising she was staring, and he was staring back. She quickly looked away. She recalled Dot telling her about his ex-girlfriend killing herself and trying to take him with her, and paled slightly.

Dot's parents enveloped her in a warm embrace and their daughter's friend was immediately placed next to them and everyone was told to make room. Maud wished the ground would open up and swallow her whole. She was mortified to make these glamorous people change seats for her. Tom happily squeezed in beside her and stroked her leg to let her know he was fine, which made her jump and bang her thigh on the underside of the table, before he turned to speak to the stunning redhead on the other side of him.

Maud took a steadying breath and wished for once that she had worn something more sophisticated and adventurous than the cream lace blouse and pretty but uninspiring black skirt she had chosen. She wondered if anyone would mistake her for a waitress, then realised all the servers were dressed like supermodels, so no worries there. She grimaced, whilst trying her best to smile. She had worn her sexy black shoes with the roses painted on them to give her courage, but even they were failing her now. Dot was positively glowing, probably at finding someone interesting that her parents hadn't met yet, and they were now practically clambering all over each other to find out what was so intriguing about her that Dot had brought her into their family sanctum.

Cosmo propped an elbow on the table, effectively blocking his wife's view, and gave the new arrivals a warm smile. Maud was mesmerised by his dark eyes and could see where Nate got his smouldering gorgeousness from. Dot's mother was one lucky woman! She was currently trying valiantly to join in the conversation by leaning over her husband's arm, but he was skilfully preventing her in a manoeuvre that had probably taken years to perfect.

Cosmo took in every detail of Maud's appearance and she blushed under his leisurely scrutiny. She was very nervous and hoped he would reassure her and not dissect her personality, but Dot had explained that it was difficult with this family, as they all tried to outdo each other, gobbling people up and expressing their feelings so openly, that outsiders sometimes took it the wrong way.

'How did you meet Dot?' Cosmo asked with interest.

'We met through a love of art,' said Maud quietly, looking wide-eyed and breathless.

Cosmo seemed genuinely interested in her but looked surprised that she appeared fairly timid and restrained. He patted her hand with affection. 'You seem a little nervous. I know from experience that the quietest of women can be complex creatures underneath, although there don't seem to be any of those in my family, unfortunately!' he sighed as he body-blocked his wife again. 'You paint?'

Maud smiled at his interest and warmed to his friendly nature. He had such charm that she felt instantly at ease. 'I try to.'

Cosmo was surprisingly candid. 'I know Dot has an amazing eye for talent and I've been worrying that she is feeling constrained by us and will want to break free soon. It isn't a pleasant thought, but was one Camille and I have talked about more and more recently. Do you exhibit your work?'

Maud blushed and stared at his jaunty cravat and the black and grey hair that was still thick. She met his gaze and shyly smiled as if the sun was shining on her and she'd just woken up. 'I've been painting since I was very small, but I'm not very good. I'm enthusiastic, though,' she tried a feeble joke.

'That's what Dot always says,' he said with a sigh of frustration. 'You shouldn't beat yourself up. Art is so subjective.' His eyes twinkled with mischief, 'although in my daughter's case,' he glanced at his offspring with obvious affection, 'it seems that it's true. I think it's because she tries so hard that her frustration appears in her work. It's slightly painful to see, to be honest.'

Maud grimaced in blatant sympathy with her friend. 'Perhaps that's why we became friends so quickly. A mutual inability to paint the work we feel in our hearts.'

Cosmo leaned forward and gave her a quick hug, which made her skin flush dark pink. 'I'm sure you're both better than you think and that your own unique style will find you one day,' he sympathised.

'I have a definite style,' said Maud, cringing a little. 'My parents think my work is rubbish too,' she said without thinking.

'Ouch!' he laughed heartily as Maud's face flamed red.

'I'm so sorry!' she said, horrified at her own lack of tact. Tom turned to see what Maud was talking about and saw Cosmo with tears running down his face and laughter in his eyes, whilst Maud was hiding her burning face in her napkin.

Maud smiled at Camille, who looked as though she was becoming increasingly bored with being shut out of the conversation. Maud could see she had been watching her son with interest, as he had been ignoring his date and straining his ears to hear his father's conversation too. Camille's eyes were alight. 'Dot bringing a new couple to the table is now doubly interesting…' she indicated with a nod of her head towards her son, as Cosmo looked across the table with interest, 'even if my husband is rudely hogging the guests,' she joked, poking him in the ribs and making him jump. She leaned forward to catch a passing waiter's attention to order more wine and food, as Dot stood up and motioned for Maud to tell Tom she was leaving the table and follow her to the ladies' powder room to freshen up. Camille smiled at Maud conspiratorially. 'Dot will be desperate to find out what amused her father so much. Tell her to mind her own business and to stop ignoring the wonderful man we introduced her to earlier. He's a sculptor and a real catch.' Maud jumped up gratefully when Dot drew nearer, and Camille saw her opportunity and sprang into Maud's vacated seat with a victorious glare at her husband and skilfully began grilling Tom on his credentials.

Chapter Fifteen

Dot ushered Maud through a set of delicate archways that were subtly lit, so that they felt that they were walking into something out of a posh interiors magazine. The bathroom was an oasis of calm, with grey granite sinks and mirrors perfectly placed above them. More sparkling bowls were bursting with softly-coloured flowers, adorning every surface and scenting the air with blossom. Toiletries were on the glossy surface of a dressing table, which sat next to the furthest wall and had a little stool tucked underneath it, in suede matching the restaurant seats. Maud gasped in pleasure and ran her hand along the walls, covered in more illustrations. This time they depicted people dancing with flowers scattered around them and in their hair. She was sure she could live in here and die a happy woman.

Dot pulled out the stool and slumped onto it, which made the petticoats of the striped dress she was wearing bunch up around her like a colourful cloud. 'Maybe this wasn't such a good idea,' she apologised. 'I guess I wanted to show them all that I can meet my own interesting friends, not just ones they have vetted first and foisted on me. I shouldn't have dragged you into it.'

Maud pressed her lips together in a grimace and was slightly offended that Dot had so obviously only asked her there to annoy her family. To be fair, Maud had insulted her parents, upset her brother in some way just by being there and she hadn't even ordered any food yet, so perhaps Dot did have a point.

Dot slumped even further on the stool, which must have been difficult as it was so small, and Maud had a feeling that it was just the voluminous skirt that was holding her up. 'I wanted to show them that I'm big enough to control my own life and I can pick nice friends.' Maud felt her cheeks flush again and she felt happy this time that Dot had chosen her, so she decided not to nudge the stool to one side, as she had been debating.

'They should stop organising me,' said Dot in frustration. 'I practically run their whole lives for them, but they still keep foisting strange people on me. They bought two extras tonight,' she ranted and threw her hands up in exasperation when Maud looked blank and continued, 'The redhead next to Tom and the token bloke they always sit next to me, as if I'm a spinster, or just desperate.'

Maud pictured the face of the 'friend' Dot's parents had picked out for their daughter and sympathised. He was about ten years older than her and, although he looked quite nice in a lanky, beardy sort of way, he had halitosis when he had said hello to Maud, and no front teeth either.

Dot was raging now, her face scrunched up as though she was sucking lemons. 'Apparently he's having his teeth replaced at the dentist in the morning, but knowing my mother's friends, they will probably be blue with a pattern on them. Where on earth do they find these people? He'll likely be living with us all and under my parents' watchful patronage by the end of next week. They adore impoverished artists and find them everywhere!'

Maud tried to smother a laugh and Dot sent her a very cross stare, so she perched her bottom on the surprisingly comfortable edge of the dressing table, wishing she didn't have quite so much padding of her own. 'Your family are wonderful, but they are slightly unusual…' she said, carefully choosing her words. She walked over to the tap and tried to smooth out a stray kink in her hair and topped up her neutral lipstick, making sure the gloss was even.

'Tom seems nice,' said Dot absently. 'I'm still mad at my parents and trying hard not to waltz back into the restaurant and strangle them both with my father's stupid cravat.' Maud thought that was hilarious as Dot was still wearing a parrot on her head, but it had slid down and was nestled just above her ear, with its beak in her hair. Maud's eyes started to water as she tried to supress her mirth, as Dot was visibly upset and she was being a bad friend.

Maud wiped her eyes and sighed, before pulling up a spare stool from along the wall and trying to sit near Dot, but the skirts surged forward as Dot moved to make room and there was little space. Maud stared in awe as Dot puckered up and applied bright orange lipstick to her lips before smacking them together, checking her face for imperfections and straightening the parrot on her head. She looked perfect to Maud. Remembering what Dot had said about Tom, she paused for a moment and pictured his face. 'I haven't had much of a chance to talk to him yet. On the way here he grilled me about Nate and you guys.'

Dot shrugged sympathetically. 'My family to tend to hog the conversation.'

Maud stared at her reflection in the mirror and wished her flushed cheeks would stop being so embarrassing and showing her up, and that her clothes weren't so boring, for once. 'I'm not sure Nate is thrilled to have me here either.'

Dot slapped her palm to her forehead and rolled her eyes. 'I forgot about him. That's my fault too,' she explained apologetically.

'It is? Maybe you're right and you shouldn't have invited us, although Tom's having a blast.'

'I should have just invited you,' sighed Dot theatrically, waving her feet around in circles, as her funny square-toed shoes with buckles were pinching her toes.

Maud looked confused. 'Don't you like Tom? I think he's gorgeous,' she said defensively.

'He looks nice... I haven't had a chance to speak to him yet, but if you like him, I'm sure I will too.' Maud looked even more confused now, but Dot carried on. 'It's just that I was a bit fed up with Nate for giving our work number to random women and then expecting me to field his calls, so when he asked me who you were, I promised to try and remember where we met. As I told you, I don't often forget a name.'

'So…?'

'I looked you up and arrived on your doorstep, as a favour to him. Then when you said you had a boyfriend, I thought it was good that someone could show him not every female on the planet fancies him and will fall at his feet because he asked them to.'

Maud was horrified, and she saw the realisation dawn on Dot's face that her big mouth had gotten away with her again. 'You used me!'

'I'm really sorry, and for what it's worth I feel like a complete bitch,' said Dot, looking contrite. 'I didn't mean to drag you into this. I really like you and was surprised that we got on so well. I didn't want you to be another notch on his bed post.'

Maud sat back in shock. 'You really don't like him, do you?'

Dot looked astounded at this thought. 'I adore him. It's just that he's used to everyone fawning over him, and for a little sister it can become tiresome. He's so good at everything and everyone worships him, even me. Once I found you, I wanted you for my own. Plus, you already had Tom. Nate seduces all my friends.'

'I'm not a pet, Dot,' said Maud, fury creeping into her voice. Dot tilted her head in interest at this new fiery side of Maud, before hanging it in shame. 'Why would Nate want to know who I was anyway?' Maud was really stumped by this. Maybe he wanted to advise her on art or something?

Dot shook her head in exasperation, as if Maud could be really thick sometimes. 'Because you're gorgeous.' She looked at Maud's glorious chest and small waist and was frustrated that all Maud could see was plainness. 'You've had been hiding your assets for so long that you don't see them, including your talent as a painter, if the competition piece is anything to go by. Your parents have a lot to answer for, but then,' Dot sighed, 'so have mine.'

Maud was still confused. 'Surely Nate doesn't fancy me?' Then it dawned on her and she wrinkled her pretty little nose in disgust. 'Does he just chat up anyone with breasts?'

Dot threw her hands up in the air in surrender. 'He only

picks women he finds interesting and wants to sleep with. They are all gorgeous and boringly in awe of him. Why do you think Tom fancies you? He's a good-looking boy.' Dot tapped her long fingernails, which had tiny bulldogs painted on them, against the marble sink, while she waited for Maud to think about it. 'For a smart girl, you're incredibly thick.'

Maud scratched her head. 'Well, almost everyone else at work is either married or seeing someone, so I guess he didn't have too much choice.' Anger blazed in Dot's eyes and she strode over, grabbed Maud's hips and swivelled her to face her reflection in the tall gilt mirror over the sink. As Maud tried to turn away, Dot held her still, then on impulse reached in front of Maud's blouse and heard her gasp in shock as she undid the top three buttons. Maud's chest surged forward and then settled comfortably into the deep V shape of the fabric. The effect was immediately sensual and changed her look completely from tight-lipped to pouty. Maud's eyes went wide in surprise and embarrassment and she quickly tried to do the buttons up, but Dot slapped her hands away, which made her skin blaze red.

Dot grasped her hand and was about to leave, when she plainly had another idea and rummaged in her handbag for a red lipstick, slicked some onto Maud's protesting lips, ran her hand under the tap and scrunched her hair into soft demi-waves and stood back to admire her work. Maud's jaw dropped in horror, as Dot knew her hair had taken ages to tame earlier, but she clearly didn't care about someone else's time. Refusing to acknowledge the fury rising in Maud's eyes and grabbing her hand once again, Dot ignored her dragging feet and pushed her friend towards the door. 'It's an experiment,' she said breezily. 'I bet Tom talks to you now, however famous my parents are.'

As they approached the table, which was by now heaving with fragrant dishes of mouth-watering food, Maud hesitated as she hadn't ordered anything, didn't have a clue what the choices were and everyone had moved seats so that the only spaces left were next to Nate and the cute blond man beside him. She glanced sideways and noticed Dot enjoying the look of surprise on both Nate and Tom's faces when they saw her transformation. Tom stood up when they arrived, but then sat down again when he realised he was penned in. He gave in with good grace and a shrug in Maud's direction. She was happy to see he was enjoying himself and returned his smile as the redhead to his left touched his arm and leaned in to hear more about his teaching career.

Nate's eyes turned almost black as Maud approached and he stood and pulled out a seat so that Dot had to sit next to Elliott, who happily poured them both a huge glass of rich red wine and drew Dot into a conversation as soon as her bottom, and voluminous skirts, touched the seat.

Nate's gaze wandered over Maud and she felt her skin grow hot and uncomfortable. 'What happened to you in there? You went in virginal and came out as if you'd been ravaged.'

Maud blushed furiously. 'I was… by Dot!' She plucked up the courage to raise her eyes to meet his. She wasn't used to being the centre of such intense scrutiny, then remembered she lived every day with her mother's watchful interference and her shoulders sagged a little. She noted that Tom had stopped talking and was watching them with interest, so she mustered up a smile for him. Why had she let Dot talk her into embarrassing herself again? She knew it was a mistake and should have stood her ground for once.

Nate relaxed back into his seat and watched the emotions play across Maud's face. 'Ah… Dot's a freak of nature. I know how controlling she can be. I've had to put up with it for as long as I can remember.' He smiled to show he was joking and it was said without malice to put her at ease. 'She's a whirlwind that keeps us all under control. She thinks I'm a lost cause in the fashion department and tells me I look like a tramp.' Maud looked at him from under her eyelashes and noted his crisp dark shirt and trousers. He looked far from a vagrant to her, but she did giggle and look up finally.

'So who is your date?' he asked.

Maud was surprised at his candour. Surely he wasn't flirting with her? Dot must have been mistaken when she said he had the hots for her. Maybe he didn't like strangers arriving at a family dinner unannounced and decided to play with them as punishment? She gripped her hands in her lap and tried to stem the confusion he made her feel just by looking at her. He was only Dot's older brother.

'Who's yours?' she countered daringly, trying to look stern and stop herself panting and shaking when he stared directly into her eyes.

Nate leaned even further back in his chair, so she thought he might fall off, and he laughed uproariously, as his father had earlier in the evening, which made everyone stop talking and look their way. Maud shrunk into her seat a little. She hated being the centre of attention.

'Touché,' grinned Nate, openly enjoying himself, his earlier anger seeming to dissipate. 'I wouldn't have brought a date if I had known you were going to be here,' he moved forward near to her ear, so no one else could hear. 'Dot didn't tell me she had found you. You've been on my mind a lot and I've been wondering where you came from. I thought maybe I'd dreamt you,' he said, his warm breath touching her neck so that she wanted to curl into him and savour his words.

Her pulse began beating erratically and she licked her lips. She didn't know if he was arrogant, wishful, in lust, or enjoyed playing games with feeble women. What the hell had happened to her life? 'Surprise,' she said feebly and sent another smile to Tom who was looking her way again.

Nate grinned in satisfaction and spooned some of the sizzling meat and fluffy rice from the pretty serving dishes onto the artisan china plate in front of her, not asking what she liked to eat or if she wanted any food. He was evidently so used to people acquiescing to his will that she began to feel a bit mutinous. He faltered when he saw her look and, for some reason, this seemed to amuse him further. 'You don't like the food?'

Maud raised her nose haughtily. 'I'm sure I'll love it. Luckily I eat anything, I was a feral child,' she joked. She felt like she'd scored a point, but he was still smiling at her, which made her salivate for more than the food and her palms began

81

to sweat. 'What is it?' She gestured towards the dish on the table with a tip of her head.

Nate seemed to find this hilarious and forked up some of the fragrant meat and began to feed her, so that she had no choice but to be gracious and not stamp on his foot. Flavour burst into her mouth and she immediately wanted more. The marinade sent spirals of ecstasy into her tastebuds and beads of sweat formed on her skin as she almost groaned out loud.

Maud flushed. Nate looked like he really wanted to kiss her, but he bunched his fists and glared at Dot instead. She seemed to be able to read his mind and gave him a triumphant look, before sending Tom a mega-watt smile that made him cough. She quickly jumped up to sit in the seat next to him as the redhead left the table in search of the ladies' room, turning away from Nate.

Nate trapped Maud's eyes again. 'You're wearing my favourite shoes.'

'Huh?' she looked down at her feet. 'You have a pair?'

Nate laughed loudly again. 'They're my favourite – on you…'

'Oh.' Maud blushed furiously again. What was it about this man that made her behave like a rampant teenager? She wanted to climb over the table, sit on his lap and snog his face off. How rude of her, as her new date was sitting just across the table.

'So tell me, how do you know my sister?' He poked his tongue out affectionately at Dot who had moved further down the table. She turned and saw the gesture, then returned it with glee, which finally made Maud smile. She'd lost out on sibling rivalry and affection as she was an only child, but Daisy had two sisters and a brother and they were constantly arguing, hugging, supporting and annoying the hell out of each other.

Maud thought about telling him how she had really met Dot, as the story would probably make him laugh again and she was already addicted to the sound. Instead she improvised carefully. 'We met through our love of art. We're both passionate about what we do, but we're not very confident in the results.'

Nate frowned at this and Maud thought he was going to take her hand, but he reached for his wine glass instead and took a sip. She was strangely disappointed and took a huge gulp of her own wine, almost snorting it back out again as it was so strong. She usually bought the cheap stuff from the supermarket and had thought there was no difference from an expensive bottle, but now she knew different. This wine was heaven.

Nate was looking across the table at Dot again as she threw her head back and laughed at something Tom said. 'Dot's not short on confidence. With her art, she just hasn't found the right medium for her style yet. She can express herself well, but she needs to stop trying so hard with her painting. It's completely forced and it shows in her work. She's vivacious but her paintings are not like that.'

Maud looked across at Dot too, but she knew that the bright exterior hid a soft centre. Dot pretended to be so outrageous. 'She's not as confident as you think.'

Nate looked stung by her words and Maud could have kicked herself. Who was she to tell Dot's bother that she knew her better than he did? 'Sorry,' flushed Maud. 'I didn't mean to be insulting. It's just that Dot is a bit in awe of your talents. You're hard to live up to.'

Nate fleetingly put his hand on her leg, seemingly without thinking, which almost made her jump out of her skin in shock, before he gently kissed the back of her wrist and then placed her hand back onto her lap. 'Dot doesn't need to live up to me. She's perfect as she is.' Maud could see he meant what he said, but the skin where his hand had touched her leg felt like it had just been branded.

He moved closer and whispered into her ear again and his mouth, oh so close to her neck, made her shiver. 'So are you...' he whispered daringly.

Chapter Sixteen

Maud woke up with a throbbing headache and winced as she tried to pry her eyes open. They felt like sandpaper had been wedged between the eyelids and her eyeballs and she drew in a sharp breath of pain. Nate had been refilling her glass of wine all last night and she'd gained confidence and managed to speak to most of the people at dinner, even the redhead, who was someone Nate's parents had introduced him to the month before. It looked as though they treated him the same way they did Dot, and foisted friends on him at every opportunity. He could hardly grumble, if they looked like the redhead, whose name she'd found out was Ruby. Maud had a sneaking suspicion she had died her hair to match her name, as the colour was just too perfect. Perhaps she would have enough courage to dye her hair one day, but to be honest, she quite liked her natural golden tones, with the wispy lighter highlights that she was born with, she just wished her hair would behave and stay poker straight, so that she didn't have to waste hours taming it.

She couldn't remember getting home or even saying goodbye to anyone, but she vaguely recalled a fleeting sound of raucous laughter as she regaled them with the artistic abilities of her class of seven-year-olds and then flinched, as she hated being the centre of any crowd and had never held anyone's attention with interesting tales or adventures before. Dot's parents had cuddled her and welcomed her to the family at some point too. Did this mean she was now in some sort of artist sect? She really should find out more about people before she invaded their lives and became one of them.

She groaned and tried to lift her head off the pillow, before rapidly sinking back down again into its blissful featheriness, as pain ricocheted through her temples and she started to feel sick. What must Tom think of her? He'd seemed to be pretty merry himself, from what little she could recall. Then she remembered him pulling her onto the little dance floor at the back of the restaurant. It had been a dark and sensuous place and she had melted into him, although he had been virtually propping her up and laughing into her ear as he drew her to him, but then Nate had appeared, shaken Tom's hand and told them the party was leaving. It had been so embarrassing as Tom had tried to pay for their meal, as had she, but Nate had waved them away and said they were his family's guests, which made Tom glow with pride and her feel a bit dizzy. Tom seemed relieved, but Maud hated being indebted to anyone and would rather have paid her own way.

She tried again to lift her weary head and she managed gently to pull herself into a sitting position with her hands tucked under her backside for extra stability. She waited a moment for the room to stop spinning and then noticed a glass of water on her side table. She reached for it gratefully, proud of her foresight, then frowned as the glass was sitting on a folded, hand-written note.

She leaned forward slowly and tried to focus on the slanted handwriting, then huffed and picked it up to hold it in front of her nose to work out what it said when the words stopped moving around on the page like little ants scurrying home. That didn't work either, but then she realised that she'd automatically put on the glasses that sat on her bedside table and she must have fallen asleep in her contact lenses. Yuck. She took the glasses off and cursed herself for being so lazy and forgetful. She never slept without taking her lenses out, as she was half blind without them but they stuck to her eyes if she left them in too long.

Squinting at the note again, she saw that it said, 'sweet dreams. Thought you might need a glass of water in the morning. I have a feeling I may be a thorn in your side. I left your shoes by the bed as you tried to throw them out of the car window. Love the mural in your bedroom, by the way. The bed looks comfy too...' It was signed Nate in a lilting text and had

85

a small kiss just under his name. Wincing, she peeked over the side of the bed and saw her shoes with the roses winding around the heels sitting prettily next to her bedside cabinet. She groaned out loud and slumped back onto the bed. It was all coming back to her now.

She recalled dancing with Tom and rubbing herself up and down his body, then Nate refusing to let them pay for the meal and offering to give them a lift home as he was driving and had only had one small glass of wine. She had protested and tried to recall if she'd seen Nate actually take more than a sip of wine, as she'd been focussing on his mouth quite a lot, but she hadn't. Tom had been ecstatic about the offer of a chauffeured ride home and jumped at the chance to get Nate on his own as they hadn't spoken at the dinner party. His face was flushed with the excitement of the evening and he went on and on about how extraordinary Nate's work was and how he had started his own modest collection of art and was a patron of local artistry. It should have made Maud cringe with embarrassment, but she had for some reason found it ridiculously funny. She had joshed Nate about his big ego as if they were the best of friends and, instead of getting angry with her, he seemed to find everything she said or did highly amusing. He had drawn the line when she had tried to throw her shoes out of the window, though, and had given her a stern look, which she had giggled at. Then he'd handed her his coat and she'd immediately fallen asleep and probably dribbled all over it as Tom was already passed out on the back seat and snoring loudly.

The whole evening had been a bit surreal and she picked up the note and read it again. She hoped she'd been gracious enough to thank Dotty and her parents for inviting her to the dinner in the first place, but had a feeling that she'd just noisily kissed them all on the lips and then rubbed noses with them as Nate had jokingly told her that this was how they greeted each other. On the way home he'd told her he had been messing with her and that his parents would never forget her. Once again, she should have been mortified, but was so sloshed that she'd laughed out loud and grabbed his face and kissed his lips and rubbed noses with him while they waited at some traffic lights, before she passed out. Oh man, why was she such an idiot?

Nate must have dropped Tom home and then come into her house. She wondered what he thought of it, after the amazing places he must usually hang out in. The house wouldn't tell him much as it kept her secrets well. Her bedroom, on the other hand, was her inner sanctum and it represented everything she loved: nature, the sea, colours and textures. It must have been a shock coming in here after the stark white walls outside. The thought of him lying her in bed and taking his time to look around her bedroom made her face flame and her stomach protest, so she grabbed it and rubbed it gently to try and ease the ache inside.

She had caught the train to the restaurant and the gallery opening. She presumed that Nate lived near both, so why would he drive her all the way out of town? Maybe he saw Tom as a new customer, although Dot had suggested he wanted to play with her. Maybe he enjoyed picking up waifs and strays as much as his parents did?

She gingerly looked down at her body and let out a hiss of air when she realised Nate had eased her out of her dress. She hung her head in shame as she remembered flinging her arms around him as she stood there in her very colourful underwear, thanking him for bringing her home. Ever the polite school teacher. Bloody hell. What would he think of her? He had been so kind bringing her home, but she had a boyfriend... of sorts… and had literally thrown herself at another man on their first date. Plus, although she wore boringly plain clothes on the outside, her magpie tendencies didn't stop at dresses and jumpers, all of her underwear was stunningly beautiful with delicate lace and intricate designs in strong, bold colours. No one had seen her underwear in a while and this particular habit had only begun fairly recently anyway, as she decided that she was the only one likely to see it, so she could be as bold and racy as she liked. Nate must think she was some sort of secret dominatrix.

She held her breath and turned the note over to the back and saw he had drawn a quick sketch of a very sexy lady in red-hot knickers and bra. How un-gentlemanly of him, she fumed, but then decided he'd had the good grace to refuse her sort of offer, when she'd draped herself all over him. She didn't know whether to be affronted that he'd turned her down or grateful that he'd left her to sleep. The little sketch was sultry and suggestive, and oh, so personal, so she took one last look at it and opened her side table drawer to slip it inside. She wondered how many women woke up to this type of note from a famous artist. With a sinking heart she realised that it was probably quite a lot.

Chapter Seventeen

Stripping off the offending underwear and throwing on her old dressing gown, Maud slowly walked into her kitchen, before frowning and retracing her steps as her mobile phone rang in the black handbag next to her bed. Picking it up she flinched at the bright, breezy, and very loud voice.

'Maud? It's me.' Maud trundled back into the kitchen and felt her muscles tense at the excruciating noise from the voice on the line. She felt her way along the kitchen counter until she reached the medicine drawer and grabbed a packet of headache tablets, before ramming them into her mouth dry and then gagging on the chalky taste.

'Me who?'

'It's Dot. Did I wake you up?' Dot sounded far too spritely to have been at the same dinner as Maud the previous evening. Maybe she was used to drinking buckets of wine? The delicate glasses had practically held half a bottle each and Nate and Elliott had topped her glass up all night. Maud thought of Elliott's boyish good looks and kind humour and wondered how Dot could be so lucky, surrounded by such masculine beauty every day. Maud tried to clear her head and think.

'Uh, no... I don't think so...' How the hell could Dot be awake so early in the morning? Maud very slowly turned her whole body towards the round clock on the wall, as she knew moving her head was not such a good idea right now, and realised that it was actually past midday.

Dot suddenly sounded concerned. 'Are you ok? Do you need me to pop round?' Maud felt a wave of nausea overcome her and she leaned an arm on the cold granite surface of her countertop to steady her heaving stomach.

'I'm fine,' she ground out. 'How can you sound so perky?'

'Well, I didn't drink as much wine as you, although Nate did have to hide the last bottle after you tried to dance on the table,' she laughed.

'Nate was the one filing up my glass all night. Well, him and Elliott, who is so hot by the way.'

Maud could imagine Dot frowning and picturing Elliott's face. 'I suppose he is pretty gorgeous, but I've never looked at him that way. He's my 'other brother'. Loads of women like him, but he's a bit more selective than Nate.' Maud flinched as Dot carried on, 'I haven't seen Elliott with a woman for a while. Do you fancy him?'

Maud grabbed a glass and ran it under the tap for a fresh drink, in the hope of soaking up some of the residual wine, or diluting it at the very least, then gulped it down and pressed the cool glass to her face. 'He's certainly easy on the eye and such a sweetheart, but I've just started dating Tom. I got the impression Elliott has his eye on someone special.' She downed the last dregs of the water and slid down onto the floor with her legs out in front of her, and tapped the speaker button on her phone before placing it gently on the floor next to her. She kept her back straight and pressed into the cupboards for support and held her palm to her forehead to see if she had a fever.

'Really?' boomed Dot, making Maud wince again even though the phone was on the floor. 'He hasn't mentioned anyone.'

That's because the lady in question is you, thought Maud. It was so obvious to everyone else, even an outsider could see how smitten he was with Dot. Unfortunately, it seemed that Dot was totally oblivious to his ardour. Poor Elliott. 'What can I do for you, Dot?'

Dot paused for a moment as if she couldn't decide what to say. 'I know we've only known each other for a month, if you count the gallery opening and then me turning up on your doorstep. I admire your artwork, even if it doesn't quite hit all of the criteria for its own gallery show,' she babbled candidly, having no idea how her words were like a punch in the guts to Maud, who was incredulous at how rude Dot could be without realising. 'I believe that you're honest with everyone other than your parents, which makes you and me almost twins! I need you to sober up and come to my studio, like we agreed a couple of weeks ago. I've got something to show you.'

Maud's ears picked up on the importance of that last sentence and she grabbed the phone and put it to her ear, before realising it was still on speaker and biting her tongue in shock when Dot spoke again, making her jump and drop the phone on her lap. 'Maud… are you there?'

Maud let out a breath when she saw how lucky she had been that her phone hadn't bounced onto the floor and quickly turned the speaker off before answering. 'I'd love to. Tell me the address and when you want me to come and I'll rearrange my busy schedule for you,' she tried to joke, head pounding.

'Wonderful.' Dot seemed really excited now, reeling off the address of her studio and the time she wanted Maud to arrive. The details went in one of Maud's ears and straight out the other as she tried to concentrate. 'Text me,' was all she said as she slumped even further down, using her arm as a pillow and rested her weary head.

Chapter Eighteen

Dot touched her head against the cool glass of the window and decided she must be mad like the rest of her family. She hadn't even let her own brother into her studio space for weeks, and now she had recklessly invited Maud, whom she barely knew. It was weird how they were so different, but the feeling of having a family that confused the hell out of them connected them in some way. They had grabbed onto each other like they were kindred spirits, even though they were actually polar opposites, but they had discovered they kept each other sane and enjoyed each other's company. Dot usually made friends with people from the gallery or hanging around her parents' house, as this was easier than making an effort with strangers, but it was getting monotonous and she was desperate for change.

She had made sure that her brother and parents were out on appointments with the media and clients before she asked Maud over. Her eyes darted up and down the street from her vantage point at the first floor window of her studio, which was one above Nate's, in the trendy, Bohemian end of town. He had a flat above the gallery too, but the family tended to descend there if they had an exhibition on, which she knew drove him mad at times, so he'd bought this place and offered the other studio space to her.

It would be just like her parents to turn up unannounced today, or for them to ignore an appointment, if they were distracted by something else on their way there. They were notorious for drifting into little galleries and cafés, making the best of friends with the owners and leaving a complete furore in their wake as people recognised them and began taking photos. She loved them dearly, but they were not easy to live with. Her mother was constantly checking on her and second-guessing her work, even though Dot had proved her worth time and again. Her dad said it was because they were worrying she was overstretched, but she felt they were just running scared in case she left and represented someone else, when she was the only person who knew their work inside and out.

She understood and was quite flattered that they wanted to keep her to themselves, but they were suffocating her. She wondered what they would say when she finally showed them her current work and explained that she dreamt about representing other artists, including her own work, whether they appreciated it or not. Surely she could find someone who could see promise in her designs?

Finally, she spotted a worried and slightly tired-looking Maud slowly walking down the street, examining the door numbers above each one she passed, before moving on. She was dressed in a knee length black skirt and a lightweight black jumper, which came up to her neck. She would be horrified to learn that this disguise actually accentuated her bountiful curves and made it difficult for anyone to look anywhere else but her heaving bosom. Maud's chest wasn't that big, but as she had a small waist, womanly hips and wore tops that went up to her neck most of the time, her boobs looked enormous.

Dot opened the window and hollered down the road until Maud finally stopped and glanced up to see where the noise was coming from. She smiled and seemed to sigh in relief before hurrying Dot's way. Dot braced herself for another disappointment once her friend stepped over the threshold and appraised her work, but gritted her teeth and went to buzz Maud in and open herself up to the possibility of failure once again.

Chapter Nineteen

Maud, whose hangover had abated slightly, had a wide grin on her face when she raced up the steps and came in, but then stifled a laugh when she saw the big square holes that had been cut out of Dot's long-sleeved top, revealing a bright orange and green fitted vest underneath. The combination was hideous.

'Don't laugh at my outfit when you're wearing that top. It makes every man in a twenty-foot radius stop and drool over your bazookas,' sniped Dot, who seemed fidgety and looked ready to run for the hills. Maud's face fell in shock and Dot had the grace to hang her head in shame briefly, before she laughed to show she was joking and pulled Maud further in, slamming the sleek metal door behind her. Maud started to stutter about her clothes, but Dot shut her up by handing her a full glass of white wine that she'd poured and turned her towards her studio area.

Maud stared in awe, studying walls full of the most awful artworks she had ever seen. She hadn't wanted more wine after last night, but changed her mind and took a hefty slug. Poor Dot.

'I know, I know,' said Dot, as Maud scrunched up her face, then tried to flatten it out again with a neutral look so that Dot didn't get such a walloping punch of rejection. Dot steered Maud forward, covering her eyes until they stood at the end of the room in front of a little workstation and pedestal. Dot told Maud to stand still and dropped her hand. 'This is the reason I bought you here.'

Maud opened her eyes slowly and then they went wide and she nearly fell over in surprise. Dot looked absolutely crestfallen. Maud guessed Dot felt she'd finally found her creative muse, and once again she'd failed. 'It's awful, isn't it?' Dot asked in a flat voice, looking like her world was crashing down. Maud could almost see her dreams evaporate before eyes that were brimming with glistening tears.

Maud rocked back on her heels and tried to steady herself before she dropped her wine. She took another hefty sip, then realised the torture Dot must be going through. She herself felt the same thing every time she unveiled a new painting before her parents' critical eyes.

In front of Maud was a tall white pedestal stand with a single piece of jewellery nestled at the centre. It was an exquisitely crafted belt buckle in bronze wire, but the disturbing thing about it was that it was a near replica of one of Maud's own paintings. The central wire was wrapped intricately to form the face of a badger, like Maud's most recent work, and splashes of enamel had been used to bring it to life. She took a steadying breath. 'It's beautiful, Dot.'

Dot let out the breath she'd been holding and her eyes lit up. 'Really?'

'But...'

'Oh, you've seen them then?'

'Them?'

'The gorgeous little paintings that have been left round, in the name of love.'

Maud smiled, as this sounded far more romantic than her idea of finding someone who didn't hate her style. 'Um... Yes, I have.'

'I suppose most people will have seen them by now. I was going to ask you to help me find the artist, as they seem to be local to you.' Dot frowned, as Maud appeared really alarmed by this titbit of information for some reason.

'They do?' she squawked, her mouth suddenly bone dry.

'I cross-referenced the drop off points and your home village is central. I thought maybe they were starting from a base and working outwards. Of course I could be completely wrong, but I decided that it was a good place to begin, as I had nothing else to go on. The artist is a complete mystery for now.'

Bloody hell. Maul felt her stomach curl up and die. If Dot had virtually found her, so could everyone else with half a brain. Maud had been so stupid to mess about like this. She envisaged people gossiping about her, and knew she would have to stop this stupid and dangerous game she was playing right now.

Dot spoke quietly. 'I was trying to find my confidence as an artist, but this has made things worse. I feel like a fraud and a copycat,' she tried to explain, a pleading note in her voice, which was so unusual for an exuberant character like Dot, who usually did as she pleased. 'It's weird, but I've been hiding up here and trying to release some creativity by making jewellery for a while now. I don't let anyone into my studio.'

'Not even Nate?'

'Especially Nate! I don't want him to see me with another failed attempt to fit in.'

Maud felt the knot of tension in her shoulders begin to ease a little. At least no one else had seen Dot's work. 'Why emulate the paintings?' She really wanted to know, as the detailing on the buckle was so beautiful that Maud's hands were itching to pick it up and study it from every angle.

Dot sighed and pulled out the chair next to her soldering desk and flopped down onto it with utter despondency. 'I tried my own style, but as usual it was awful. The paintings inspired me and this was the first piece I've been proud of, but I am an idiot as it's a rip-off. I, of all people, should know better – I'm the one who sells original art by talented people for a living. I know how bad my family feel if another artist tries to copy their work. It's happened to more than half of them. I wasn't going to sell this, I just wanted to make it and enjoy looking at it.' She gulped a huge mouthful of wine and swung her legs up onto her workstation, which wasn't easy, as it was set up quite high and she almost toppled off.

'I hoped it might inspire me to use nature or animals in other pieces, if you thought my new style was good enough,' said Dot, through another big mouthful of wine.

Maud took a thoughtful sip of her own wine and tried to decide if she was annoyed or incredibly flattered that finally someone thought enough of her work to emulate it. Sighing, she decided it was annoying, and Dot would need nurturing to find her own unique style. She was definitely a gifted artist if this piece was anything to go by. No one had even liked Maud's paintings a few weeks ago and now here one of them was, gilded and made into something women might wear. The thought gave Maud a thrill of pleasure, as maybe one day in her wildest dreams, she might be able to commission someone like Dot to create a collection of jewellery based on her art.

She gently started to pick up the buckle, then stopped and turned to Dot to see if it was ok to touch her work. Dot's cheeks were flushed with embarrassment, but she just shrugged her shoulders to acquiesce. Maud brought the delicate piece of art to her face and studied it carefully. It really was charming and she couldn't believe her own art had inspired such refined work. 'I think that it's a real likeness to the painting in the paper,' she said carefully, 'but there's no mistaking the craftsmanship, Dot, it's exquisite.'

Dot spun round in her chair and stood up in surprise. 'Really?'

Maud smiled gently to her friend, knowing how important her next words would be. 'Really. You don't need to emulate anyone else, Dot. With talent like this you can make designs of your own. I bet if you drew some leaves or animals, they would look gorgeous as buckles.'

'That's the problem,' Dot grimaced and plonked herself down again desperately. 'I can't draw.'

Maud was taken aback and thought about the dilemma for a moment. 'But you can draw with wire. Look at what you've created. I'm a teacher and I draw, so I can help you.'

Dot looked astounded and hopeful. 'You'll teach me? My parents tried to foist loads of their painter friends on me, but they just scared me witless with their own ability. It can be so intimidating drawing in front of a proper artist.' Dot cocked her head to one side and considered Maud. 'It's a great idea,' she said sloshing more wine into her mouth. 'I should have tried having lessons from someone who isn't a great artist, no insult intended,' said Dot without malice, as Maud almost choked on her wine.

Dot continued speaking her thoughts out loud. 'I mean, I'm sure your art is good and all that, but it's not like my family's art... no offence.'

Maud leaned on the pedestal in exasperation. She'd just offered to help Dot after she'd copied her work, and now she was insulting her talents like everyone else, and thinking that by saying 'no offence', that her comments were magically not massively offensive. Maud had fleetingly considered trusting Dot with her secret, but she definitely wasn't telling her now. She thought about letting her stew on her own too, but the teacher in her had found a new pupil. She wanted to prove to Dot's parents that their daughter wasn't a lost cause, the way she wished there was some way she could prove it to hers.

Chapter Twenty

Maud dragged her feet as she walked along the path to her parents' house. She stopped and looked up at her childhood home, but didn't feel any real connection to it. The front garden was manicured and the house was clean and solid, but there was nothing to inspire an inquisitive mind here. Everything was rigid and had its place. Even the shed at the bottom of the square garden was freshly painted every year and, as her dad wasn't much of a handyman, the only tools in there were for the garden, alphabetically organised and hanging on the wall. Even the fold-down mower hung its head in shame every time it coughed up a mouthful of grass and deposited it on the shed floor.

Reaching up and pressing the doorbell, Maud could hear tinkling laughter from inside and her stomach sank further. Her mum had summoned her to Sunday lunch, which would last for hours and have three formal courses. Laughter inside meant that they had guests and guests meant Maud would have to sit there and listen to her mother's bragging and not vomit. Her shoulders ached from all of the drawing she was doing lately and she smiled at the memory of the few times she had sat in the park with Dot and taught her how to simplify what she saw and capture it in a sketch that she could interpret with wire. Maud hadn't considered teaching adults, and had certainly never thought of giving art lessons, but it was a new possibility she might explore one day. She was already qualified as a teaching assistant, but could take some classes herself first to make sure she had the skills to set up structured lessons. A strange thing had happened through working with Dot. She realised she really did have the ability to paint and draw. By walking through the steps of line and form with Dot, she had recaptured the basics and knew she had them mastered. From now on, her parents' opinion wouldn't hurt so much, she had decided, but standing waiting for them to answer the door, she wasn't so sure she had the confidence to tell them yet.

Dot was still so wrapped up in her newfound skill that she was oblivious to the turmoil Maud was going through with her own art. Although Dot was working hard on her designs, she had persuaded Maud to sketch some square buckles with plants and animals hiding inside for her to use in her first exhibition and had insisted Maud keep the first belt she had made, as she would never be able to sell it anyway. Dot had said it would act as a sort of barter system for the drawing lessons Maud was giving her, as she refused to take any money from Dot for her time. Maud had eventually taken the buckle and reverently hidden it in her wardrobe with her other treasures, but she often took it out and sat and stared at the beauty of Dot's craftsmanship and the painting which seemed to have sprung to life on the surface. Maud hoped Dot's new collection would be as good. If only Dot knew she had handed the treasure back to original artist. Maud hadn't plucked up the nerve to tell her yet and the timing had just never seemed right to bring it into conversation. Maud had now left it too long.

She was jolted out of her reverie when her father opened the door. She had no idea of how long they had left her standing on the doorstep whilst they chatted merrily, but she was sure they hadn't hurried along. She gave her dad a warm hug as he welcomed her inside and was surprised to find her mother almost on the edge of her seat, and straining to hear what the other couple in the room were saying. Maud recognised them as fairly new residents to the street, about her parents' age or maybe a bit younger, but from her mother's bright-eyed look as she shushed her and made a waving motion to the seat by the window, Maud could tell the gossip was good.

Marcy and Don stood up politely and broke their conversation to greet Maud and her mother suddenly jumped up and followed suit, swooping in and checking Maud's appearance, then giving her a quick hug and sitting back down again, looking expectantly at Marcy who giggled and rushed back too, as if she had the most exciting news to share.

'Well?' asked her mother. Maud scooched to the edge of her seat too. She was here now, so she might as well hear what they were all talking about and, from the aroma coming from the kitchen, it seemed that her mother had timed dinner impeccably as usual and the first course, prawns in a seafood dressing gently placed on a bed of crisp lettuce, or prawn mayonnaise as Maud called it, would be ready within the usual twenty minutes of guests arriving. Neighbours being here could throw off a normal Sunday lunch, but her mother had either invited them to join them, in which case it had been planned for weeks and no one had told her, or the gossip was so good that they would sit down exactly two minutes late.

'Well,' said Marcy with a complicit smile. 'Have you heard all of the talk about this incredible artist who is leaving their work on park benches?' To Maud's surprise her mother nodded earnestly and her even her dad looked interested. 'People are staking out parks to try and find out who it is and photographers are hiding in bushes,' she continued, waving her hands around with glee, making Rosemary edge even closer while Maud's stomach began to churn. Maud started wringing her own hands in her lap and hoped she wouldn't be sick on her mother's taupe carpet. She'd been too busy to leave more than one artwork out lately, as Dot was so demanding. Maud was enjoying having an artist friend in her life, so she'd put up with it. She'd been a bit slapdash this time as she'd been in a hurry, and had left it in a really local park.

'The latest update from Nev...' Marcy paused for dramatic effect and Maud's mum cut in and mentioned that Marcy knew a well-known journalist who often told her stories while she styled his hair at the town's fancy new salon, 'is that they think they've worked out that the artist is from Twigleston!'

Maud sprang up at the same moment as her mother. Rosemary clasped her hands to her chest in glee, while Maud looked on in horror and confusion. Her mother hated art. 'How exciting to have such a talented artist in the area. Maybe it will bring other celebrities into Twigleston and the house prices will rise, benefitting everyone.'

Maud felt bile at the back of her throat. Her mother would never move from the house she had spent the last thirty years making perfect and she had mountains of Maud's paintings in the wardrobe upstairs, which Maud had found when she went to her old room to collect a book the previous year. The sight had cut her heart in two and she'd quickly shut the wardrobe door and rested her head against it briefly, before rushing back downstairs lest anyone noticed she had gone anywhere other than the bathroom.

Excusing herself as Marcy and Rosemary prattled on, and marching into the kitchen to see if her anniversary gift had been shoved into the cupboard too, she was slightly mollified to see it had been placed, as promised, in the darkest corner of the kitchen on a little shelf, but her mother had placed a plant pot in front of it and the fronds of the fern pretty much obscured the surface of the painting. Maud quietly seethed in anger. She was thinking of telling her parents that she had had some success with her work, but hearing them go on about a visiting artist making money for the town and how it would benefit the area, she decided that she might actually have her work evaluated by a professional. If it was worth anything at all, then her parents could be sitting on thousands of pounds of art that would never see the light of day. While her parents were distracted she squared her shoulders and decided it was time to act. Running up the stairs two at a time, she flung open the wardrobe doors, grabbed as many canvases as she could safely carry and did repeated journeys to her car, until the boot and whole back seat were covered in pieces of art. She flung the pale blue woollen rug she had on the back seat of her car over the ones there and then shut the door and doubled over as she was out of breath. Making herself stand up, she rushed back inside to see if anyone had missed her. They hadn't. She'd only been gone for a few minutes, but it had felt like an age. She would make a useless spy. If anyone asked her where she'd been, she knew she would break down and tell them what she'd done.

'Maud paints, as a hobby, you know,' said her mother from

the other room, as her guests seemed to hold art in esteem.

'How lovely,' said Marcy. 'Can we see some of her work?'

Maud imagined Rosemary's face suddenly blanching and she heard her tell them that they needed to get on soon, as the food would be ready, and maybe another time. Maud popped her head round the door as they left and said a polite goodbye and brushed her dusty hands down her jeans from the sides of the canvases that she had just stored in the back of her car. She assumed there were more in the loft, but this little act of defiance made her feel a bit better and took the sting out of them being hidden in the dark. She fleetingly thought of all of the beautiful clothes she had tucked away in her own wardrobe at home and gritted her teeth. She decided that the time would come soon for her to bring them into the daylight too. She was doing them a disservice by hiding them, the way her paintings had been stashed out of sight, and she was determined she was going to become less of a doormat.

Chapter Twenty-One

Tom checked that the children were outside and then came up behind Maud and grabbed her round the waist for a cuddle. She backed up in surprise, almost bumping into his face and knocking his front teeth out. She apologised profusely and then turned to give him a quick peck on the lips, which was highly inappropriate, but felt so damn good. They hadn't had much chance to see each other lately as Maud had been so busy but, as she was helping Dot with an art project, he didn't seem to mind. He kept asking what they were working on and she just told him she was assisting Dot researching a local artist, and wished he would stop going on about it.

They had managed to meet up to go to the pictures. They'd seen a horror film, which meant she'd been scared stiff and almost had to sit in his lap, which he'd seemed to enjoy, as he'd taken the opportunity to feel her backside as she got up. They had also grabbed a quick drink after work one night, but Daisy and the rest of the staff had turned up and heckled them from across the bar until they joined them, which didn't exactly count as a sexy date night.

She checked her watch to see if the bell was going any time soon, and then dared to give him another, slightly longer smooch. She would have loved to spend a night in at her home, so they could get to know each other better, but for some reason Dot always had something else for her to do. Maud seemed to have become the gallery errand girl and, although she did feel indebted to Dot for the gorgeous jewellery, no one else could wear it, as it was plagiarism. Maud decided to give her a wide berth for a little while and concentrate on her own paintings and love life. Maybe tonight would be Tom's lucky night!

Maud's phone buzzed in her bag again and she ignored it. Dot had been calling her incessantly and she'd had to put her phone onto silent mode. It was getting towards the end of the day now, and her back was hurting from bending down to explain things to the children all day. They had returned from playtime and were now busily reading their storybooks. Robbie had been a real handful today, and Becky had been even worse. She'd asked so many questions that Maud's head had started to pound and her legs felt like lumps of lead. She called out for the children to grab their schoolbags and there was a mad scurry of footsteps as they bumped into each other and chatted away. The end-of-day bell pealed and Maud breathed a sigh of relief and swung open the glass classroom door, sending the children off in the direction of their parents. She noticed that lots of people were huddling together and looking behind them. Maud groaned as she noticed a wave of purple hair with several bright feathers nestled jauntily at one side, fanning out like a rainbow. As the sea of parents parted to a buzz of gossip, Maud quickly ushered the last child from the room, gave the parents a jaunty wave, as if this brightly coloured person was a usual occurrence in her daily life – which to be honest she was these days – and quickly ushered Dot in, before slamming the door shut behind her with relief.

Tom looked up from his desk in surprise and delight. Bypassing Maud he swept Dot up into a warm hug and sloppily kissed her on the lips as if they were the best of friends. Dot gave a weak laugh of embarrassment as Maud looked on in confusion. Maybe the night they had all met they had chatted more than she thought? To be honest she had been so drunk she still couldn't remember the finer details. Some of the parents were hovering by the door and looking in, so Maud gave Tom a quick shove in that direction, said her goodbyes, much to his obvious disappointment, and grabbed Dot's hand to lead her out of the building via the infants' entrance, as they vacated the site ten minutes earlier than the juniors.

As they walked out to the road, Maud spotted Dot's snazzy sports car. The only way she could think of getting her away from the gossip of the school playground, and finding out why she had descended on the school like a demented peacock, was to take her back to her bungalow. For once, Dot wasn't wearing frothy underskirts and she slid behind the wheel without a word, as she'd obviously noticed that Maud seemed desperate to get home and was upset for some reason.

As they moved away from the curb and headed home, Maud finally relaxed a little. 'Why did you come to the school?'

Dot looked confused and took a moment to answer. 'I needed you. To be honest I've got myself into a bit of a panic. I'm so grateful that you've been helping me and my confidence is growing, but I need you again.'

Maud sighed heavily and didn't know how to respond. This flamboyant friendship seemed to be a bit one-sided, suiting Dot's schedule, while she obviously thought nothing of turning up at her friend's place of work, expecting to see her immediately without notice. It was beginning to grate on Maud's nerves. She realised that Dot was often surrounded by people who pandered to her every whim, but Maud's life was more reserved and far less exciting. It had skyrocketed from being borderline boring to overwhelmingly busy and most of that was because of Dot. Her own life, what there was of it, was being side-lined aggressively and Maud was feeling steamrollered. 'What do you need my help for?' she asked, rubbing her temples and wishing her headache would take a hike to someone else's head, preferably Dot's, and leave her alone.

Dot pulled up outside Maud's bungalow and turned the engine off. She swung round to face Maud and batted her eyelashes at her. 'That won't work on me,' said Maud, letting her shoulders sag in exhaustion.

'It's those little paintings that are being left everywhere. Remember I said that I came to see you originally to see if you could help me, as you must know the locality better than me? It's getting worse. More people want to find the artist now and I really must get there first. The press is saying the same thing I did, that the artist is here somewhere.'

Maud's stomach began to hurt again. This was becoming a

bit of a habit, and she was worried she might have developed an ulcer with all the stress. 'Let's go inside and I'll see what I can do.'

Dot clapped her hands in glee and jumped out of the car, grabbing Maud's bag from the back seat. She rushed to the door, delved into the bag, helped herself to the keys and opened the door before Maud had set a foot out of the car. Maud wearily slammed the car door, heard it beep behind her as Dot locked it from the hallway, and trundled inside her own house like a guest, noting that her belongings had been taken into the kitchen and not left on the hook by the front door.

Dot was opening cupboards and grabbing the tea to put in two mugs, happily switching on the kettle and making herself at home. She seemed so much more relaxed now that Maud had agreed to help her, but Maud was tired after a long day, and irritable that Tom had been so exuberant around Dot when he'd never looked quite so pleased to see her. Maud knew it was petty, but Dot had barged in and laid siege to most areas of her life and, although it was exciting, it was also exhausting. Maud took in every detail of the outfit Dot was wearing and felt cross that the parents at school would now be gossiping about her and wondering how she knew this uncouth interloper. They would know she wasn't a parent at the school, as the mums and dads were pretty well known for having cliques. The local area was very conservative, which was why her parents fit in so well here. There were no wild parties and loud music from the teenagers and boob flashing or snogging behind the bike sheds from the parents, although she had heard from a teacher friend in another area that this had happened at her school after a parents' fund-raiser. One of the children had caught them and taken a picture for posterity on his phone camera and shared it on social media. The staff had talked about little else for weeks.

She saw Dot tug at her skirt and scratch her ribs as the fabric she wore rubbed. The movement exposed her tummy and Maud could see red marks where the material had hurt her delicate skin. Maud felt tired suddenly, and the anger she had built up bubbled to the surface and burst. She didn't know why

107

she was taking her frustration over her own situation out on Dot. Dot was vivacious and ran her life at full pelt. Maud's own life was gradually changing and she felt as if she was sitting aboard a rocking ship. 'Dot. Why do you wear clothes that burn your skin?'

Dot stopped what she was doing, on the point of opening more cupboards to search for biscuits. Her tummy rumbled loudly and Maud guessed that she'd been too busy persuading Nate to hold another private view in a few months, capitalising on his rising celebrity status, to eat all day.

Dot self-consciously pulled her top further down and blushed to the roots of her purple hair, looking defensive and scowling at Maud. She then started banging cupboards closed, her hackles clearly rising. 'I like wearing these clothes,' She quickly poured hot water over the teabags and splashed in some milk.

'No, you don't. You told me when we first met that you dress for your parents, but we haven't discussed it since. Isn't it about time you grew up? If you want to find this artist and be independent so badly, why don't you start with the way you dress?' Maud had a terrible feeling that she had just repeated a recent conversation she'd had with Daisy.

'What about you?' Dot answered angrily, slamming her mug of tea on the counter top so that it sloshed over the rim, and Maud fought the urge to rush over and clean the surfaces. 'You can draw a lot better than you first let on, and yet you dress like a nun and don't paint.'

'I don't dress like a nun!'

'You do!'

Maud looked down at her buttoned-up blouse and A-line skirt, in a soft but boring brown suede, and grudgingly admitted Dot might have a point.

'I'm really fed up.' Maud threw her tea into the sink and opened the cupboard to set up two wine glasses, before going to the fridge and selecting a crisp, chilled wine. Pouring two almost overflowing glasses, she slugged back hers in front of Dot's shocked face and then poured herself another one.

'Maud! What's got into you?'

'Drink up,' said Maud. 'We're getting drunk and you can stay the night if you behave.'

Dot giggled, then thought about it for about two seconds before gulping down her first glass and following suit. 'I don't have any spare clothes.' Maud eyed her friend up and down, saying, 'thank goodness for that!' Both women burst out laughing, so Maud grabbed the wine and pulled Dot towards the garden. 'How much does it mean to you to find this stupid artist? Are they really that good?'

'The work can rival Nate's,' said Dot earnestly, spilling the wine, which splashed over the rim of the glass onto Maud's grey kitchen tiles as she followed her friend. 'I wouldn't be so bothered otherwise.'

Maud's step faltered. 'You have got to be kidding me?'

Dot looked at her incredulously. 'Have you not seen the work? Having a client like that might mean I could start being myself and finding my own voice.' Dot sighed. 'I've been working really hard on my collection and you're right, it's about time I stopped trying to be someone I'm not. I'll try if you will,' she dared.

'We should start trusting each other,' said Maud. 'I've been hiding myself away for so long that I've forgotten what it's like to share things. My friend Daisy is the only one who sees the real me.'

Chapter Twenty-Two

Dot felt a pang of jealousy towards Daisy, but shook it off as she could feel she'd been crowding Maud lately. She'd tried not to, but she'd been snowed under at work and Nate had kept giving her extra jobs to do. He'd said that Maud had offered to help, but seeing how frazzled Maud was today she had a sneaky suspicion he had ulterior motives and wanted Maud to be too busy to see a certain dishy teacher. How underhand was that? She did grudgingly admire his tactics though.

'If we're being truthful,' said Dot, 'I know I've been taking up too much of your time lately...' She thought about dumping her brother in trouble, but she'd never seen him pay much attention to a woman before, so she cut him some slack. 'I've been overworked, with the drawing classes, managing my family's art and trying to find this artist, and I've been leaning on you too much. We haven't known each other long enough for me to do that yet,' she joked.

Maud raised a smile and clinked glasses with Dot, suddenly looking much better now that they were friends again. 'It's ok, but don't do it again,' she chided. 'Seeing as we're sharing confidences, I didn't just bring you out here to admire my tidy bush.'

Dot raised an enquiring eyebrow and Maud laughed and ran to the end of the garden and disappeared through the hedge. Dot frowned and went after her, discovering a small gate. Not pausing to wonder if she should go through, as she really didn't care and was desperate to find out what Maud was on about, Dot opened it. She stopped short when she saw the beautiful studio with big glass windows and an easel set inside. She gawped as she drew closer and saw the delicate little artworks, with spidery line-drawn animals and splashes of vivid colour. 'What the hell is going on?' Dot felt totally confused at how Maud could have all of these here. Had she stalked the artist and pinched every single one of the artworks he'd left in the parks? Surely that wasn't fair on the local people he'd left them for? She stepped beyond the open double doors and saw a half-finished work on the easel. Maud was sitting in front of it and, as she looked at Dot, everything was suddenly sliding into place, and Dot was kicking herself for not guessing her secret sooner. Now that she could openly gaze around at the various pieces of art in the studio, the resemblance to the prize-winning artwork Maud had submitted was obvious. She hadn't copied the style – she was the style. The trees in her bedroom... she had painted them too.

Dot turned around in awe and couldn't stop staring at the detailing in the creatures' faces and eyes. It was exquisite work. 'Why didn't you send these into the competition? I know you won anyway, but this work would have earned you an agent and a fight over who represented you.' Dot could barely contain her excitement.

Maud sat back and for once she didn't hesitate. 'Enough has been said in the press for me finally to have the confidence that my work is good.' She hesitated and blushed, brushing her hair across her face. 'Not just good, but really good, no matter what my parents think,' she sighed.

'People finding out the artist is me, isn't a problem from an art point of view, it's just that it could possibly alter my quiet life, and I'm not sure if I'm brave enough for it. I've kind of just decided that if you can change, Dot, then so can I. Daisy sent in the entry to your competition. She didn't think I would kill her if she submitted one of my earlier works, but knew I was precious about these ones.'

'I can see why,' said Dot reverently, then remembered something and looked at her strangely. 'You've been leaving your beautiful work all over the region. Why? You could have made thousands from those paintings. Was it a publicity stunt?' she couldn't imagine something of this magnitude from a timid girl like Maud, but nothing else made sense.

Maud scoffed at that idea and set her wine glass down,

almost knocking it sideways and giving Dot a heart attack, as it just missed the canvas on the easel. Maud's cheeks were flushed and she seemed decidedly tipsy. 'I might regret my decision in the morning, but I don't think so. I'm not clever enough to plan a media-frenzy like this, but I wanted to show someone. It scares me a bit,' she half-joked, reaching her hand out to have another mouthful of wine and looking confused that it had all gone and the glass was empty.

'I wish I'd thought of it,' sighed Dot, glugging some more wine, then setting her glass down too, to go and pick up a little painting of a fox to study at close range. 'It's a perfect marketing idea that will go viral pretty soon, I'm sure.'

'Viral? Oh crap. I just wanted someone to like my art. My parents hate it.'

'They won't when they realise one collection could buy them a new house,' said Dot, affronted that anyone could not love this work. 'They really are stupid,' she said blandly, which made Maud splutter and laugh loudly. Dot grinned too and rushed forward to hug her friend. 'You're incredibly talented. I was so desperate to represent the artist who created this work, but now it's you, I can see you should consider all the offers you will most certainly get and take your time checking the contracts. I'll help you.' Her shoulders sagged in defeat. 'I'll just have to discover the next Maud Silverton.'

Maud hugged her friend fiercely back. 'I don't like the limelight and I'm not ready to tell anyone else about my work yet, but if you can somehow work around that, then I'll happily sign your contract and be your first client.'

Dot stepped back with tears in her eyes, and stared at Maud in wonder. 'Are you sure? You can check out my contract,' she delved into the bag over her shoulder and produced one, like a magician pulling a rabbit from a hat, and Maud doubled over and held her sides with mirth.

'Bloody hell, Dot. You brought it with you?' Maud was rubbing tears from her eyes and her shoulders were shaking uncontrollably as she giggled.

'I carry it everywhere, in case I ever find him or her,' she said innocently, batting her eyelashes again.

'I told you, that move doesn't work on me,' Maud held her stomach and gasped for air after all the merriment. 'You really are a one-off, Dot. I've been thinking about it a lot lately, though, and we would work well together. What are the terms?'

'It's a fair contract,' said Dot seriously now, 'but take your time and check it out with a professional. No hurry... but I'll help you choose one tomorrow!'

Both women leaned into each other and stood with their arms looped around each other's backs, but an impatient Dot moved forward and was picking up and examining every last piece, before Maud pulled her away, locked the studio door and returned to the kitchen to open a second bottle of wine.

Chapter Twenty-Three

A few hours later, they were lying on their stomachs on the floor of the lounge. They had just poured out the remains of the second bottle of wine and found a third hiding at the back of the fridge. Maud winced as she rolled over to look at the ceiling. Her head was spinning a bit, although she quite liked the hazy sensation of seeing everything through a white fog. It meant she didn't have to think too much about the contract she had agreed to sign with Dot, or the plans they had been drunkenly mulling over.

Dot finally noticed that Maud had gone quiet, but was evidently too wound up to sit around for long, so she heaved herself up, using Maud's bent knees as a support. 'I've had the best idea ever to stop you thinking things over too much,' she squealed in delight at her own brilliance. She paused while she tried to stop her stomach growling by rubbing it, as they hadn't bothered with food. 'Now I've stood up I've realised I'm famished, too.' She ran and collected a pizza flyer she'd seen neatly squared up next to Maud's fridge earlier, hit a button on her mobile phone and called in for delivery to Maud's house, while Maud sat and stared at her in bemusement.

'Great idea,' said Maud, easing herself up and slowly going to get a glass of cold water. 'You have all of the best ideash.'

'I know I do... sh,' Dot parroted Maud's slurred words and they both spluttered with laughter again. The whole evening had been full of wine, plans and more wine, and tiredness from a full day at school was starting to make Maud sleepy. Gabbing Maud's hand, Dot shuffled her into her bedroom and shoved her none too gently onto the bed.

Maud giggled. 'You can't have your wicked way with me,

if that's your idea. You fancy men and I've got a vagina!'

Dot snorted merrily and looked at Maud's ungainly sprawled figure on the bed and her soft blond hair fanned over the bedspread. 'I think my brother wouldn't mind finding that out, but as the thought is disgusting, it's a good job you've got a boyfriend. Speaking of which, I really should find one for myself sometime soon. Work takes over my life. That's why this is a good idea.'

'What is?' Maud got up on her elbows and frowned as Dot opened her wardrobe doors and started picking out clothes and holding them up against herself.

'We're going to swap clothes.' Dot looked down at her own attire and started to undress, making Maud squawk and hide her eyes. 'Maybe what I wear is a bit too far for you to go in one sitting, but let's live dangerously for once, Maud. We're just about to do a joint showing of my jewellery and your paintings... we need to start being ourselves.'

'By wearing each other's clothes? Doesn't that make us each other?'

Dot threw a sparkly top with delicate flowers sown all over it at Maud's head and carried on stripping off. 'No, it makes us discover who we want to be, not what everyone else wants us to be.'

Maud fought with the top and threw it on the bed. 'Isn't this a bit deep after three bottles of wine? Can't we just eat pizza and fall asleep in our own slobber?'

'No,' said Dot decisively. 'Ley's try on some clothes.'

Maud thought for about twenty seconds. Then, mainly due to her lost inhibitions from the alcoholic haze, she flew off the bed with an athleticism she didn't know she possessed, and began pulling her own clothes off until both girls were standing almost naked, curiously looking at each other's bodies. Dot had beautiful black lingerie that sculpted her small breasts and knickers that whispered over her lean hips, Maud had her brightly coloured underwear on and the sight made Dot gawp. 'Blimey, Maud,' she gasped. You wear pale clothes that you button up to your neck, and then have that hiding underneath? It's enough to give a man a heart attack.'

Maud blushed furiously as she hadn't shown anyone her purchases, even Daisy. She did fleetingly remember that Nate had seen them, and hoped Dot wouldn't find his note. 'I decided that now is a good time to start being a bit more adventurous, but I haven't found the courage to do more than wear the underwear that I had hidden away. It's been sitting there for so long that I felt it was about time I went out and found some fierce.'

Dot stood in awe. The colourful garments lovingly caressed Maud's full breasts and womanly hips and the strong pinks and blues that were interwoven in lace drew your eyes immediately. 'I wish I had big boobs,' she sighed dramatically. 'I bet Tom loves these wisps of lace. How does he keep his hands off you at school knowing that this is what you wear underneath? Do you do it to drive him nuts?'

Maud looked appalled at the idea. 'I'm not trying to tease him... well, maybe I do like the idea of him panting at my feet, if he ever sees them.' She visualised Tom staring at her lustfully and quite liked the idea. 'But I haven't had a moment alone with him to find out. You keep me too busy. My old boyfriends didn't see them as I just wore plain black and white. I thought you would see the other colours through my clothes, but the fabrics are all quite thick, as the weather hasn't properly warmed up yet. You're right that I've been hiding behind a boring alter ego. I want to be a butterfly,' she slurred, flapping her arms in the air.

Dot looked momentarily guilty for giving Maud so many jobs, but then explained her plan. 'Ok, look. If we start by bringing out your inner butterfly by adding some colour to your wardrobe, then your outside will match your amazing pants and Tom will move heaven and earth to get inside them.' She threw some more clothes Maud's way. If Maud had been sober, she would have felt faint with the mess, but as she wasn't, she delved in and started pulling the wispy fabrics over her arms. Dot's top didn't go past her shoulders, which they both found hilarious, so Maud turned to her own clothes. Looking up and seeing Dot wearing one of her A-line skirts and a loose lace blouse, she fell about laughing, before remembering she hadn't pulled her top over her arm yet. She promptly tripped and fell face-first onto the bed, making Dot roar and go to help hoist her painfully back up.

Looking at Dot in the demure clothes, Maud could see how wound up she must appear to everyone else. The clothes shouted go away, but on Dot, still wearing a few crazy accessories, Maud could finally see there was a middle ground somewhere. Dot waited for Maud to finish getting dressed and they stood side by side in the mirror. Both women stared mutely at their reflections in awe. Maud was wearing a white blouse with lace detailing which cut into a low dip at the front, with a khaki jacket over the top with delicate little flowers sewn all over the shoulders. Below that, she wore fitted dark denim jeans, skimming her legs, and turned up mid-ankle. On her feet were sky-high black ankle boots making her legs look endless and sexy.

Without the vivid colours and very weird sculptural distractions, Dot looked a lot less exotic and confusing, but on her tall, slim frame, the clothes took on an ethereal quality and she looked very beautiful and angelic. 'Wow, Dot! You look like a fashion model, though hell knows how, as the clothes are so damn boring. On you, they drape as if they've been sewn by angels. How can you make them look so damn good?'

Dot was still gazing at her reflection in shock and then cocked her head to one side to squint at them both really closely, as she was having trouble focussing, and Maud remembered that they really needed some water to drown out the wine.

'What the hell have we both been doing all these years?' Dot asked quietly. 'We've been dressing up in someone else's clothes. Ok, this isn't exactly how I would choose to look, but I've never really considered anything other than appearing like a serious artist.' She gave Maud a hard stare when she saw the corners of her mouth twitch at the thought of Dot's mad clothes and how they made her look anything but serious.

They heard the doorbell peal and Maud pushed past Dot and ran to answer the door. The deliveryman smiled as if his day had just got more interesting when Maud opened the door and Dot peeked out behind her. He'd delivered to Maud many times, and his sister had been at school with her and Daisy. He'd never seen her looking ready for a night out, with her hair tumbling wildly about her flushed face, though. He must think he'd arrived in a parallel reality, Maud decided, although he gave her a big grin in response to her new look. His sister had once told Maud that he thought of himself as a bit of a lady's man. He gave her a lascivious wink and handed the pizza her way. 'You girls going out somewhere nice tonight?' he asked, staring at Maud's chest, as if hoping they would invite him to join them.

Dot reached past Maud and grabbed the pizza, pressing £20 into his palm giving him a dazzling smile in return, which almost knocked him sideways. He was obviously shocked to realise that Maud had such glamorous friends.

'We just had our own party,' she winked at him cheekily, making his smile go wide then falter as she shut the door in his face. 'Keep the change!'

Chapter Twenty-Four

The following weeks were hard on Maud, keeping up the pretence of normality, when in reality Dot had taken over her life. Maud's stomach buzzed with excitement, and not the boredom she normally felt, but trying to paint enough art for her first exhibition, with one or two extra canvases to leave around to keep up the press momentum, was taking its toll on her sanity.

She'd confided in Daisy, who had been suitably impressed, jumping around the office again. Daisy had then basically taken credit for sending her art to the gallery for the competition in the first place, and crowed that she was the one who'd discovered Maud's talent. It had all been said in jest, but Maud had made a show of hugging and thanking Daisy none the less. She'd promised tickets to the opening show for Daisy and Ryan, and she'd need them there to help calm her nerves. Living a double life, helping children to read during the day, then furiously painting at night, was exhausting. She was worried her art would suffer.

Tom was being very patient with her and she was enjoying flirting for the first time in years. He seemed to be an expert in it, giving her more confidence and bringing out her personality to make her feel a bit happier about her appearance. She knew she'd never be supermodel-gorgeous like Dot, but with every bottom stroke in the staffroom when no one was looking, or every time he brought her a cup of tea in class and gave her a dazzling smile, she had begun to unfurl and stand straighter. She didn't hunch over her chest anymore and she'd begun to loosen up over her clothes, and experiment a bit. She had been doing it so gradually that hardly anyone noticed so far, but Tom seemed to appreciate the delicate accessories she now wore and the slightly lower-cut necklines.

Dot had been arriving at the bungalow every other night, to check on Maud's progress and sometimes to ask her opinion on her own work, which she was trying to fit in between her usual family commitments. Maud could feel how frazzled Dot was, but as she had no energy reserves of her own, she decided Dot would just have to manage, the same way she was. It was all Dot's fault this had happened anyway. Seeing Dot slump onto her sofa and grab a bowl of spaghetti Bolognese that Maud had whipped up for them from a jar, Maud decided she was being mean, as Dot was working so hard to make this exhibition a success for both of them. She tried to recall a moment when Dot hadn't been in her life, and although it had only been months, if felt like they were best of friends now and had known each other since playschool, where true bonds were formed.

Maud sighed and rubbed her temple. Her forehead was aching and she felt a migraine coming. Wavy lines danced in front of her eyes. She slurped a long drink from the glass of water on the little white wooden side table by the sofa and threw a couple of headache tablets in her mouth, fished from the bag at her feet. Daisy had said she might turn up later and, although Maud had been sworn to secrecy by Dot, Daisy insisted she was included in major decisions about which paintings would be shown. Dot had been annoyed that Maud had told anyone, but she could see Daisy was jealous of her new relationship with Dot and was just marking her territory. The problem was that Dot knew very well what she was doing and when she privately swiped at Daisy for interfering, Maud got defensive and they grumbled at each other.

'Dot...'

Dot looked up from spooning another big mouthful of the meaty spaghetti into her mouth, as if she hadn't eaten for days, and raised her eyes.

'I know Daisy can be a pain, but could you be a bit gentle on her? She's my oldest friend,' Maud kept from saying best friend, as she had discovered Dot was quite possessive over her friends and family. Maud was hoping she would bring

Daisy into the fold, but it just hadn't happened. 'She has my interests at heart and spends most of her time with Ryan anyway, so she won't trouble us too much.'

'She's been here poking her nose into our plans for our joint exhibition ever since you told her. Why did you do that?' demanded Dot.

Maud felt exasperated and rubbed her sore head again, before resting it on the back of the sofa and looking up at the ceiling for strength. 'She's the one who sent my work to you in the first place...'

'As she often tells us.'

'She's proud, as she should be. I've noticed she's not her usual sunny self lately and I think this is what's bothering her. She's been by my side for years and has tried to get me to show someone my work. She's been my biggest supporter.' After a glare from Dot, Maud corrected herself, '...after you, of course. But she knows about our collaboration and if we want her to keep it a secret, then we have to keep her onside.' Maud hoped that by playing to Dot's business mind, she could make her ease up on Daisy.

Hearing the doorbell chime and pulling her heavy bones up to answer it, as Dot was stuffing her face again and going nowhere, Maud decided she'd have to leave them to it. Walking to the door and hearing Dot call out for second helpings of pasta, Maud wondered how such a slim person could eat as much as ten men and still look like the wind could blow her over. Maud just had to look at a bag of crisps and magically the equivalent calories appeared on her thighs. She'd been desperately dieting to be able to wear a pretty dress to her exhibition, and she had shed some pounds, her clothes were looser, but it had been mental torture. Especially with the amount of chocolate biscuits that were always offered round in the staffroom at school, and the box of chocolates that Tom had surprised her with at lunchtime the previous day, even though she'd told him she was trying to get fit. He'd parried that she was gorgeous as she was, as he liked something to grab on to, and she'd almost thumped him in the face with the chocolate box. Maybe he was a bit frustrated as they hadn't

121

had a lot of time alone, but she'd not known whether to be insulted that he thought she had love handles, or complimented that he fancied her. They weren't an 'official' couple yet, as they had avoided the subject for the first few months and just flirted a lot and gone out occasionally. Lately, they had agreed not to date anyone else while they were getting to know each other.

Opening the door to Daisy, she smiled and pulled her into a hug, loving the feel of her friend's warm body, but noticing she had lost weight too, which made Maud concerned as Daisy was open about loving her curves. Daisy was so different to Dot, but they could both be darn bossy when it came to their friendships and Maud was determined they would get on.

'I've saved you some pasta. Dot's in the lounge.' Seeing Daisy's face scrunch up in distaste, she placed an arm around her waist in a show of solidarity and shepherded her in. Dot actually smiled up and acknowledged Daisy for once and Daisy's eyebrows shot up in surprise. 'Dot was looking forward to you coming round, weren't you, Dot?' Maud gave Dot one of the stares she gave naughty pupils in her class and Dot sighed and got up to make room for Daisy to sit down next to her.

'Of course! We were just saying how great it is to have your input, as you were the one who got us all together in the first place, weren't we, Maud?' she parroted.

Maud brought Daisy a steaming portion of Bolognese, thankful that Dot had left her a small bowlful, and they all leaned forward to begin making decisions about the upcoming show.

'Are you keeping up the mystery of who you are, all the way to the show?' Daisy asked.

Maud was about to reply but Dot jumped in. 'We are, although it's amazing really as Maud didn't have a clue what she was doing,' Daisy and Maud exchanged glances. 'She managed to create an incredible media buzz. It would cost thousands to buy that kind of publicity and, for a first time artist, it's like gold dust.' She barely paused for breath. 'We need to keep the momentum going, but from now on Maud is going to consider her work as valuable property and not leave quite so many free samples around.' Dot tried to match Maud's hard stare from earlier, but only managed to look like she'd been hit by a spade as her eyes went a bit cross-eyed. The others tried not to laugh, but for once Maud could see that Daisy heartily agreed.

Maud couldn't believe they were on the same side for the first time ever, and just had to let them get on with Maud-bashing, if it helped them bond into some weird kind of friendship group.

'Can I see some of your work, Dot?' Daisy asked suddenly. Maud realised that Daisy had decided she might as well cash in on Dot being nice for once, as she hadn't found the courage to ask to see the jewellery before and it had been grating on her nerves and making her grumpy at being left out.

'No,' said Dot firmly, then saw Maud's face and tried to soften her tone. 'I don't let anyone into my studio.' When she saw Daisy was about to protest that Maud had seen her work, she played the family card. Maud wished she would stop blaming them for her shortcomings. They weren't like Maud's family, who didn't even give her work a moment's consideration. Maud thought Dot was selfish about her whole family. They actually tried to see her vision, unlike Maud's parents, who trashed her dreams even though she did have some talent, as it didn't fit with their own plans. Dot knew her family would be there for her if she told them she was moving on to becoming an agent for other artists, and would support her in any career she chose. Maud's mum and dad told her what friends she could have, what to wear, where to work and how to behave. What a mug she was. The fact that Daisy had tried to help Maud for so many years should have made Dot warm to her, but because she hadn't intervened or stood up for Maud against her parents, Dot was angry instead.

Dot tried her best to look innocent but it didn't work. 'My parents haven't seen the work yet, as they don't know I'm trying something new. They'd be devastated if I let anyone see it before them.' Seeing Daisy about to protest, she ploughed on, laying it on thick. 'To be honest, Maud, I've been a bit stupid about this and felt jealous about your friendship with Daisy.' She batted her eyelashes at Daisy who visibly softened, much to Maud's disgust.

Maud gave Dot a mutinous look and sighed in exasperation, as it now seemed like Dot had decided the best way forward was to get Daisy onside. She continued sweetly, 'We need to have the element of surprise at the show and, as you've been so supportive of Maud and me, how about me keeping back one of the pieces I practiced on, just for you?'

Maud and Daisy were stunned to silence. 'Really?' Daisy gasped. Maud had told her how beautiful Dot's work was, and Maud knew she'd be thrilled to own a piece, as she could never afford to buy one.

Maud smiled at her friends, who seemed to have finally broken the ice, however unconventionally, and sent Dot an appreciative air kiss for trying to be more pleasant for once. Her headache was easing off and she decided it was time to break out the wine. 'Dot's earlier pieces have such charm, Daisy. You'll love them. Dot, that's so kind of you.'

Dot shook herself out like a proud peacock. 'I know.'

Maud grinned, collected three glasses and started pouring, before slowing down on the amount after remembering what happened last time she had shared wine with Dot. The pizza guy, Rob, had tried to ring the doorbell to get back in, and by the night's end they'd climbed into every last item of clothing in Maud's wardrobe and Dot had tested her by telling her she wasn't allowed to pick a single thing off the floor, which would have been excruciating if she hadn't been so drunk. They'd then found Rob asleep under the heap of clothes, snoring into a second, half-empty pizza box. Maud vaguely recalled him being let in by Dot after his shift at work, and them all getting even drunker by playing a game which involved wearing a pizza slice on their foreheads. It had taken her ages to persuade him to leave, and then to tidy everything away the next day.

Maud scrunched up her face and tried to think back to remember maybe snogging him, Dot snogging him or worse, but she had little or no recollection of events past two o'clock in the morning at all. She hoped she hadn't, as although she and Tom weren't boyfriend and girlfriend yet, they had agreed to tell each other if they wanted to see other people before doing it. Her nether regions were feeling fine and didn't show signs of energetic frolicking with a naked man, so she had to assume they had stayed platonic. She was going to have to cut back on her wine consumption, before she became a lush or a hussy. She looked at her wine glass and wrinkled her nose. It would be a shame to waste such good grapes though. She'd start the plan tomorrow, as surely one day couldn't make a difference?

Envisaging Daisy joining in their party the night before and trying to fit her ample curves into the sparkly collection of clothes hidden in Maud's wardrobe, made her giggle and spill the wine. Daisy jumped up to help clean the tiny mark on the table, but Maud waved her away, which left the other two girls open-mouthed in surprise. 'Right, ladies, we have an exhibition to plan, so drink up and let's get the party started.'

Daisy and Dot stood up and clinked glasses with Maud and, after taking a sip of the deliciously cool wine, they grabbed bowls and handbags and congregated around the central island in the kitchen where Dot had laid out some provisional plans for, hopefully, the most exciting night of Maud's life.

Chapter Twenty-Five

Maud's mood lifted over the next few weeks, as at last Dot and Daisy had called a truce and were getting along. Daisy wasn't interfering so much and had gone back to spending practically every waking moment outside of work with Ryan. Maud thought she looked at bit ill, but she'd assured Maud that she was fine and just felt she'd been neglecting her boyfriend and wanted to make it up to him, so Maud had let the subject drop.

Maud had found it a struggle to keep dealing with the smiles, tears and tantrums of the children at school when her mind was clearly elsewhere, but she'd tried her best to be professional and not shout from the rooftops that she was an artist now and needed to be in her studio painting. She was far from being a diva, but for once she wished she had some of the bravado that came with the job. She craved the solitude of the artistic space in her garden, where no one bothered her. Dot had been confined to the house, as she kept disturbing Maud's concentration with her pacing. Maud enjoyed the bustling environment of the school, but understood now that she had used it as a buffer against the outside world. She'd cocooned herself inside, with the gentle people and gregarious children, and had been content to coast along on the shirttails of her oldest friend.

Pausing to look up at the façade of the building she had arrived outside, Maud remembered how nervous she'd felt the first time she'd walked up this street. The gallery looked so different in daylight. It welcomed you inside with wooden sliding doors, currently open, and a metal post and rail with printed fabric in between depicting the work of the family of artists housed inside. Maud thought how fabulous the fabric would look on a dress, and drooled at the prospect of having one to add to her collection. She fleetingly wondered if Dot would kill her if she snaffled the length of fabric nearest the door and had it made into a handbag, or something? Maybe that was a future product collaboration she could suggest to her dotty friend.

Stepping inside and gazing in awe at the splendour of the current exhibition of paintings, a selection of Dot's cousin's work, she stopped and examined the nearest one in detail. She smiled first at the smartly-dressed young man who was sitting at a metal reception desk, which seemed to have been hammered to within an inch of its life, but looked so textural and interesting. Maud recalled the table had been covered in crisp white linen and lined with rows of champagne bottles and glasses at Nate's show. If she'd seen it like this that night, she would certainly have wanted to take a closer look, or run her hand along the surface at the very least. She wondered if all artists were like her? She couldn't pass something textural or interesting without wanting to take a closer look.

Maud's fingers also yearned to touch the art on walls and she felt incredibly inadequate, thinking of her own work next to Dot's family's masterpieces. She knew that Dot was desperate to make her own statement, but was Maud making a mistake getting involved in family issues? It could destroy her own family, if they found out what she was up to. What if Dot was wrong and her work was useless?

Waving to the young man, she saw him acknowledge she was there, but he indicated that he was on the phone. She smiled, showing she was just browsing, and he bent his head and returned to his call. Dot was supposed to be meeting her there at ten as it was Maud's day off, but Maud wanted to be greedy and look at the art before Dot realised she was there. Dot got to stare at this any time she pleased, and Maud guessed she could too, now, but she felt so privileged to be able to get close to the work. There were only four or five people milling around the gallery, so she decided to savour the peace and quiet before Dot crashed in and took over. Maud wondered if Dot had changed her way of dressing yet, and was apprehensive to see which way she would go. Dot might not realise it, but Maud suspected she was a closet magpie too.

Feeling warm breath on her shoulder, she turned and looked up into Nate's smiling eyes. She jumped and took a step back, as he was invading her personal space. Maud knew his flat was above the gallery, so she shouldn't have been surprised to see him. Why the hell hadn't she thought that he might be here? As she recoiled, she tripped on her own feet again. She'd been standing with her legs crossed, a terrible habit, she realised. Nate reached out as if he'd been expecting her to fall at his feet, and placed warm hands around her waist. She was gratified to see that his hands fitted perfectly – her love handles of fat had disappeared. He frowned before pretending to chastise her. 'You've lost weight. Why?'

With surprise, she noticed he kept his hand on her waist in a familiar way, but for once she didn't blush and make a fool of herself in his presence. 'Working too hard to eat, I guess,' she said simply, making him look upset, while a deeper frown creased his brow.

Maud had avoided Nate at Dot's studio, as being near him scared her a little. Dot had been so scathing about his prowess with women and Maud wanted to give her fledgling relationship with Tom a chance. Things had definitely been hotting up, as Tom tried to touch her at every opportunity after the school bell had rung, when the class was empty, which she sometimes found embarrassing if a parent passed by the window. She had enough to deal with, with the nervous exhaustion of keeping everything a secret, which was becoming more difficult now that everyone seemed to be looking for her. Leaving artworks around was so cloak and dagger, she'd started dressing in black and trying to make herself even more forgettable when she made drops in the parks. No one would think a normal girl like her could be the one in the news. They would be looking for someone like Nate or Dot to appear.

Knowing Dot better now, Maud wondered if her animosity towards Nate was just familial jealousy, as she slated him at every opportunity. Maud couldn't shake off the hurt from her last boyfriend seducing someone from a neighbouring village behind her back, so she was wary of Nate's attention. Dot had told Maud over several glasses of wine, that Nate was her parents' favourite and he could do no wrong in their eyes. Maud had seen the way they idolised both of their children, though, and didn't think this was a fair assumption. It was probably just Dot being grumpy.

Chapter Twenty-Six

Nate was staring at her with a wide grin on his face, and his hand was still resting gently on her waist as he turned her towards Dot's office at the back of the gallery.

'You know I'm here to meet Dot?'

'She told me. Unfortunately, though, she's just been urgently called to see our parents, as they feel she's been neglecting them of late for some reason.' Nate conveniently forgot to tell Maud that he'd phoned and told his parents that Dot was disregarding them as soon as she'd mentioned that Maud was meeting her today. As he'd predicted, their parents had been aghast and decided he was right and that Dot should come and see them immediately. He didn't usually play hardball, but Maud had been to see Dot loads of times and she'd managed to avoid him somehow, he could feel it. He wanted them to be friends at least, as his nerves were both soothed and riled up when she was around, after the turbulent years where Lena had dominated his life, and the barren times in between when he hadn't let himself feel a single good emotion for anyone. Maud didn't fawn all over him but blushed anytime he got near and, even though he knew there was a spark between them somewhere, she valiantly battled it. He understood that she had a boyfriend, but he hated the guy. No one was good enough for any of his sister's friends, but Maud was even more special and he had no idea why he felt this way. He'd had to use guile to keep her away from Tom and he'd never done anything like this in his life. He'd made Dot keep Maud busy by giving her underhand tasks that were irrelevant. He was being domineering; a trait he deplored, but he couldn't help it. He wanted Maud, and he intended to have her.

He wasn't sure what it was about Tom, but Nate didn't like the way his eyes had darted around the room at dinner the first night they had met, and the way his arm had been casually slung around the shoulders of Nate's own date, when Dot and Maud had gone to the powder room.

Maud faltered for a second, and he jolted out of his reverie as she spoke. 'Oh... right. I'd better get back to my own work then, I suppose.'

'I thought you had a day off? Dot said you'd kept the day clear for her? She asked me to take you to lunch as an apology for messing you around.'

Maud looked aghast. 'You don't have to do that! It's a treat to come here and look at the art.'

'How about your own work? I saw your competition entry, and it was lovely.' Nate pushed open the office door and guided Maud to Dot's chair, while he picked up the phone and made a reservation at a restaurant along the road. He glanced at Maud's feet and was disappointed to see she was wearing simple flat shoes, although he had noticed her formal look had gone and she was softening the edges and adding colour. Today she was wearing a delicate almost-blue top, which hugged her shoulders and spread wide across her chest. The sleeves had little ties at the wrists and she wore several loose chains around her neck with charms hanging from them. Moulding her hips were fitted jeans that were turned up to reveal her ankles. Although she had lost weight, she still had curves at her hips and bust, and he wanted to bite into her soft shoulder and lock her in his sister's office and bury the key. Then he'd gently spank her for not eating properly and feed her strawberries covered in chocolate... Man, he was losing it!

He watched Maud carefully, which made his pupils dilate and his head spin. He felt the air grow warmer and Maud sat up straight before she realised that her new top afforded him a glorious view of her chest and sprang up, almost crashing into him. 'Sorry,' she gasped as he steadied her again.

'Maud, if you keep throwing yourself at me every time we meet, I might have to take you up on your offer,' he joked, but her face flamed in embarrassment. He laid a gentle hand on her face and stroked her cheek. 'Maud... I'm joking.'

'Oh, ok,' she stuttered, picking up her bag and preparing to leave.

He grabbed her hand and opened the office door, quickly telling Mario on the front desk where they would be. Maud tried to break away, but he held firm and ushered her with him, so she had no choice but to comply.

Turning to face her, he held her chin with his fingers and made her look up at him. 'I know you have a boyfriend and it seems for some reason that my beloved sister doesn't want us to be friends, but I don't care what they think. I like your company and I think you enjoy mine. Let's go to lunch, talk about your art and then you can go home. Ok?'

Maud sighed and tried to move away, but as he was gently holding her hand, she couldn't. He saw that she had noticed the sliver scars snaking up his wrist, but she didn't flinch away and, for once, neither did he. He looked down at her and gave her no choice but to stare up into his eyes and see that he meant what he said.

Her stomach grumbled and that made up his mind. She'd probably forgotten to have breakfast. 'You're coming with me.' He tucked her hand under his arm and hugged her to him, which was something he never did. He let Dot hug him sometimes, but she was the exception. Ever since Lena, he'd avoided familiarity with anyone outside of the family, and Dot would keel over in shock if she saw them. He wanted Maud to trust him and decided that she would have to make up her own mind about him, and not go on the put-downs Dot often slung his way.

Maud linked her arm around his waist, which surprised him, and for a split second he drew away, then pulled her further into his side as he regaled her with stories of his family's antics as they walked up the road to the little French bistro that he favoured.

Nate felt some of the frustration that he had been swamped with at work drain away. He'd been immersing himself in a new style, and it almost felt like the devil was inside him when he was painting. Because of this, he'd been unable to approach Maud directly, which would have been his usual way. He wasn't one for playing games or wasting his time. He'd thought about Maud and her sexy rose shoes more than he liked and the fact that Dot was interfering, for some reason, intrigued him even more. It appeared that Maud was harbouring secrets, and he knew only too well how that felt. He had nightmares about the day Lena, his ex-girlfriend, had died and he'd pretty much steered clear of any emotional entanglement since. Maybe that was why he liked Maud, because she was off limits and he didn't have the pressure of trying to please her, even though he wanted to. He felt a desperate urge to seduce Maud and get her out of his system. He needed to scratch the itch. That was all it was. He should really stop mooning over her and go out and get laid. The thought of what an idiot he was being made his shoulders tense. This was someone else's girl and he'd have to learn to let her go. One meal and he'd send her on her way, but today was theirs.

Nate tried to shake off the rage he felt when he got close to someone, but it was brimming inside him and always seemed to be just below the surface, about to erupt at any time. He'd tried being kind to Lena, but she had thrown it back in his face and ruined his life. He ground his teeth and was glad Maud hadn't noticed how tense he was. She was on his territory now and he wasn't one to waste an opportunity. He wouldn't let her get under his skin and then take over his life. He'd done that before and had been burnt emotionally. He thought about the silvery scars on his arms, but the damage to his mind had been worse. The scars were a reminder every day to keep others at a distance, as life was much simpler that way. The problem was that he wanted to touch Maud. It was a compulsion that wouldn't go away. It annoyed the hell out of him, but excited him at the same time. He hadn't felt like this in so long that it was torture.

As they reached the restaurant, Maud smiled into his eyes and his mood softened again. She looked like an excited child about visiting somewhere new. He reached out and opened the door to the bistro, and enjoyed the delight on her face when she took in the Parisian detailing in the furniture. He hadn't taken much notice before, but the tall, high-backed stools at the bar and the little tables with granite tops and dove grey chairs tucked underneath, did offer a certain charm. Maud was looking in awe at the rows and rows of French wines that lined the mirrored back wall and then rushed over to gaze at the plethora of daintily-iced cakes and macaroons that were displayed in various-sized glass domes near the front window. Baskets full of freshly baked bread nestled to one side of the bar and staff dressed in crisp white shirts with grey aprons and black trousers offered menus to the guests dotted around. He couldn't help but grin at her fascination. For a teacher, she wasn't very worldly if a small bistro could produce such delight, but maybe she saw something he didn't, the same way she'd seen passion and excitement in his paintings on that first night at the gallery opening. Perhaps he was the sheltered one who should get out and experience life more? He'd pretty much locked himself away for years and held no emotional attachment to anything he did. He enjoyed painting and being with Elliott or his family, but they also drove him mad with their nagging to get out more. He only ever took dates to one restaurant or the little flat above the gallery, it never occurred to him to do anything else. They preferred getting him naked to going out, so who was he to complain?

He pulled out a chair for Maud to sit and their knees touched below the table, making her jump. He was sure the tables here were designed for love as you had to sit near each other and he was rather enjoying the feeling of making Maud nervous. He opened the menu, but he had been to the restaurant on so many occasions, he knew which dish he would choose. He wondered what Maud would pick and watched her eyes dart about the page before she sat back and placed the menu onto the table as a waiter stopped beside her, order pad and pen at the ready, and a welcoming smile for them both. He nodded a greeting at Nate and then turned to Maud to ask for her selection.

She smiled up at him. 'What would you recommend? I was

thinking of something light.'

The waiter thought for a moment, then decided he had the perfect dish and opened the menu with a flourish and pointed to the full description. 'We have a beautiful three cheese soufflé, with a vibrant green salad?'

Maud smiled delightedly. 'That sounds divine.' The waiter appeared thrilled that he had made her so happy and pointed to a wine that would complement the meal, whilst telling her it would taste like nectar from the Gods, which earned him a pat on the arm and another wide smile. He then turned to Nate, who was sitting back in his chair and glowering at him, making him briskly straighten his back and move away from Maud.

'For you, Monsieur Ridgemoor?'

'I'll have my usual, thanks, Tony.' Nate tried to soften his words as he realised he'd been glaring at poor Tony, who was only doing his job and couldn't be blamed for warming to Maud. It appeared to him that most men fell under her spell as soon as she met them but she didn't have a clue what she did to them, the poor suckers. She seduced them with her smile before they even noticed her ample chest and the soft curve of her hips. That was just an added bonus.

Tony, who had begun to sweat under Nate's piercing gaze, scribbled on his pad. 'Of course, Sir. Would you like a glass of wine to accompany the cassoulet?'

'I think I'll try some of the nectar of the Gods,' Nate said drily. 'Bring a bottle and we'll share it.'

Maud nudged his foot with hers and he knew he was being rude, but she appeared to be enjoying herself and hadn't stamped on his toes yet. Nate ran his foot along hers and she jumped and glared at him. 'I thought you wanted to play footsie?' he drawled with a suggestive wink.

'You know I didn't. Stop annoying the waiters, and you look like you've got something in your eye,' she giggled, treading on his toe this time, making him yelp in pain, while her grin spread wide in satisfaction.

He held his hands up in surrender. 'Ok. I'll behave myself and apologise to Tony for behaving like a child.'

'Thank you, young man.' She said primly, but with a wink of her own.

Tony reappeared with their wine, and Nate was very gracious in accepting a glass before telling Tony it really did taste like he was drinking nectar, which made Tony very happy and Maud's face flush, when they both turned and smiled her way. Nate grinned with satisfaction that the day was working out the way he wanted it to, and his mind began to plot other ways to meet Maud 'accidently', all earlier resolutions forgotten.

Chapter Twenty-Seven

Nate had obviously decided he'd better stop winding Maud up because he spent the next couple of hours charming her and finding out more about her life. He seemed so interested that she didn't question what he was up to. Tom did enquire about her past occasionally, but he began talking again before she'd finished a sentence and then changed the topic after a few minutes. She hadn't really paid much attention to it before, but talking to Nate was so refreshing.

As they ate, Nate began telling her a story of how his parents had inadvertently set off a hotel's fire alarm when they had been trying a new tantric sex position, and had fallen and crashed into a panel on the wall in their room. 'I mean,' he laughed, visibly cringing at the memory of their candour, 'what parent would relay this to their own child?'

Maud gasped with laughter. 'And now you're telling me, so that I have that picture in my head too?' She could imagine Camille and Cosmo entwined in a tangled mass of limbs and tried to squeeze her eyes shut and block the picture out.

'Closing your eyes won't help you. Welcome to my world,' he joked.

Maud spooned another mouthful of the heavenly soufflé and tried to distract herself. It worked for a while as the flavour burst and she almost groaned in pleasure.

Nate stopped in his tracks and his pupils dilated. 'You're making my mouth water. I could literally lick your lips and die of ecstasy right now,' he leaned forward and whispered huskily, making her blush bright red. 'I haven't wanted a woman so badly in years, if ever, and you're slowly driving me insane.'

Maud was speechless, but couldn't take her eyes from his

lips. He waved Tony over to add the bill to his account, as Maud looked on in embarrassment at his sudden urge to leave. She quickly spooned another bite of delicious food into her mouth as, however nervous she was about his words, she'd never eaten a plate of food that had almost left her as aroused as his sultry words, and she needed time to think before she grabbed his gorgeous face and pressed her mouth to his. She placed her cutlery neatly on her plate and, brushing a stray crumb from her lap, dared to look into his fiery eyes.

'Am I holding you up?' she asked carefully, not knowing what to do.

Nate glowered at her again and then sighed. 'You're not, but I can't watch you almost have an orgasm over a cheese soufflé and not pull you over the table and take a taste for myself.'

Maud wrung her hands in her lap, feeling completely ruffled. 'Nate! You can't say thing like that.'

Nate ground his teeth and looked like he was struggling to control his emotions. 'I know, and it's bloody frustrating.'

'But you have a girlfriend.'

'Do I?'

'I... Uh...' Maud's brain was muddled and she couldn't think straight. She was sure Dot said he had a girlfriend. 'Well, I have a boyfriend,' she said simply, almost wishing it wasn't true.

'And therein lies the problem,' he said honestly.

'I don't know what to say...'

'That you'll bin the boyfriend and then we can get to know each other properly?' he grinned suddenly, a glint lighting his eye.

'Nate!' Maud couldn't believe he was being so blatant. His words were really hot, but she wasn't that kind of girl... was she?

Nate took her hand from her lap and ran his fingers over hers, feeling her racing pulse at her wrist. He dropped a series of searing kisses on the delicate spot and then gently placed her hand back, leaving a scorching heat there, too. 'I don't like competition, but I'm willing to make an exception for you. I won't touch you again, though,' he looked deep into her eyes, 'until you ask me to.'

'I won't ask you to,' Maud gasped, feverishly dabbing her neck with her napkin

'Won't you? Are you sure?'

'I'm with Tom.'

'So dump him.' Nate looked like he had never wanted anything more and the fact that she was loyal seemed to be something he hadn't encountered before. Maud guessed that if he liked a woman, he wouldn't have to try and take them from someone else, they would probably leave of their own accord anyway. It would take a strong woman to turn down an offer from a red-hot man like Nate. He sent a woman's pheromones into overdrive. He'd said he wouldn't cross the line, but she could clearly see that he sure as hell wanted to.

Maud stood up shakily and smiled her thanks to Tony. 'Can I pay for lunch?'

Nate got up too and ignored her question at first. 'I apologise. I will try to learn to control my temper and stop myself from kissing you senseless and dragging you back to the gallery and upstairs to the flat.' Maud stood open-mouthed in shock, then shut up in case he did as he said and kissed her. Part of her wanted him to grab her and kiss her anyway, but that would make her a cheat, and she abhorred that kind of behaviour. She'd been burnt by it too many times. She'd just never been in the position of being the one who could cheat before. No one had declared how exciting she was, or how much she turned them on, just by eating food in front of them. In fact, they usually made her feel invisible, and she had assumed this was normal. It was a bit of a revelation to feel so desired. Even Tom didn't make her feel this womanly and aroused. Plus, it was broad daylight – and they were supposed to be having an innocent lunch.

Nate was getting restless and began running his eyes over her soft curves. 'I invited you,' he insisted. 'You can pay next time.'

Maud gave him a look she kept especially for the naughty children in her class, but he grinned, as he knew he'd got her.

She was too polite to not return the favour.

'You are incorrigible.'

'I know,' he smiled, as he put a warm hand on her waist and guided her back to the gallery, to call a car to take her home.

Chapter Twenty-Eight

Maud woke up a week later and decided that Tom deserved more of her attention. Her dreams were full of Nate and she felt terribly disloyal for being this way. Nate had kept his word and they hadn't seen each other, but they had exchanged a few texts and had one or two late night phone calls. She'd also had a few dates with Tom the previous week, and had refused to do any more trivial tasks for Dot or Nate. Nate had called her just to chat, and she had enjoyed speaking to him, but he hadn't flirted with her at all and, if anything, it had left her feeling deflated after their meal out together. She felt confused about her feelings for him, as he'd been pretty blatant in letting her know that he wanted sex with her. She was sure he'd be great in bed and it was time she had more than she was currently getting from Tom. For some reason she was holding him off and he was easily distracted.

Tom had tried every trick in the book to get her to sleep with him, and she was wavering, but his moods changed so quickly sometimes that if she didn't jump his bones when he wanted her too, then he blew cold and brushed her off. Even when she tried to explain how tired she was at work, she knew he was getting annoyed with her and she'd have to up her game or lose him. He'd told her more than once that he could pretty much date any woman he wanted to and that she was a bit frigid, which had made her want to cry, but she'd refused to let him know how his words stung.

Maybe he was right? He was so good-natured, usually, that he must be frustrated with her behaviour and she couldn't blame him. She was feeling pretty frustrated and confused herself. They'd almost fallen into bed last week. They'd spent the evening at the pictures and had cuddled all the way home, but Dot had been sitting on her doorstep with a huge pizza when they got back to the bungalow and, for a second, she'd been relieved.

Tom had been glad to see Dot and had regaled her with snippets of their night and the film. He'd slung his arm affectionately over Dot's shoulder and whispered something in her ear, which had made her scream with laughter. Dot had been suitably impressed about their night out, but had refused to go home, and then snored quietly in Maud's immaculate spare room and had strewn the covers all over the floor in her sleep. Tom had been uber-affectionate and asked to stay too, but the thought of Dot behind a paper-thin wall in the next room made Maud cringe, however much she thought she might like him to stay. But they had made out a lot... and things had definitely heated up.

Over the next week, Maud hadn't had a spare moment to go on more dates with Tom, but he seemed happier after their night of 'almost sex' and things were progressing. She was still feeling tired and on edge, in case her phone pinged with a notification, telling her Nate had left a message. She found herself looking forward to the texts that he sent with things she might find interesting. Once it had been a photo of a little painting of the sea he had found in a tiny gallery and another time a picture of a dog that was smiling straight up into his phone, which made her laugh and send a smiley face emoji back.

Tom had asked her for Dot's number so that he could speak to her about some art, and Dot had mentioned in passing that he'd called her a few times, which was odd, but she didn't dwell on it as she had too much to do.

To be honest, Tom was being super-affectionate to her at school, and had asked her out often. It had got to the point where he was suffocating her a bit. Then suddenly he was hardly around as he'd apparently had to spend a lot of time back near his family. He hadn't told her much about it, other than his brother was having relationship problems, and he was going to travel home fairly regularly. He seemed to spend a few days at school, and the rest of the time he was nowhere to be seen, and certainly didn't have an hour or two for her. A full-time contract wasn't available at the school yet and Zoe had come back from maternity leave, then asked to work only half the week so she could spend time with her new baby girl, so Tom had agreed to stay. He was a little more stressed and he wasn't always in the same classroom as Maud, but the new hours suited him whilst his brother needed him.

She knew it was probably her fault for keeping him hanging on without letting him know where he stood. She'd decided she would just have to make a decision and either commit to him or let him go, but the pressure he was applying was making her back off. She knew that she would usually have slept with a new boyfriend by now, but she hadn't had a chance with Tom, and recently she wasn't completely sure she wanted to. The initial burn of desire had worn off, as his constant touching made her edgy instead of alive. It was almost creepy, but she knew this was just her inexperience and not his fault. He was trying really hard with her and she would have to sort herself out and stop mooning over Nate. Nate wasn't a good option for her as he was definitely a womaniser, so she'd be safer with Tom who was solid and dependable.

She thought of the amount of times Dot had told her about different women coming out of the flat above the gallery and her stomach turned over. She shook her head to clear it and tried to focus on work. Dot had come round last night and they had decided that the belts looked much better with simple coloured fabrics behind them, so Maud had been gradually changing her style so that she would be comfortable wearing one at their gallery opening. She felt like her soul was unfurling and the real person inside was gradually shedding her skin and reaching for the light. Dot was still wearing clashing colours and said it was because people expected it of her, but Maud knew she had bought some different clothes too and was waiting for the right time to experiment and not scare off her clients with the new demure Dot. Maud snickered at this as, although the latest clothes were toned down, they certainly weren't that much better, and she secretly wondered if Dot was having difficulty changing her style because it was either ingrained, or it was more of a reflection of her actual personality than they had both realised.

Planning the exhibition had been exhausting but hilarious, with Dot's sharp wit and constant new ideas for another wacky addition to their show. Maud had needed to rein in some of the plans as they were completely bonkers, but between them they had come up with something pretty good. She couldn't believe the amount of work that went in to one show. She had a renewed respect for Dot and would be forever in her debt for becoming her agent and supervising her first exhibition, as Maud would have run for the hills long ago if Dot hadn't stood firmly in her way and shouted at her to stop being such a coward.

They had been thankful that the painting drops were still generating publicity too. The stories had slowed down, but reporters were still hanging out in parks and a few really dedicated ones were determined to discover the artist's identity. It had seemed strange to Maud to be planning art drops with Dot rather than hiding in bushes on her own, but it felt good to have someone on her side. They'd had to plan the launch in record time as Dot wouldn't let Maud give too many more paintings away, now that they knew how valuable they were. The exhibition was shaping up and the nearer it got, the more she began to quiver with fear inside.

Chapter Twenty-Nine

Nate rammed his booted foot into the waste paper bin and sent it crashing across the floor. Elliott, who'd been sitting with his feet up on Nate's huge dark blue suede designer couch, looked up from his newspaper and swung his feet to the floor. He looked like he was going to comment, then obviously thought better of it and buried his nose back into the paper with a shrug.

Nate was frustrated that Maud had walked right into his lair and she'd slipped through his fingers. He'd heard she was still with Tom, which infuriated him, but he intended to change that. He'd heard from his sister that Tom had been sending slightly inappropriate texts to her, and the thought made his blood boil. What was Maud doing wasting her time on such an idiot? She seemed like a bright girl. Couldn't she see he was a player? Dot had begged him not to say anything, as she was embarrassed and said she'd probably misunderstood the context of the texts, but Nate wasn't so sure.

Dot had told him that Maud's best friend Daisy had noticed Maud's style evolving and was jealous that Dot has been able to make her change when she'd tried for years with no success. Dot was spitting mad that Daisy was making Maud feel guilty, but what could he do?

He'd tried to arrange to meet Dot to talk about Maud, but she kept foisting him onto Elliott, which made poor old El mad too. It wasn't that they didn't like spending time together, but Elliott knew all about Maud and seemed to find the whole situation gut-wrenchingly funny. Nate hunched his shoulders and sunk down into his chair in defeat. Maybe Maud wasn't the one for him, and he should let her go.

Elliott glanced up in sympathy for his friend and went to

make them both a coffee from the shiny new machine Dot had bought Nate to keep him awake and painting when he was tired. 'You know she bought me that so I could be more productive, not as a sisterly treat for her hard-working brother?' said Nate to Elliott's back.

Elliott smiled and walked towards Nate with two steaming mugs of fragrant coffee. 'Yep. She told me. I said she was mercenary, but she just laughed and said that she's your agent and has to get the best from you. She said you're grumpy and need coffee to paint.'

Nate shook his head in exasperation. Dot really was a one-off. It was good to know she was thinking of him. 'I don't know what you see in her.'

It was Elliott's turn to look glum for a second, but his sunny nature wouldn't let him stay down. 'You love her as much as I do and you should be used to her madcap thought processes by now. Didn't you stay up and paint all night?'

Nate grudgingly nodded and stretched out his long jean-clad legs.

'It worked then, didn't it? You're being more productive as you can't sleep on a coffee high,' said Elliott.

'You really are an idiot.'

'Says a man who is also in love with a woman who he can't have,' Elliott jeered, happy finally to have someone else in the same predicament as him, even if it meant that Nate was miserable for a while.

Nate was shocked and jumped up, almost sloshing half his coffee onto his hands and looking at the slivery scars that were burned into his skin. 'I'm not in love. I just think Maud's boyfriend is an idiot, and I like her company.'

'Sure. You carry on telling yourself that.' Elliott took a satisfying sip of coffee and went to pat a stunned Nate on the shoulder before reaching down and picking up the bent waste paper bin, and setting it back on its base.

Chapter Thirty

Dot rummaged around a drawer she had in her office, which was crammed full of designer clothes. She advocated non-wrinkle fibres as she was quite messy at home, but her parents' housekeeper, Tandy, usually told her off and then rushed away to wash and iron everything for her, so it didn't really matter either way. She'd begun keeping some of the designer samples she was sent by fashion houses, who wanted her to wear their clothes to gallery openings. Usually she was too busy to look at them and just shoved them into this very deep drawer, but today she needed to change out of the rather heavy and sweaty fake feather blouse she'd been wearing all day.

She pulled on a burnt orange crop top and hot pink denim skirt, which just skimmed her bum, and called out to Nate, who was sitting perched on her reception desk, chatting away to one of her part-time receptionists, Rob. Nate was looking relaxed and comfortable in dark denim jeans and a white shirt, open at the collar. She sighed at his movie star good looks and then took a quick glance at herself in the tall mirror on the back wall. Deciding she looked just fine and jauntily grabbing her bag, which had cake sprinkles glued all over the front in the shape of flowers, she nudged him on the shoulder and they walked amicably to the local wine bar.

Dot smiled to a few people she recognised and Nate ignored them all, as usual. As soon as they were seated at their table in the dimly-lit but decidedly snazzy bar, Nate began to draw her into a conversation about the secret artist. Dot gulped a big mouthful of the delicious ruby-red wine that had appeared in front of her and almost choked on it. She laughed with false merriment and waved to a man two tables away to say thanks for the bottle he had just sent over. He was a riotous artist who wanted her to represent him. She'd been considering it until she met Maud, and might sign him at a later date, but currently she had enough work with her family and the surprise show. She liked the fact that he was fearless, as not many people would approach or interrupt a meal at a table where Nate sat, unless they knew him well enough to be growled at in good humour. Most people liked the fact that Nate spoke his mind and loved him anyway, but he could walk a fine line with his banter sometimes. He really was a grizzly bear, but for once she was happy to not have the interruption.

Surprisingly, Nate wanted to chat and all he could talk about was the way the mystery artist captured the eyes of the animals they drew, and he wished he could express emotion like that in his work. Dot almost choked on her wine again. This was getting stressful. Was Nate stupid? His work was rammed full of emotion. It almost made her cry to look at the beauty and pain shown there. He obviously didn't know how open he was within his work. It was why people respected him so much, not just for being a talented artist, but because he didn't talk about his past, he painted it. She'd never heard him put down his work before but she was fascinated to hear what else he would say. She supposed she should comfort him, so she picked up his hand, which he looked at in surprise.

'Nate... we all know your work is sublime. The new artist is good, but you paint from the heart.' She squeezed his hand and he didn't pull away but looked confused.

'What do you mean?'

'You don't talk a lot, but you express your feelings in your work.' Dot smiled up into his eyes and he still looked perplexed, even though she was being sincere for once.

Nate took a sip of the wine and thought for a moment. 'I don't express my feelings. I just paint landscapes that people seem to like,' he tried to joke.

Dot grinned with genuine warmth and her heart melted a little. She loved him so much, but he could be a royal pain in her backside. He was macho and boorish, but he'd become a bit reclusive over the years and it was hard to get him to

148

express himself vocally, so she didn't want to scare him off when he was finally seeking out her opinion. 'You show your emotions by painting troubled scenes of fields or buildings with deep swirls of colour or underlying details that people spend years trying to fathom, but above all you show your own inner turmoil. Lena did a great job on you. When she set fire to herself, she took your soul with her.'

All colour drained from Nate's face and Dot realised she'd gone too far. She'd wanted to talk to him about the way he was cocooning himself from the world, and his emotions, and only letting a few people in. He needed to realise that Lena was a psychopath and not worth the years of suffering, making him into the fragmented man he was now.

Dot turned to the waiter who had just arrived at their table and ordered for both of them, as Nate had gone deadly quiet and was staring into space. She leaned in and wrapped her arms around him to make him snap out of it. 'I'm sorry if I upset you, but it's about time you realised it wasn't your fault and started living again.'

She rubbed his arms and the silvery scars that ran up them were reflected in the candlelight. 'She chose to do what she did and she's left you with both physical and mental scars. If she wanted to punish you for some stupid misdeed she believed you'd done to her, then enough. Just because you wanted to break up with her when you were both only nineteen, it doesn't give her the right to destroy her own life, then yours. You've suffered enough, Nate, and it should end now.'

Nate hung his head and Dot hugged him even harder. He looked into her eyes and softly kissed her cheek before hugging her back and then reaching for his wine. Dot hoped Maud would forgive her, but she was going to tell Nate what they were planning. He needed something else to think about and she hated lying to him.

Dot had practically had to pull teeth to discover the truth about the day Maud had visited the gallery, but she had finally admitted that she'd spent the afternoon with Nate. Nate had promised Dot that he would call Maud and tell her Dot had

149

cancelled their meeting, but the cheeky sod had 'forgotten' and taken Maud out to lunch instead. Dot was also sure he'd phoned their parents just to get her out of the way. Maud had eventually confided that he'd plied her with wine and flirted with her. Naughty boy. Dot grinned at him suddenly and decided that someone like Maud was just what he needed, someone who wouldn't hurt him, but would make him smile again. It was kind of unfortunate that Maud was happy with Tom, but she was definitely taken.

Dot knew Nate was jealous of Tom and Maud's relationship, but Maud told her Nate had decided to stay out of it and hope that the relationship fizzled out. The man was delusional. The problem was, Dot knew that Maud was an all or nothing girl, and not very experienced with men. Nate had no idea, but he probably scared her half to death with his full-on manliness, and Tom had lucked out and found her before Nate had.

Just as she was about to tell Nate what was going on, a stick-thin blonde woman came rushing over to their table and draped herself all over Nate. He looked annoyed at the interruption, but then obviously decided to behave like a gentleman for once and had the good grace to stand up and introduce her to Dot, who was speechless at the way the woman was running her fingers through Nate's hair, until he caught her hand and brushed it away. He politely tried to suggest they meet another time, as he was with his sister, but the girl just gushed about how much she wanted to meet Dot, and plonked herself down on an available chair, signalling the waiter for another wine glass. Dot was about to stamp her foot and grab the wine from her reach when she saw Nate's warning raised eyebrow, and she realised that this was either a girlfriend, which meant he was the rat she thought he was, and Maud had had a lucky escape, or this brash woman was a customer of the gallery and she needed to play nice.

Chapter Thirty-One

Nate was feeling really fed up, but he had a plan and thought it inspired. Maud had been avoiding him. She'd replied to some of his texts, but hadn't answered any of his calls. He'd been talking to Elliott about it and had decided that if idiot Tom was Maud's choice, then he would have to accept it and should get to know the guy better. Maud was one of Dot's best friends now, and would be in his life for a long time unless they fell out, which with Maud's gentle nature, he couldn't picture, so he needed to think of another idea.

He'd managed to coerce Dot into giving him Tom's number and had sent him a text to invite him on a boy's night out. If the man was so amazing, then it was about time that Nate and Elliott found out why. Nate grinned suddenly and his mood lifted as his phone pinged with a message, saying that Tom would be back from visiting family that day and could join him and El later.

Nate glanced at his watch and wondered how much hardball to play? He could ask a few of his beautiful women friends to arrive and surprise them, to see how Tom reacted, or he could play it cool and see where the battle lines were drawn. He was pretty sure that Tom wasn't aware that he liked Maud, or that Nate knew about the texts he'd sent Dot, so it would be interesting to see if he was as confident out of his comfort zone.

Deciding that he wouldn't play too dirty, Nate grabbed his jacket and headed for the studio, to put any residual emotion into his work.

Later that evening, Nate ordered the drinks from the bartender and leaned on the counter while he watched Elliott and Tom chat in the booth they had chosen. They were in a trendy bar, conveniently just a few streets along from the gallery, which meant Elliott and Nate hadn't had to travel far. The place was buzzing with conversation, and a four-piece jazz band were playing in a corner. People were already huddling in groups and talking loudly, while some were swaying to the music on the little dance floor surrounded by booths.

Nate was oblivious to the interest he was generating from the women in the room and he grabbed the beers that had just been placed in front of him and walked Elliott's way. Elliott gave him a grateful glance, took the drink and gulped some of the chilled amber liquid down with a sigh of satisfaction. Nate soon found out that Tom had been bragging about how easy his job was at the school where he worked with Maud, and regaling Elliott about how he spent half of the week travelling now and didn't have a spare moment to see her, even though she was a 'nice girl'. He'd begun speaking as soon as they'd reached the booth, telling Elliott he was planning on working as a substitute teacher at a selection of schools until a permanent job came up and, although the women in the bar were decent, sometimes you couldn't beat the desperate and womanly charms of a school mum. Nate had arrived at this point and El had brought him up to speed. Tom had winked and explained he could take his pick of the single school mums, and most of the teachers, too. He loved being surrounded by women all day. It was a perk of the job.

Seeing Elliott's eyes narrow and his fists bunch, as one of his friend's wives was a school mum, and he didn't think she'd be too happy being described as desperate when she wouldn't touch someone like Tom if he was the last man alive, Nate intervened. He clinked his bottle with Tom's and sent Elliott a warning glare. They needed to keep Tom onside for now, while they found out more about him. Tom laughed heartily and slapped Elliott on the back, saying he'd just been joking, but Nate sensed that he was doing some groundwork to test what type of boys' night out this would be. Nate had already warned Elliott that Tom had sent sleazy texts to Dot, so he was walking a fine line before he'd even arrived.

Elliott sent Nate a look to tell him he'd been right about the slime-ball next to him and Nate rolled his eyes behind Tom's back, before slipping into the booth opposite him and smiling like a tiger about to pounce. 'How's your day been?' he asked Tom, appearing friendly and sociable. Elliott knew this wouldn't last long though, as Nate's shoulders were tense and poker straight. He was smiling but his eyes were like heat-seeking missiles on Tom's face.

'I've been travelling; I only work a few days each week at the school now. I often pop and see my brother, as he's having woman trouble,' Tom looked to the men for solidarity and found it lacking slightly, so he just shrugged and ploughed on. 'It's great to be invited on a boys' night, it's ages since I had time to go out.'

Elliott cringed, as he knew what was coming when Nate spoke. 'You haven't been out with Dot or Maud lately, then?'

Tom looked confused, then slightly suspicious. 'I haven't seen much of Maud, as she's working hard on some mystery project with your sister, and our schedules have been crazy. We have managed to get some special moments alone, though,' he drawled, obviously hoping Elliott would be impressed and Nate jealous. 'You have to make time for your special girl.'

Nate curled his fingers into his palms and Elliott could see he was trying to think about anything else but planting his fist into Tom's smug face. 'Have you seen Dot?'

Tom's smile faltered and he took a slug of his beer, taking a moment to process the fact that Nate and Elliott obviously knew he'd been texting Dot. 'Why would I have seen Dot? I barely have a minute to see Maud during the day, as I'm in such demand in different classes. Sometimes I am only with Maud for a day or two before moving on somewhere else in the building. Keeping up with classwork during a job share means that I can't socialise in class. I have to keep that for lunchtimes, but Maud often rushes off-site to meet Dot for lunch now.'

'So you and both girls are just friends now?' asked Elliott, holding his breath for the answer and hoping Tom said the right thing, before either he or Nate called him out for trying it on with two friends.

Tom flushed and then tried for bravado. 'Maud and I decided a while ago to keep things casual. She's not ready for a commitment and neither am I. We don't get many hours together, so we can see other people if we like.'

Nate knew this was a lie, as Maud was loyal to him. Maybe she was getting bored with him and backing off? The thought made Nate feel suddenly chipper. The guy was a jerk. It looked like Tom was sensing Maud was hesitant, too, and was covering his own back. Nate looked like he'd just been handed a priceless gift. He crossed his arms, which bulged with muscles, and made Tom look his way. 'So you are happy for Maud to text other men and go out on dates?'

Tom gulped and shifted uneasily in his seat, looking like he wished he'd kept his big mouth shut. 'I... um, I hadn't really given it much thought. I guess I need to clarify the situation with her.' Tom was about to say something else when three beautiful women approached their table and his eyes lit up, as he casually grabbed his beer and sat back further into the booth, giving them a cocksure stare, all thoughts of Maud forgotten.

Elliott waited for Nate to send the girls politely on their way, but he couldn't have looked happier with the interruption and invited the girls to join them. Nate knew that Elliott would fleetingly wonder if Nate had set this up, but the timing was too perfect, and Elliott should know better than to think that Nate needed to ask women to join them. He usually had to fend them off.

Nate spotted his sister the minute she entered the bar, and he glowered as he noticed who she was with. Tom had his arm round a stunning blonde woman with long hair and a tiny silver dress and Nate held his breath to see if Maud would notice this and bash Tom over the head with her handbag. He'd spent the evening getting steadily drunker, stroking the blonde's hair and whispering loudly in her ear that he loved women who told him that he was great in bed, while she batted her eyelashes flirtatiously. It was turning Nate's stomach and he was glad for an excuse to stand up and move away from him.

Maud was giggling and holding on to Dot's arm for dear life as she bent down to straighten her shoe. Nate saw she was wearing his favourites and blood rushed to his head. What was it about this woman? Why couldn't he just grab one of the stunners who'd been trying to sit on his lap earlier and take her home, instead of trying to sort out Maud's love life? Maud turned and saw him, and her face lit up. He felt his stomach tighten and heat fill his loins. He smiled into her eyes and then his gaze flicked to Dot in question, as he could see by the way Maud was weaving towards him that she was pretty drunk.

Dot rushed after her and Nate reached in and caught her hand, just as she fell over her own feet and launched herself at him. He caught the fragrance of her perfume and then realised she was hugging his elbow for support, so he pulled her tighter into his side, just as Tom saw who it was and sprang apart from the blonde, who pouted and melted away into the crowd. Dot gave her a filthy stare and then shared the same look with Tom, who ignored her and pulled Maud's hand, until she fell onto the booth beside him with a laugh. Nate was furious that she hadn't seen Tom's behaviour and then his mood thawed as he realised how cute Maud was when she was drunk. It was hard to stay mad when she was around. She was staring goofily at him and trying to prop her elbows on the table before sinking down to rest her head on the cool surface. Dot cringed and Nate smiled as the table was sticky with spilt drinks. Dot stood next to Maud to hoist her up again. 'I think I need to get Maud home,' she said, looking at Tom with distaste.

Nate was desperate to offer to help, but Elliott signalled towards Tom. There was no way he was letting her go home with him in her drunken state. Tom was getting up and offering to take her, but Nate quickly drew his phone out of his jeans pocket and called the girls a car to drive them. 'Stay at her house, Dotty,' he said with steel in his voice. She looked as though she was going to argue, then decided against it when she saw Tom get up and grab his coat.

Nate quickly signalled for the bartender to bring them another round of drinks. It didn't take much to persuade Tom that he couldn't abandon his first proper boys' night with them so early, and he'd glanced at Maud and seemed to realise he wouldn't be going anywhere with her tonight, as Dot was practically glued to her side. Maud had her arms linked around Dot's neck while Dot looked pretty pained, but she sighed and put her hand on Maud's arm as she giggled and waved happily to the men, blowing them kisses and then planting a smacker right on Dot's face, barely missing her nose.

The blonde girl watched them from the bar. As soon as they left the building, she sidled over and slinked back in beside Tom, who gave her a knowing smile that made Nate and Elliott realise that this was going to be a really long and painful night.

Chapter Thirty-Two

Dot was freezing. She rolled over in Maud's spare bed and realised she'd thrown the covers on the floor in her sleep. She'd been cross with Nate for expecting her to take Maud home the night before, but to be honest she'd been glad to get away from Tom before she let slip to Maud that her boyfriend was sending her inappropriate texts and threw a drink straight into his smarmy face. Why Nate and El had wanted to go out with him, she'd never know. Nate was supposedly hung up on Maud, and yet there he was on a night out with her boyfriend. She'd never understand that man, she sighed, reaching down and snuggling into the duvet again.

She looked around and was happy to see some of Maud's older artworks displayed on the walls in the otherwise stark spare room. Dot had stayed there many times now, and could see why Maud loved it. Maybe she should buy her own bungalow and create a hidden studio in the garden?

She was surprised Maud had had the courage to put her art up here, as she'd got really drunk on Mojitos the night before and morosely told Dot that her parents really disapproved of her new look. Her mum had said her hair, which now fell in soft waves to her shoulders, was a mess and that her clothes, which were feminine but had an artistic edge, were inappropriate for a school teacher, and that her new friends were obviously a bad influence. She also kept ringing Maud to tell her she felt unwell, and had taken to her bed for a week. Maud's mum was more of a drama queen than Dot herself. Who'd even known that was possible?

Bad influence. If anything, Dot had changed the most since meeting Maud. She knew she was a little kinder to other people now, albeit only the ones who didn't really annoy her like Daisy did. Dot's own clothes were less outrageous and she'd stopped dying her hair. She'd visited a top salon and had one of those trendy new blow-dries where your hair was semi-permanently ironed with ceramics, or some such nonsense. She'd sat there, bored stiff, for a couple of hours under the heat, and then walked out of the salon with silky-smooth blonde hair that reached below her shoulders, with sun-kissed highlights.

Dot swung her legs out of bed and cringed when she remembered how Maud had sung at the top of her voice all the way home in the car. She would have to ask Nate to apologise for them, as the poor woman driving their cab had probably gone out and bought earplugs that morning after going to bed with a headache.

Elliott had asked Dot to meet him for a meal this evening, and Dot had stupidly asked Maud to bring Tom, as she'd felt nervous about being alone with El at the moment for some reason. After seeing Tom leering all over that woman in the booth last night, she'd changed her mind and would rather be alone than in his company. Unfortunately, Maud had already accepted.

She took a blissful sip from the glass of water that she'd put on the bedside table last night, after trying for over an hour to get Maud to go to bed, and then giving up and leaving her snoring on the couch in the living room. She was starting to feel more awake now, and recalled she'd tried to cheer Maud up last night after she'd become morose about her parents being so mean, and never seeing Tom. She'd also confided that he was being a bit pushy and suffocating when Maud did see him. Dot had been so tempted to confide in her about the texts from Tom, but she'd heard the phrase 'shoot the messenger,' and didn't want to fall out with her new friend and superstar client. She did casually let slip that Nate had gotten rid of his super-bitchy girlfriend a few weeks ago, though. She'd decided that, even though Nate was popular with women, at least he was a nice person and a better bet for Maud than trashy Tom. Dot thought that she should probably be a bit kinder to Nate, and if he and Maud liked each other, then maybe she should be a bit more sisterly and give them a helpful nudge in the right direction.

Dot felt really mean, well... a tiny bit mean, as she quickly shut her phone and looked innocently at Maud. Maud had taken ages to wake up and shove into the shower that morning, but she was finally looking presentable in a tonal grey dress that had flowers sewn all over it in different shades of blue. She looked fresh and pretty and Dot's stomach did a somersault as she wondered if she was right to interfere.

Maud smiled at her and then walked to her bag as her phone bleeped to tell her she had a message. She looked crestfallen suddenly. 'Oh no! Tom has just said he can't make it tonight.' Dot felt terrible, as Maud appeared genuinely upset.

'Uh, why is that?'

Maud sat down heavily on the couch and looked despondently at her phone. 'He says that something has just come up with work. I can't really complain as I've not spent any time with him because of my art.'

Dot pulled a face and looked away but she seethed at the lies, even though she realised she was being hypocritical. She had asked Elliott to give Tom the number of the blonde girl from last night, as she was someone they both knew. Elliott had been confused, but done as he was told. True to form, Tom had obviously called her and made plans for that night.

Dot was momentarily upset she had ruined Maud's night, but then her phone buzzed as Nate answered her earlier message. 'You'll have to go on your own with El,' said Maud, slumping over and dropping her handbag to the floor.

'Maud,' said Dot carefully. 'Nate has just offered to step in so our night isn't ruined. His own plans have just fallen through and I hate to think of him sitting in on his own...' she wheedled, crossing her fingers behind her back and sending silent thanks that Nate had answered her quickly. She'd decided that it was a good idea for her to see Nate with Maud, to decide whether there was a possibility for that relationship to progress, if Tom was out of the way. She knew it was sneaky, but her brother's and her best friend's happiness were at stake, and it was time for someone to do something about it. If Tom had been a nicer man, she wouldn't have got involved, but as things stood, he deserved all that came to him.

Maud looked embarrassed at the idea of Nate joining them. 'Surely Nate has better things to do than babysit me while you are on a date?'

Dot jumped up in shock. 'I'm not on a date with Elliott! We're just two friends having dinner.'

'Sure you are,' said Maud with a smile as she contemplated her choices for the evening. 'So it's either join you and your brother on a weird sort of non-date date, or sit here like a sad loser on my own?'

Dot recovered well and smiled back at her. 'Yes. Don't be a sad loser all your life.'

'Ok,' Maud said, grabbing her bag and picking up the keys to lock up behind them. 'Let's go.'

The evening had turned out to be a great success, and Nate had been on his best behaviour, as if he'd decided to become Maud's best friend. He was charm personified and had them all holding their sides, aching from laughing at the stories he told them about some of his clients. They had chatted until the sky turned dark and they noticed the clock on the wall, realising that needed to get home for work the next day. Dot and Elliott had enjoyed themselves too, and she was beginning to become a bit girly and confused around him, which was weird. Nate had asked Maud to join him in checking out some new gallery space. Predictably she had blushed, but been unable to refuse as it was the golden 'art' word, which she was addicted to.

Nate looked so happy that Dot's heart melted a little. She'd even grabbed Elliott's hand and given it a squeeze, which had made him beam from ear to ear and bring her hand to his mouth for a kiss, which had made her blush too. She didn't know what was happening, but suddenly Elliott was morphing into a hot man before her eyes, even though he'd been the same person all her life. She didn't know why she was behaving this way, but could only assume she had a silly crush on him as he was always so nice to her, and she'd been too busy to really notice the wonderful man he'd grown into before.

She'd whispered to Maud that going to view art with Nate was a good idea, as they needed to check out other gallery spaces for their own work and they had the final details of their first show to organise. 'It's got to be bigger and better than any other I've done for my family,' she hissed vehemently.

Elliott paid the bill and grabbed Dot's hand to walk her to a taxi, where she seemed to have lost the power of speech, which Maud and Nate seemed to find hilarious for some damn reason, she huffed, haughtily sticking her nose in the air and prancing towards the car.

Chapter Thirty-Three

Nate opened the shiny black car door and Maud felt a frisson of excitement about going out for the day with such a glamorous man. Her neighbours had met him a few times now when he'd popped round to collect Dot, so there was no curtain-swishing when his car pulled up. He'd taken her to four galleries and they'd talked about the little paintings that had been left on park benches, which had made her feel slightly nauseous. He'd told her that the artist had a gift and he'd love to see more of their work. Maud felt like a complete heel for not confiding in him, but Dot had been adamant that they kept it between themselves and Daisy. Dot said she was really proud of their new work and wanted to surprise her family. Maud couldn't argue with that, although she'd purposely chosen a date for the art show when her parents were on their yearly holiday. Their plans were identical every single year, and they returned to the same place time and again. As a child, Maud had loved visiting friendly places, but as she had grown older, it had become monotonous. She'd tried to make them see the joy in experiencing different cultures, but they'd looked at her as if she was an alien and then patted her head in sympathy for her not understanding the benefits of familiarity, as if she was a pet dog. The last thing she wanted was for them to stand in the middle of a crowded room and look horrified as she opened herself up to the world and presented her collection of work. It would ruin the evening she had spent many restless nights over and, although it was harsh, she just didn't want them there.

Nate had been inspiring to listen to. As they'd viewed the different styles of art, he'd explained how each artist worked and the techniques they employed to capture their subjects.

Maud didn't have to pretend to be fascinated, as the timbre of his voice made her bones feel like warm honey and he kept gazing into her eyes to see if she was enjoying the visit, as if her pleasure meant something to him. She felt like a precious gem in his hand, as he made sure she was happy with every decision he made about where they would visit next. Tom would have just dragged her along anywhere that suited him. She hadn't heard from him since the boys' night out, but presumed that she'd embarrassed him with her drunken antics as he was such a responsible man. She'd never seen him falling over tables in an alcoholic stupor or spewing his guts up onto the pavement after a heavy night out. She supposed she should have called him to apologise, but she was a bit miffed that he hadn't checked to see if she got home ok, before cancelling their only date night for ages.

Shaking her head to clear it, she tried to concentrate on her current dilemma. She was rapidly falling head over heels for her best friend's brother. She knew he liked her too, but she was wary of having her heart broken again, or ruining the wonderful friendship they had discovered with each other. Nate had nudged her shoulder to get her attention, as he'd found them a traditional café and they had eaten the most divine little sandwiches and dainty cakes. It had been funny to watch Nate trying to eat the iced fancies when he had such huge hands.

She took a deep breath and smiled into his eyes. 'How did you get your scars?' She looked at his arms. He was wearing a casual blue shirt and jeans, but the shirt was rolled up a tiny bit at the wrists. Nate usually wore long sleeves, but she'd noticed he was being a bit less careful about it lately, and she sometimes got a glimpse of the marks. It made her heart break to think of someone hurting him. Dot had told her the basics, but hadn't elaborated, which had been frustrating.

Nate glanced down at his arms and looked like he was having an internal battle about how much to tell her. She hoped he wouldn't back away from her now that they were forming some sort of friendship bond.

'When I was nineteen I was a bit of a jock,' he said quietly.

163

'I had been dating a girl called Lena for about a year, but she was so possessive and jealous of everyone, especially Dot and Elliott.' Maud understood how someone could fall out with Dot, as she was such a whirlwind and so bossy, but Elliott? He was the kindest man Maud had ever met.

Nate saw her confusion and ploughed on. 'I need to explain while I have the courage.' He took her hand in his and his fingers aimlessly trailed across her skin, making it tingle with very inappropriate lust, considering this was a serious conversation. Nate wasn't even looking at her now but staring into space with a troubled frown, as if remembering a terrible time. 'She didn't like anyone taking my time from her. She was Dot's best friend, but tried to set us against each other by telling me Dot was sleeping around. I got overprotective and she screamed at me for not believing her. It took years for the damage to heal.' Maud hadn't known Dot for long, but they had talked about past boyfriends and she knew that Dot hadn't had that many for a woman her age, so this Lena had done a right job with Nate, sullying her name at such a young age. Poor Dot.

'When I realised how delusional Lena had become, I tried to break it off with her, but she cried and pleaded, then she would appear in my student flat half-naked and embarrass my friends. Eventually she persuaded me to get back with her. I'm only human,' he sighed and rubbed his tired eyes. 'But it got too much, and I explained I couldn't be with her again. Looking back, I should have had more sensitivity and been kinder, but she was suffocating me. She told me she'd slept with Elliott, which I shouldn't have believed as he's the most loyal friend you could ask for. I was so burned up by anger, I still didn't see how ill she was, and I punched Elliott.' Maud gasped and held her hand to her mouth in shock.

Nate hung his head in shame. 'Elliott didn't speak to me for years after that. I didn't realise that Lena had a mental illness until it was too late. She was fixated on me and felt that the only way she could be happy was when she was alone with me. She alienated my friends and family until I didn't know which way to turn. I blamed them for not supporting me. In the end my parents spoke to hers, and they made me see she was ill. Her parents had tried to get help for her for years, but she'd seemed calmer after she met me, so they had let it slide.'

Maud felt so angry with Lena's parents for being irresponsible and not warning Nate or his family. She could understand their need for a fulfilled life for their daughter, but not at the cost of someone else's happiness. She held his hand in her own and he seemed surprised by the gesture, but he didn't pull away, just gave her a sad smile.

'Lena called me and asked me to meet her at the end of my parents' garden by the boating lake. She said she wanted to apologise, as she'd made up the things about Dot and Elliott, because she was jealous of the relationship I had with them. I was so angry that she'd caused me all these problems, but I still cared about her, so I agreed to go.' He looked up at Maud as if he expected her to be disgusted with him, but she only had compassion in her eyes.

Maud felt tears brim over her lashes and Nate used his thumb to gently brush them away before leaning in and kissing her cheek, and resting his forehead on hers. He continued speaking quietly and Maud tried to hold onto her emotions for the poor teenager he had been, but in the end she let the tears flow. 'When I arrived, she was sitting in our rowing boat wearing a long white chiffon dress. She looked almost angelic and was apologetic as she asked me to row her to the middle of the lake so that no one else could hear her apology.' Maud wiped her tears away and picked up a napkin to blow her nose very messily, which made Nate smile and sit back, still holding her hands across the table like a lifeline.

'When I had finished rowing us to the middle of the lake she asked me to reconsider my decision about leaving her. I was astounded. I thought she'd realised it wasn't going to work, as I'd told her often enough. I said no. She raised a glass of what I thought was wine, and then threw it into the bottom of the boat. When I looked down I realised that the whole inside of the boat was wet. She'd doused it with petrol.' Maud was horrified and sat back in alarm, her gaze going to the scars snaking up his arms.

'Before I could react she'd lit a match and thrown it to the floor. The boat burst into flames and my first reaction was to jump.' He hung his head in shame and Maud moved her chair round the table to hug him.

'Anybody would have jumped from a burning boat!'

'I should have grabbed her with me,' he said sadly. 'I've replayed the situation a million times, but I felt the heat of the flames and jumped. When I hit the water, I turned to see if she'd jumped too. I thought she'd been messing around with a lethally dangerous game, but I didn't think she was trying to kill us both. I swam nearer and tried to reach her,' he looked morosely at his arms, 'but the flames fought me back. I hear her screams in my nightmares, that scene haunts me, but I never manage to save her.'

Maud wiped more tears away and kissed Nate's cheek. She turned his face to make him really look at her, and stared right into his eyes. 'You can't change the past, but you can change what happens now. From what you've told me, Lena was troubled and needed professional help. This isn't about you trying to save her, Nate, it's about saving yourself from this hell now. You didn't leave her to die, she tried to kill you both and you survived. I, for one, am eternally thankful that you did, and so are your family and friends.'

She stood up and threw some money on the table to cover the meal and pulled him up beside her. 'Come on. It's time we went out and had some fun. Both of us have been living in the past. We should start on our futures.'

Nate gave her a half smile. 'Thanks for understanding and not calling me a freak,' he joked, trying to shake off the embarrassment of sharing his story.

Maud led him out into the sunshine. She linked her arm around his waist as they walked in a companionable silence to the next gallery, trying to pretend that their friendship hadn't shifted to a different emotional level over the last couple of hours.

Chapter Thirty-Four

Maud had left Nate that evening with such regret. She'd wished that she could invite him in as he pulled up outside her bungalow, but they were both emotionally wrought and they had work the next day. They'd carried on talking as they walked around the last gallery of the day, and had agreed to meet up again soon. Nate had leaned across his seat in the car and given her a tender kiss on the lips before she got out. She'd almost burst into tears again, but hadn't wanted to upset or confuse things more than they already were. How had her life suddenly turned upside down, in such a short space of time?

The phone had been ringing as she opened her door and she rushed to answer it, hoping that Nate had decided to overrule her and was about to tell her he had turned the car around and was coming back for her. Instead Tom's voice came on the line and she sighed and opened a cupboard door to pour herself a glass of wine, as she was exhausted.

'Where have you been all day?' he demanded to know. Maud had thought that maybe Tom would be annoyed with her for spending the day with Nate, but after all they had shared, she really didn't care what he thought anymore. He had been getting pushy lately and they had begun to argue. When she wearily told him where she had been, he almost hissed down the line. 'He can't keep his hands off you, can he? He obviously likes going after women who aren't available and have boyfriends. You shouldn't hang around with him and Dot so much. They trade on your sweet nature for their own benefit. They're users.'

Maud ignored his comments as she was too darn tired. She changed the subject and told him how worried she was about

Daisy, to try and distract him from the topic of Nate. She was surprised when Tom laughed suddenly. 'Daisy is so clingy, and then ignores you when her boyfriend wants to see her. He's all she ever talks about at school, and I've tried to talk about us to her a few times, but she just talks over me and waffles on and on about her incredible sex life. It's pretty disgusting and not appropriate for her to talk that way in front of her friend's boyfriend,' he said with disapproval in his voice.

Maud felt upset about what he was saying, as she didn't realise Daisy was as open with other people as she was with her. Maud had thought it was because they were best friends, but now she wasn't so sure. She had felt special that Daisy confided in her about her relationship, now she realised that Daisy spoke the same way to everyone.

Tom was right that it wasn't appropriate for Daisy to say things about her sex life to Maud's boyfriend. Maud would rather die than tell Ryan about her personal business. She liked him, but that was overstepping the line. She'd been wondering what was going on with her friend lately. Daisy only had time for her when Ryan was busy. Perhaps she was having relationship problems of her own? All of her friends seemed to want her to fit into their lives and be there whenever they needed something, but the reverse wasn't true. Spending special moments with Nate that day had made her realise that none of her other friends made time for her unless they had nothing else to do. She wasn't a priority to any of them. The thought hurt like hell and she slugged back a huge mouthful of wine and winced at the bitter taste while Tom ranted on.

He was right, though, as Dot was totally obsessed with the art gallery and producing enough pieces of her jewellery, without a thought for Maud's punishing schedule holding down two jobs. Daisy only worried about Ryan and when she could get him alone for another marathon shag-fest. Maud was feeling resentful, and was actually glad that Tom had helped her see the light. She would start spending more time with him, and see how the girls like it. Dot was only ever available when she wanted something from Maud, so Maud would be the same. She finally managed to get a word in and told Tom she was tired and would see him the next day at work, before sinking into her couch and switching on some mindless TV to distract herself from thoughts of her selfish friends.

Chapter Thirty-Five

Dot frowned when she heard the buzzer to her studio sound in the other room. She placed the soldering iron she had been working with back into its fireproof stand, and firmly shut the workroom door behind her. She wouldn't be surprised if her parents had suddenly arrived and were trying to get into her studio space again. They'd run through every trick in the book until she'd finally had to change the locks, as her mum had pocketed the spare key and Dot had noticed it wasn't on the hook by the little kitchen where it usually hung.

Pressing the intercom, she was surprised to hear Tom's voice asking if he could talk to her about Maud. How did he find her address? She walked over and opened the door, letting him into the sitting area with trepidation. He was wearing a smart shirt and pressed trousers, and appeared to have made an effort with his appearance for some reason. Maybe he was going on a date afterwards, she thought sourly.

She didn't ask him to sit down and he began pacing the room like a caged tiger, which made her step back towards the kitchen. 'I want you to stop pushing Maud so hard,' he demanded, looking at Dot as if she was some kind of monster. 'Maud has told me she's giving you drawing lessons now, but surely that's a joke and you can draw, coming from a family like yours?'

Dot's face flamed and then her eyes narrowed in on him like lasers. 'What is your real problem with me seeing with Maud? Are you worried I'll tell her about the sleazy texts you sent me?'

It was Tom's turn to flush red and he stopped pacing, and then smiled cockily. 'I sent you those texts because you gave me the come-on when we met, giggling in my ear and draping yourself all over me. Don't play innocent now, when you're worried Maud will hate you for it. Go on... tell her,' he goaded. 'Let's see who she believes.'

Dot's knuckles went white where she held onto her hands to try and stop herself from scratching his eyes out. 'You just want to keep Maud apart from my brother and me. Why are you so threatened by us? Is it because Maud prefers our company to that of a lying scumbag?'

Tom's eyes grew angry and he started to approach her. He was just about to reach for her arm when Nate walked through the open door. 'What the hell do you think you're doing?' he demanded.

'Tom was just leaving,' spat Dot angrily, moving to stand with her brother.

Tom looked from Nate to Dot and then went to push past them, before turning and putting his face right near Nate's, who didn't back away. Nate moved even closer and spoke quietly in a voice Dot recognised as meaning he was on the brink of losing his temper, which was never a good thing. It took a lot to make Nate lose his cool. 'Tell Maud about the texts you sent Dot, or I will.'

Tom backed away but sneered at them both with bravado. 'I've got Maud exactly where I want her, and I can have her any time. She wouldn't believe a sex-starved artist who can't get a girl of his own, or a crazy lady who dresses in her nan's old clothes.'

Nate growled and swung for him, but Dot grabbed his arm and held him back.

Tom moved quickly out of the way, but Dot saw fear in his eyes. 'So what if women like Dot and Maud want to shag me?' he demanded to know. 'They like pretending to have a respectable job and being seduced, so what's the problem? They were all very willing. You must shag loads of groupies,' he spat at Nate, who still looked like he wanted to throttle him. 'It's the same with hot teachers and parents at the school. They simper suggestively and hand me their numbers wherever I go. What else am I supposed to do with them?'

Dot couldn't imagine anyone other than Maud choosing to

sleep with Tom, and that was only because she had no confidence and he'd paid her the slightest bit of attention. 'What did you want from Maud?' she really wanted to know, before she asked Nate to throw him out on the street where he belonged.

Tom leered and Dot felt sick. 'I like her. She's zipped up but red hot inside. Have you seen her sexy underwear? I know you want to,' he taunted Nate. 'You're no better than me. I've made her come out of her shell and now she's great in bed! If you ever finally get into her knickers, then I'll have done you a favour.' Nate actually landed a punch this time and Dot was nauseated that Maud had slept with this joker.

Tom got up and wiped his nose before spitting blood on the floor and looking at them both with distaste. 'I'm going to sue you for that. I'm a grown man and I date a few different women. There's no law against that.'

Nate leaned towards him menacingly. 'Get out of my sight.'

Dot slammed the door shut after Tom and put her palm on it to make sure it was firmly closed before hanging her head in exhaustion. 'Are you ok?' she asked Nate, who had gone to the kitchen and was running his hand under the cold tap.

Nate looked up and grinned. 'I'm feeling much better than I was yesterday.'

'Nate,' she admonished. 'You can't go around hitting everyone who insults Maud and me. We're big girls now. I could have handled that situation myself.'

Nate raised his eyebrows and she had to admit that she had been a little intimidated – but not scared. Tom might be a toss-pot, but he was a teacher and she didn't think he would have hurt her. He just wanted her to stop and listen. She understood that he could date whom he liked, but she wasn't about to let him ruin Maud's self-esteem by treating her the same way her previous boyfriend had. She sighed as she realised that it was already too late for that, and she would have to be there to pick up the pieces when Maud found out he'd cheated on her. She'd never really bothered worrying about a friend's emotions before, and she quite enjoyed the feeling of being the responsible one for a change. She could grow to like this

172

being-nice-to-others lark.

Nate frowned. 'We'll have to break the news to Maud that her boyfriend was seeing other women. She's going to be angry with us, so I'll do it, then you can have an easy life,' he joked, mock-seriously.

'Then she'll be angry with you.'

'Dot, you've been angry with me for years, so one more woman mad at me won't make too much difference.'

'I haven't been mad at you,' Dot said in confusion.

Nate led her to sit on the small grey couch near the door. 'You've been mad at me for being able to paint when you can't,' he said carefully. 'It's not my fault that I can. I love you, but you take your frustration out on Elliott and me so often. We both have pretty thick skins where you're concerned, but the other 'brother' is crazy about you.'

Dot sat in stunned silence and digested what he was saying, but didn't comment about Elliott as she needed a second to think about what to do. 'Since the accident you've kept me at arm's length, Nate. You won't let the scars heal inside like the ones outside have. I apologise for being such an annoying brat, but maybe it's time we both put the past behind us, and started behaving like grown ups?'

Nate grinned at her and her heart melted. 'Do we have to?'

'Yes we do,' she said with finality, leaning over to kiss his nose.

Chapter Thirty-Six

Dot hitched her feet up onto the edge of her desk and admired her new shoes. They were glittering boots, with skyscraper heels and ankle-hugging zips, but for once the design was understated. There were no adornments, apart from the softly shimmering surface. They made her ankles look pretty and her legs endless, so she was finally coming around to the idea that a little less drama might be more effective. Her dress was simple for her, with a plain neckline and fitted bodice, cinched in at her tiny waist with a thin red belt. She couldn't wait until she could add one of her own designs. The skirt of the dress fell in waves to mid-calf, and for once she felt creative, but understated.

She was flicking through photos of the date night with Maud, Nate and Elliott on her phone. Tom's behaviour yesterday had really shocked and upset her, as she'd been fooled into thinking he was a nice guy. She usually trusted her instincts, but he had slipped through her vetting process and it worried her. Nate had always hated him, but she'd assumed it was because he wanted to get into Maud's knickers and Tom had got there first. Dot was hurt that Maud hadn't confided in her that she'd slept with trashy Tom, but Maud was shy. Maybe she realised she'd made a mistake and was embarrassed?

Dot stared closely at a photo of them all and squinted in concentration. Was there a difference between the way Maud gazed at Nate and the way Dot herself saw Elliott? Dot thought not. Maud might not realise it, but she definitely had feelings for Nate. The longing in her brother's eyes shocked her too. The dude actually liked someone for once, but she was taken. Dot wished Maud would dump Tom and put them all out of their misery.

She could understand why Nate fancied Maud so much, as Dot was pretty enamoured with her too. She'd never had a friendship where she could be so open and honest. Dot made a bit of a performance of most situations and had never been herself with her friends. She felt they expected so much of her for being from a family like hers, and she behaved accordingly, shockingly badly sometimes, she now recalled with a slight tinge of shame.

She had always had to fight for the spotlight, as everyone adored Nate, for goodness sake. Although, to be fair, what was not to like? He was actually a great bloke, she realised. The jealous haze she'd carried since childhood had begun to evaporate over the last few days. It wasn't his fault he was so amazing at everything and she was so useless. Dot grinned wickedly as she remembered that Nate was rubbish at something, he couldn't get the girl he wanted. She snickered into her hand and then straightened her back with a little cough as she remembered she was supposed to be being nice. She decided she'd need a lot more practice. It was hard work.

Now that Maud had gently nurtured her talent with the drawing classes – and Maud really was a great teacher – Dot finally realised what a complete cow she'd been to Nate. Knowing that Elliott was interested in her, even though she had often been disparaging to him and dismissive of his kindness, showed she'd been prancing around like a princess. An entitled drama-queen. She now had so many amends to make, she cringed and her shoulders slumped. No wonder she didn't have any real friends. Most of the people she hung around with were gallery clients or friends of her parents or brother. What a sad mess.

She bit the inside of her lip until it hurt and sighed, thinking back to Tom's angry face as Nate punched him. They'd probably get a lawsuit thrown at them today and, to be honest, she couldn't have cared less. Tom had deserved to be floored for the way he treated women. She hoped he had a child of his own soon, not with Maud, and also hoped it was a girl. Then he could see how it felt if anyone treated her poorly. Maybe, just maybe, that would be the only way he would change. Then Dot remembered what an idiot he was and realised that he enjoyed flitting around with his part-time work and his family, so that he could meet more women. It was such a shame that Dot's best friend was one of them, and didn't know it yet. Tom made her skin crawl and she was determined to make Maud her first priority on her making amends list. She shouldn't have overworked Maud. For one, it might have affected her art and secondly, it made her terribly moody. This, in turn, put Dot on edge. She wondered if it would calm things down a little in her own life, if Maud finally got rid of Tom and started dating Nate but, knowing Maud, unpredictability followed her everywhere. You never knew who was going to fall for her next. She'd often told Dot she wished she looked like her, but Dot would have killed to have boobs like Maud's and some meat on her bones. However much she ate, she stayed stick thin. It was depressing. Ok, she could wear high-end fashion, and she recalled some of her old outfits and frowned, but she couldn't wear low-cut tops or anything fitted without looking like a boy.

Maud had lost some curves lately, but she still had hips you could grab hold of and a bust you could loose your face in. Dot looked down at her own tiny little breasts and sighed. She grabbed them and pushed them up, to make them look bigger, but it didn't work. She could hear Maud in her mind telling her she was supermodel-gorgeous, but she didn't believe it. She'd always been the oddity in her family, and the thought processes were ingrained.

She got up, deciding that Elliott would have to wait, even though she desperately wanted to see him. She also felt incredibly embarrassed at the fledgling feelings for him that had begun to unfurl, as if they had been there all along but needed the jolt of electricity from his touch to make them come alive. Gritting her teeth, she knew what she had to do next, and picked up the phone to call Daisy.

Chapter Thirty-Seven

Maud's shoulders ached and she rolled them around and rubbed them with her hand to try and ease the tension. She stopped at the school's reception desk to talk to Daisy, but once again she was nowhere to be seen. The press frenzy around the paintings was reaching a crescendo, with more photographers staking out parks and locals talking incessantly about who the artist could be. It put her nerves on edge in case someone discovered her before she was ready. She'd lost more weight and even her boobs were starting to look a little less humungous, which she was surprisingly sorry about.

Maud knew Daisy had lost weight too. She'd seen her scurrying across the playground earlier looking harassed. Maud had tried to contact her by phone and even turned up unexpectedly at Daisy's flat, but all she got in return was a closed front door and an over-jovial message saying she was recovering from a bug and felt awful, so she'd been off work for a few days and hadn't wanted to see anyone in case they caught whatever she had. Then she'd explained that she was busily trying to catch up on the work she had missed and really needed to get on with it, if she didn't want to lose her job. Maud frowned. The head of the school had three children and a very demanding, executive-type husband, so she was usually understanding when a staff member was unwell. Maud couldn't imagine her threatening to sack Daisy. She was just too nice.

Maud was really worried that Daisy was lying to her and that the stress of keeping her secret from her family and Ryan was making Daisy ill. Maud loved Daisy's parents and the thought of seeing them upset made her stomach feel like it was jammed full of lead. Daisy was such an open and honest person, it must be torture for her to keep the details of the artist everyone was looking for to herself, especially from Ryan. Maud felt a bit ashamed that she hadn't trusted him and told him herself. She'd known Ryan for long enough, and knew from the way he adored Daisy, that he wouldn't ever let them down. Maud decided that whatever happened, she would tell Daisy to let him in on the truth. He might be a little hurt, but surely if they told him soon, then he would still get at least a little thrill from knowing before everyone else and might forgive them both. Maud certainly didn't want the responsibility of being the person who ruined her best friend's happiness for her own.

Hearing the morning bell peal, she sighed, rubbed her forehead and tried to stand up straight. Her shoulders protested, but she'd made a decision and she felt better for it. As she turned, she saw Daisy walking rapidly across the playground with a phone stuck to her ear. Maud grimaced. How many times had they both reprimanded the children for walking along and talking into their phones on the way to school? Even though this was a primary, they saw it often with the Year Six children. She would have to scold Daisy later, but she'd check on her mood first, as she might not appreciate the gentle teasing.

She frowned and squinted at Daisy. It looked like she might be crying. Maud turned to retrace her steps and find out once and for all what this was about, or tell her quickly to include Ryan in their secret mystery art gang. Then Tom walked up behind her, sliding his hand around her waist and leading her into the classroom before they opened the doors for the children. They walked into the store cupboard where they hung their coats, and he whispered into her ear that he was going to ravish her later that night, then kissed her chastely behind her ear. She blushed to the roots of her hair and completely forgot what she was supposed to be doing, before hastily rushing to let the children in.

Trying to clear the fog from her brain as the children noisily filed into the room, she bit down on her lip to make herself concentrate and not focus on Tom or her exhaustion. Luckily it was the end of term soon, so she could get some rest then. She thought of Daisy's miserable face earlier and felt frustrated that she'd missed her again. That was Tom's fault. She began her working day with the resolution that she would go straight to see Daisy at lunchtime to check she was ok. If Daisy was having relationship problems, then Maud would be there for her. She would not be a bad friend, and she wouldn't get distracted by distracting men!

Tom had been incredibly sweet to her over the last couple of days. He must have finally realised how worn out she was trying to help Dot and do her job too. He might not be that understanding when he finally realised what she had been up to with Dot, though. She hoped he would be happy to find out she was the mystery artist, and not angry. She supposed she could confide in him too, but the thought had never crossed her mind, which made her frown a little in confusion. They had become more like flirty friends lately because of the distance between them most weeks, and she didn't see him as boyfriend material. All of her thoughts were clouded by a tall dark-haired man with silvery scars on his arms.

Tom had been really busy lately. His brother had just separated from his wife and needed Tom's support, which she totally understood. She had even been a bit relieved, as it meant she could concentrate on her upcoming exhibition plans with Dot without feeling guilty about not having enough hours in the day for him. She would have to make it up to him after the art show, and hope he didn't hate her for lying to him, and would understand her reasoning. If the worst came to the worst, she could just blame Dot, as it was her fault in the first place. She smiled, knowing she would never do this to Dot, however much of a pain in the backside she was. This thought re-energised her and gave the strength to pick up the pile of story books she had been aimlessly gazing at, and start helping with the day's lesson.

At lunchtime, Tom was marking exercise books and working through the next week's travel plans, so Maud waved and left him with his sandwiches, rushing away to search for Daisy. She stamped her foot and huffed out her breath when she got to reception and found that Daisy had gone to collect something in town and had left the site for the lunch hour. Maud stalked into the staffroom and then faux-casually asked around if anyone else had noticed Daisy being unwell or unhappy. She felt on edge, as she had to be careful whom she asked and didn't want to pile on more stress if other people started checking on Daisy too. People sticking their nose into their business would just make Daisy even more upset, as it would create more lies.

A few people walked over and commented that they'd noticed both Daisy and Maud had lost weight, before asking for dieting tips. When Maud looked confused and said she was eating less, they looked really disappointed that it wasn't a miracle weight loss plan, and then carried on with other topics of conversation, while she stood on the outside of the group not knowing what to do next.

As the final school bell rang for the day, Maud arranged to meet Tom later, as he'd told her he was setting up a romantic dinner for her and wanted her, finally, to stay the night. Butterflies fluttered in her stomach and she was conflicted about what to do. She hadn't slept with many people, and Tom was handsome, so why not just jump into bed with him and enjoy herself? She was sure he had more experience than her and would be a considerate lover. She was getting fed up with spending so many nights alone and decided she felt good about finally sharing more than just heavy groping with him. She was behaving a bit like a horny teenager around both of the men in her life and she needed to grow up. Nate wouldn't want a serious relationship with her, while Tom did, so the choice had made itself.

She rushed towards reception, with flushed cheeks and a twinkle in her eye about the night ahead of her. She squashed down the inevitable nerves over sleeping with someone new for the first time. She'd never enjoyed one-night stands. She'd tried one once and hated herself afterwards, until Daisy told her off and said it was perfectly normal for a grown woman to enjoy sex. Maud hadn't really enjoyed it though, as he grunted like an axe murderer and it was over in approximately two minutes and twenty-two seconds, not that she'd been counting. He had snuggled her into his arms, after tweaking her nipples a few times and rubbing her crotch, but after those few minutes of making her sore, he was snoring loudly and fast asleep. She shook her head to clear the ghastly picture of sneaking out of his house at the break of dawn, and then reached the reception desk, only to find Daisy had just left. Maud had literally just missed her. Hearing her phone beep, Maud grabbed it from her bag and read a text message with relief. It was from Daisy, saying she hadn't seen Maud much lately and she had sloped off work a few minutes early to grab a bottle of wine, but she'd meet Maud at her bungalow in fifteen minutes.

Picking up the bag she'd unceremoniously dumped at her feet and throwing her phone inside with glee, Maud stopped and suddenly remembered the romantic evening planned with Tom. Straightening up, she decided that she'd just have to fit two evenings into one and hope that Daisy wasn't round for the night. It seemed like she'd spent every evening with her boyfriend lately, so Maud couldn't imagine that she'd want to be away from him for more than a few hours. If not, Maud would have to find out if Daisy was ok, then rush to get the first shag she'd had in a very long time. She couldn't let Tom down again, but needed to see her friend and make sure all was well in her world first. Picking up her pace, she vaguely waved goodbye to a few colleagues she saw out of the corner of her eye from across the school car park and power-walked all the way home.

Chapter Thirty-Eight

Ramming her key into her front door and pushing it open, Maud stopped suddenly, as she heard voices coming from her kitchen. Her pulse rate jumped up a notch and she gulped in some air, suddenly frozen to the spot. Looking around frantically for a weapon, she decided an umbrella would have to do and grabbed a tall one from the bamboo coat stand by the front door. She probably should have turned and run, but the rage that someone had the cheek to invade her personal space made her move forward and raise her arm to strike. She stopped suddenly, and her eyes opened wide in shock.

Dot and Daisy broke apart from the hug they were having, and both looked her way in confusion. Maud's arm was still hovering above her head, but she dropped the umbrella, which fell and clunked her on the head, making her wince in pain and rub the tender spot where it had bounced off her skull. She wondered what the hell was going on. Was Daisy ill?

Dot kept her arms around Daisy, who wouldn't look up from the floor, as Dot led her to a seat on the couch. Maud realised she was standing mute in her own house, and sensed that something must be terribly wrong for Dot to be kind to Daisy. She rushed over and sat beside her best friend, holding her hand and stroking her fiery skin. Suddenly she frowned and took a few steps back in her mind. 'How did you get into my house?'

Dot shrugged her dainty shoulders, still looking at Daisy with concern. 'Oh I had keys cut a while ago, in case I needed to see you quickly.'

Daisy did raise a complicit smile with Maud at the barefaced cheek of the woman, before she looked like she might cry again.

'Okay,' said Maud slowly, shaking her head and rolling her eyes heavenward. 'Confess. Is the secret of my art too much for you? Am I causing you this stress?'

Daisy looked confused and burst into noisy tears. Dot sat down opposite them, biting worriedly on her bottom lip. 'We've got something to tell you,' she said to Maud.

Maud started to feel sick. What the hell was going on? She looked at Daisy in alarm, not getting any reassurance there.

'I'm so sorry, Maud,' said Daisy.

Maud held her breath. 'What for?'

When Daisy didn't speak, but began to quietly sob again, Dot spoke for her. 'It's Tom. He's a complete bastard!'

Maud jumped up and her muscles contracted in shock. This is the last thing she expected them to say. 'What? No, he's not.'

'Not only is he a complete bastard, but he's been shagging your best friend.'

Maud assumed this was Dot's warped sense of humour and began to laugh. Then she saw that Dot was deadly serious. 'Daisy?'

Daisy sobbed louder, but couldn't meet Maud's eyes, as her own were red-raw from crying practically every day for the last few months.

'What about Ryan?' Surely this couldn't be true? Maud felt bile rise up in her throat.

'Tom came to see me yesterday,' said Dot, as if this explained everything. 'He's been sending me sleazy texts and was trying to get into my pants, then told me he'd just been in yours.'

'What?' Maud jumped up and started pacing before she slamming her fist on the kitchen table, trying to make sense of what her friends were trying to tell her. 'You have to be kidding me?' Her heart started heaving in her chest and she picked up a glass to pour some wine into, and put it down again in case she threw it at Daisy. Her hands started sweating and she stood behind the kitchen counter, creating a barrier and looking at these two people, as if she'd never seen them before. Her eyes implored Daisy. 'You slept with my

183

boyfriend?'

Daisy hiccupped and raised sore eyes to meet Maud's very angry ones. Maud wanted her to really see her and understand the pain she was inflicting. She demanded that Daisy look at her, and tell her she'd betrayed her in the worst possible way.

Daisy implored her friend to understand her. 'It only happened once. Then I hated myself. I'm so sorry, Maud,' she reached out a hand towards Maud and then dropped it into her lap. 'I know I'm a terrible friend.'

'*Friend!* Friends don't have sex with their best friend's boyfriends...' Maud spat out viciously, tears streaming down her face, feeling her paltry lunch rising back up in her stomach. She barely eaten, as she'd been so worried about Daisy. Now she wished she hadn't wasted the time on this evil witch. She looked at Daisy's blotchy, red face and saw a stranger. She felt rage building in her chest, which was so unlike her usual submissive demeanour. How could Daisy, her most trusted friend, betray her like this? 'Get out,' she yelled at the top of her lungs.

Both of these women were telling her that her judgement was off, and that Tom was a cheat. Well, that much was obvious from the fact that he'd slept with her best friend. She felt the burn of humiliation as her face flamed. She wouldn't let Daisy have the satisfaction of seeing her cry, so she pressed her nails into her palms, making herself wince in pain. Once again, she'd been treated like she was worthless. She waited and turned away from her two closest friends, as Daisy grabbed her bag and ran out of the front door, slamming it behind her.

Chapter Thirty-Nine

Dot stood her ground and didn't go after Daisy, however much she'd have liked to run away too at this point. But Maud was her priority. Dot understood that Tom had seduced Daisy when she'd got very drunk, but she was Maud's oldest friend and this must be absolute hell for her. The fact that Tom had tried it on with Dot, too, made things twice as bad and really awkward for Dot.

Maud walked to where Dot was sitting in the lounge, refusing to move, and sat down heavily on the couch, tears sliding from her eyes. She put her head in her hands, sobbing quietly. Dot looked at her sympathetically, which made her cry harder. Dot cringed. She was useless with anyone else's emotions and had found the whole afternoon exhausting. First, Dot had had to console Daisy, who was half hysterical after keeping her secret from Maud, as Tom really was a complete scumbag and had said he'd deny it. But Dot had also wanted to slap Daisy's silly face for falling for his charm. Maud had told her Daisy had an amazing boyfriend called Ryan, who treated her like a princess. What was she playing at, hurting Maud this way? Especially as she often boasted what a wonderful friend she was, for starting Maud's new career. Perhaps she'd been jealous of Maud's fledgling relationship with Tom and had subconsciously wanted to destroy it?

Daisy had confided to her that Tom had turned up at her flat while Ryan was there, saying he needed to talk about work. The man had no shame. They had been about to eat, so he'd been invited to join them. He'd brought a bottle of wine with him by way of apologising for disturbing their evening and didn't seem bothered by Ryan being there. They had a great night and they'd steadily all got stinking drunk. Ryan had passed out and they'd put him to bed, laughing that he was a lightweight. Then Tom had turned on the charm. Daisy had been so drunk, she hadn't known what day of the year it was, and Tom had managed to seduce her. Daisy said the whole night was a blur, but she did remember him leaning in to kiss her and nothing after that. Tom had called her early the next morning and told her that they'd had a mind-blowing evening, before saying that if she told anyone about their 'hot' night he would blab to Maud that Daisy had been coming on to him for weeks. She'd told him to leave her alone and had cried every day since, as she couldn't believe what she had done.

Dot sighed and gently rubbed Maud's shoulder. She was still sobbing into her hands. To Daisy's credit, she had immediately woken her boyfriend and told him what had happened. He had thrown her out and she had been trying to make up with him ever since. Her whole world had blown apart, because of one bad choice in life.

Dot did sympathise with Daisy's situation, but seeing Maud cry made her resolve harden. She'd always thought Daisy was annoying and flaky, and she'd been proved right. The problem was, by telling Maud that Tom came onto her too, she only made matters worse for herself. Maud could side with Tom if he told her a different story, which would be a real problem.

Dot sat next to Maud on the sofa and put a comforting arm around her, patting her back as she had seen people do in films, where it seemed to work in the same way that mothers soothed crying babies. Maud stopped sobbing, and Dot now saw raw fury in her eyes, as she sat back in complete silence. Dot quickly explained what she had found out, with as much detail she could manage without causing more pain. Apparently, Tom was copying a tried and tested formula. Within months, he'd slept with a few of the parents or staff at the last three schools he'd worked at. The school administrators were always so embarrassed when they found out, that they sent him on his way with glowing references, as he was a good teacher, even though he was a horrible boyfriend. He had just had a lot of relationships. He wasn't doing anything illegal, just immoral, as far as Dot was concerned. The nasty pig.

Maud looked horrified and then began laughing manically. Dot rushed to the sink, located two wineglasses and grabbed the bottle of wine she'd brought along, knowing they would need it. 'I'm so sorry, Maud. I know you liked him. He told me and Nate that you just slept with him, too?'

Maud stopped laughing and spluttered, 'Nate? Although Tom tried, I was so tired that I resisted, as you and your brother made me too damn busy to go near him. Tonight was supposed to be his lucky night...' She began laughing again until she was gently crying at the unfairness of it all.

Dot let out the breath she'd been holding and handed Maud an almost-overflowing glass of wine, before taking a hefty sip from her own. 'Thank goodness for our good judgement,' she sighed, feeling much better about things, before seeing Maud's dark look and hiding her face behind her wine glass.

'Why do I always pick the shysters?'

Dot had heard about Maud's dating history and felt sorry for her. She sent up a prayer of thanks for her brother's dastardly plan to keep Maud away from Tom. It had actually worked.

'Not all men are cheats,' she said picturing her brother, and realising it was true. 'Tom zeroed in on you, you didn't pick him. You were simply desperate for some attention after a dry spell,' soothed Dot.

'Not helping,' glowered Maud. 'He sought out me, and half the population by the sound of it. I'm such a moron.'

Dot thought for a minute, but had to concede that Maud had a point. She was an idiot for falling for his chat-up lines, but maybe now wasn't the best moment to mention that. Dot was trying to keep up with her be-nice-to-people plan, but she was really struggling in the face of such silly women. 'I'm so sorry that this happened, Maud.' She wasn't really, as this meant that Maud would be less distracted and have more time for her, but she schooled her face to look concerned and serious. She quickly dampened down the glee in her eyes, before Maud saw it and threw the wine in her face.

'I was supposed to be seeing him later,' said Maud miserably.

187

'Call the bastard, and tell him you don't feel very well. Make him wait. Then we'll plan your revenge.'

Maud did raise a small smile at this. 'I quite like the idea of making him suffer.' She tore off some kitchen roll and wiped her eyes, and blew her runny nose loudly, making Dot cringe as she sniffed. Then her mouth drooped sadly.

Dot could tell Maud was exhausted, but she needed her to focus. She was visibly upset by the double betrayal, but she'd learn she was better off without Tom and Daisy in her life. She would soon be a darling of the art world and people like Daisy and Tom would be a distant memory, or at least they would if Dot had her way.

Chapter Forty

Nate decided that he'd let Maud wallow in misery for long enough. She'd been working with Dot a lot and they were always whispering in corners and scurrying off to scribble notes. He wondered if Dot had roped Maud in to be her assistant. He'd also talked seriously to his parents about the fact that they were emotionally blackmailing Dot to represent only their family's work. His mum had been insulted, and said that Dot adored representing them, and it made her feel part of the family. His dad had thought about it for all of twenty seconds before declaring that he was sure she was happy and not to give her any silly ideas.

Nate loved Dot, even though she drove him crazy with her constant nagging and, although she could be a bit of a diva, she was a gifted art agent. Nate had the feeling she was restless to discover her own clients. Her recent meetings with Maud seemed to be more than just friends being there for one another. In fact, he was getting pretty annoyed that whenever he'd arrived at Maud's, Dot had already been there.

He was completely confused over why Maud hadn't told Tom where to shove his roaming penis, but Dot had assured him that Maud would make him pay in her own way. But when? The idiot was strutting about as if nothing had happened, and Nate wanted to grind his face into the floor every time he thought about him, which was far too often. Nate had dated different women in the past, but he only ever slept with one occasionally, contrary to Dot's constant accusations, and he certainly never got into a relationship with one while bedding another. What would be the point in that? If you were going to make love to a woman, you might as well immerse yourself in the pleasure, and do the same for her.

Surely bed-hopping meant everyone was emotionally wrung out, and someone was going to end up in trouble? Knowing his luck, it would be him. It wasn't worth the headache. The thought of it turned his stomach over and made him angry, after the trouble he'd got into with Lena, Dot and Elliott when they were younger. If Nate was doing something, or someone, he did it well. Which meant he didn't need to go looking for another woman to tickle his libido.

He smiled as he hoisted two full carrier bags from the boot of his car. Things had gone on long enough and he wanted Maud to know that someone would treat her with respect and look after her. He'd meticulously planned a meal to cook for her, as he knew she was often too exhausted to go out. She needed to regain those sexy curves and stop looking so frail and gaunt. Luckily the swell of her breasts hadn't disappeared, so he still had a reminder of how luscious she had looked when she'd first fallen into his arms at his preview show. She'd looked adorable, trying to stick her nose up to the painting to get a closer look. Those artisan shoes had made her legs look amazing, he'd been secretly watching her from the moment she'd arrived.

Maud's elderly neighbours were used to seeing him and Dot arrive most days by now and Nate had checked Dot's diary, which was surprisingly full, to make sure that she was out of town with his uncle that day. He sent a winning smile to Mrs Lancy, who apparently spent an hour come rain or shine tending the beautiful array of scented roses that ran along her front wall. She'd insisted he call her Sally practically as soon as they met, and he'd planned to bump into her across the garden fence. It worked like a dream.

'Maud's lucky to have a boyfriend as dishy as you, Nate,' her eyes sparkled at him as she went inside to collect her spare key to Maud's house. 'If only I was 40 years younger,' she winked at him, making him laugh uproariously as he carried her rose cuttings inside and took the key with a quick hug and a smile.

'Thanks, Sally,' he called over his shoulder as he waved the key at her.

He hauled his purchases in and plonked them down on the kitchen counter. He had steaks, salad, and strawberries dipped in white chocolate, as he'd heard they were her favourite. He was determined to tell her how he felt, and to ask her to move on from this ridiculous game of cat and mouse she was playing with Tom. He knew she was over him already. She was bound to be angry still, but maybe this had all made her realise that her judgement wasn't so off, as she'd kept Tom at arm's length. She could so easily have jumped into bed with him. Dot had confided to Nate that Daisy had told Maud about her fling with Tom on the very night they were supposed to sleep together. Nate supposed he should feel bad that he had tried every trick in the book to keep them apart, but he wasn't, and it had worked. He understood that Maud had been really frustrated with him at the time, but when he had explained to her the other night that he'd started to have feelings for her and was jealous, she'd blushed bright red and hidden her face behind her hair. They had talked long into the night and he'd even stolen a few mind-blowing kisses in the last week, but she was still holding back. She needed to get rid of Tom once and for all. Tonight Nate was going to tell her how he really felt. He hadn't been able to stop thinking about her, from the first moment he'd laid eyes on her, and he wanted her to be his and his alone.

He put the wine he'd bought on the counter top and stood and admired Maud's home. It was simple and beautiful, yet didn't represent the vibrant woman who lived inside. His own flat had floor-to-ceiling windows and views across the river that ran alongside the town. His paintings adorned many of the crisp white walls and the furniture was all artisan, beautiful to look at and a pleasure to use.

Maud's place was simple, but pretty. It suggested creativity by the way the garden was designed to draw you to the front door, and the furniture was neutral, but comfortable and welcoming. He felt at peace here and was sure that was what had attracted Maud to the place. He remembered seeing her sprawled across her bed on the first night he had brought her home and wondered if she'd kept the little drawing he'd done of her. He hoped she had. It had been torture to leave her alone when she had been pleading with him to stay and been wearing that vibrant and sexy underwear that he'd been unable to stop thinking about ever since. Trying to clear his head, he imagined some of his smaller artworks hanging on the walls here, envisaging the whole room immediately jumping to life. The place needed more of Maud's personality, which was feminine and interesting.

Smiling and whistling to himself, he checked the black Rolex he'd treated himself to. He'd wanted to buy it after the success of his last exhibition, but held off. He wasn't one for fancy trinkets, usually, but this one had called his name and he'd fallen in love with the sleek design. Normally he wouldn't wear anything that drew people's attention to his wrists or arms, as he would immediately see horror or compassion there, which made him burn with shame. It was his fault the scars were there and he certainly didn't need anyone else forming opinions or feeling sorry for him. After another successful show, and seeing how much pleasure Maud had got from his paintings, he'd felt he deserved a present for himself and that it was maybe time to stop worrying about what other people thought of him. If they didn't want to know him after finding out how he got the scars, then that was their choice, and their loss. Maud had helped him to understand that his scars were part of his history – like a painting, she'd said, as she'd run her delicate fingers along them. He hadn't flinched away, but had taken her hand in his own and kissed her pulse gently, before letting her hand go. There had been so many moments like that in the last week that he was beginning to find it hard to concentrate on his work. He wanted to be around Maud, touching her skin and looking into her eyes. He wished she would come and sit in his studio all day and eat grapes, preferably naked, so he could look at her and feel inspired, rather than having to rely on images of her in his brain.

He knew that he had hours before Maud got in from her day's work, so he carefully placed the food in the fridge, noting how tidy and uniform everything was in there and trying not to disturb the neat rows of food. He then checked the clock above the oven and let out a big breath, trying to release some of the nerves that were starting to buzz around his body. What if she didn't feel the same way he did? What if Tom, the 'trashy tosspot' as Dot had renamed him, had caused too much damage, so that she hated all men and never wanted to sleep with one again? The thought horrified him and he quashed it quickly. He'd been dreaming of Maud in his bed for months. He knew he'd been underhand in keeping her away from Tom, but from the moment he'd set eyes on her, he'd wanted her to be his. He'd discovered a streak of jealousy he'd never experienced before, and had kept Tom and Maud apart. It was Tom's own stupid fault. If that had been Nate, he would have turned up on Maud's doorstep every morning, arrived at the end of the day to walk her home from school and spent every spare moment with her, until she fell in love, and then into his arms. Tom had been so busy shagging every other woman in sight, that he'd let the prize slip straight though his cheating grasp.

Feeling a bit smug all of a sudden, Nate grabbed a glass and poured himself some of the wine. It was still warm outside, so he decided to go and sit on one of the rattan chairs at a little table, just outside the double back doors. For some reason, they hadn't ventured outside much when he was here. He tried to think back if the weather had been bad, but shook his head. It didn't really matter anyway. He was hoping he'd spend a lot more time here from now on, and if not, he'd put Maud over his shoulder and carry her back to his flat with him like a Neanderthal.

He found the key to the back door in a pretty little ceramic dish painted with tiny flying birds on the inside, on a circular side table by the back door. Not the most security conscious idea, as anyone outside could see it. He'd have to have a word with Maud about that. Taking in all of the scenery as he stepped outside, he took a sip of his wine and then placed the glass on the garden table. He looked around the perimeter and had to admit that, unless you were actually already in the garden, you couldn't see the back door from neighbouring properties as the hedge along the back was so tall. There were fences either side, partially hidden by fragrant planting similar to the design in the front garden. Maud obviously liked plants and had a good eye for colours and shrubs that worked together.

He squinted as he noticed something towards the end of the garden and went over to see what it was. Nestled between the hedges was a pretty little gate. It was painted green to match, so unless you knew it was there, you probably wouldn't notice it. He frowned and moved closer. There wasn't a lock this side of the gate, so he wondered if it led to a neighbour's garden. They'd have to be pretty close friends to have a linking door between their properties, but Maud had never mentioned them before. Without a lock, anyone could access the garden, he thought, getting irritated again about Maud's lack of thought for her own safety. He pushed the gate open and stuck his head through. Instead of seeing a neighbour's land, he saw a white-painted wooden building, with tall windows and a veranda. He stopped short in surprise and stepped into the other bit of garden. He felt as though he was intruding, but this seemed to be all part of Maud's property, as there were fences surrounding the still-sizeable plot and similar planting around the borders.

He noted the craftsmanship of the building and immediately felt drawn to look inside. It was exciting and his heart started beating faster. Then he paused. Why was this hidden behind a huge hedge? Surely you'd want to sit on this porch and look back on the beauty of the garden? Sure, the plants were beautiful surrounding the building here, but you still looked out onto those towering hedges. He tried to open the door, but it was locked, which he was begrudgingly happy about. Then he pressed his nose onto the glass to peek inside, and the bottom dropped out of his world. Maud had been lying to him the whole time.

He felt the humiliation burn inside at how he had carefully explained how different artists worked and the tips he had given her to improve her work and become more confident. He drank in the scene before him and stood still in shock as he thought back. The mystery artist had been leaving art around way before his latest exhibition. He pictured Maud and Dot whispering in corners and thought about how Dot wanted to break out on her own. The colour drained from his face. They'd both been lying to him for months.

He retraced his steps, threw the wine in the sink, locked the doors and gave Sally a chaste kiss on the cheek as he handed the keys back and got into his car.

Chapter Forty-One

Maud was finally starting to feel human again. Nate and Dot had been so kind and supportive lately. They'd made her realise that Tom had never really been her priority. She had kept him at arm's length, even with Nate's interfering. There had always been a side to him that had put her on edge instead of making her feel warm and bubbly inside. She'd never been able to work it out before as she was too overcome with having someone show an interest in her, after a spell of feeling incredibly lonely. She wondered if Tom gave off a pheromone that was way too strong for her. Instead of drawing her in, she'd put up barriers and run a mile. Other women, it seemed, basked in the scent and rolled around with him in it. The thought made her stomach turn over in disgust, as she pictured him and her best friend in bed together, right under the nose of her loyal boyfriend.

Tom had actually had the audacity to tell her he was having to move back to his old school this week as a teacher had fallen ill and they needed full time cover, but that he'd definitely come to the gallery show she'd been helping Dot organise. He said he'd try and visit some weekends, but had to go where the full-time job was. He liked mingling with the rich and famous, he'd winked with a laugh, so he'd be back. Daisy had looked deathly pale and had cornered her in the staff toilets, where she had told Maud that she'd been checking up on Tom and he'd had to go back, as one of the dinner ladies from his last school was pregnant! Maud had been surprised as, instead of tears, she'd actually burst out laughing, and then so had Daisy. They'd looked at each other warily, made a very uneasy truce, as they had to accept they would be in the same building together, and then gone back to work.

Maybe they could rebuild a friendship, thought Maud. It would never be the same as before, but perhaps it was time they both grew up. Maud knew Daisy must have been incredibly drunk to sleep with Tom. He'd taken advantage of her. It would take a while for the wound to heal, but Maud missed her friendship so much. It was the smallest thing, like a hug when she arrived at work, or hearing Daisy belly-laugh as she drained another drink at the pub and then made a silly face to make Maud smile.

Hanging her jumper up on the coat hook and slinging her bag on the floor by the kitchen counter, Maud was surprised to see a wine glass on its side in the sink. She fleetingly wanted to stamp her feet and wished Dot would be tidier when she came round. She treated this place like a hotel lately. Maud knew she was keeping an eye on her, but wasn't totally sure whether this was because she was her friend, or a business asset. Nate, on the other hand, had nothing to gain by turning up the way he did. Other than sex, of course. She thought Tom had put her off for life, but Nate kept touching her when she least expected it. Not really in a sexual way, but he'd stroke her arm or gently tuck some stray hairs behind her ear and then come up behind her and rub her tired shoulders into submission until she was practically purring with pleasure. It was embarrassing how easily he could seduce her, even after the trauma she'd experienced lately.

She bent down and opened the fridge, then frowned when she saw the two steaks, salad and dipped strawberries. She stood up in confusion and then saw that the gate between the hedges was swinging open and her shoulders slumped in horror. Nate must have been here.

She'd really wanted to confide in him, but Dot had held her back. With a sinking feeling, she realised that this had been the wrong decision and the food and wine told her that he'd been planning a surprise. Her mouth drooped in disappointment and she felt annoyed that she'd listened to Dot once again. Now Nate would feel stupid about teaching her about art, which she had loved and would always treasure, and he would feel angry that they'd lied to him. Rightly so... unfortunately.

197

She'd been thinking about him incessantly recently and wondered how she'd feel if he had been sleeping with, or had feelings for, someone else, the way Tom had. She knew she would have been devastated and would have hidden from the world for months. No one would have been able to console her, whereas with Tom she'd just been humiliated and angry that he was such a toad. She'd formed a deep connection with Nate recently and she loved hugging him and listening to his voice. She was happy to find him at her door usually, but she assumed he'd got the key from Dot and decided to feed her up, as he was always telling her off for not eating enough these days.

She grabbed her mobile phone and called Nate's number, which went straight to answer phone. She left a message pleading for understanding and asked him to come back. Then she fired off a text to him and then to Dot, to tell her what had happened and to ask her to try and make him see sense. Maud knew he would be angry with Dot too, so she didn't hold out much hope of that working either.

Chapter Forty-Two

Dot was extremely frazzled but needed to have her best game face on and persuade everyone that she was the epitome of calm. Nate was refusing to talk to her and even though she had turned up at his flat with a personal invite to the show, he'd ignored her. She'd finally resorted to getting her parents involved. She'd eventually told them about her plans to represent other artists and, although they had thrown a bit of a flamboyant strop, they'd all shared a bottle of wine and she'd explained that she'd found an astounding new talent. Their curiosity was spiked and they'd pleaded, then resorted to trying to bribe her with fewer party guests, to make her share who it was. She was sorely tempted, as her party list was reaching mammoth proportions, but she'd laughed and revelled in being the centre of attention for once, before she told them they'd have to wait and find out at the gallery event like everyone else. They had pouted and cajoled, but she'd resisted, although it had been hard, as they'd tried to bribe her with a case of a very good vintage of wine from their cellars next. They'd also taken to popping in at the gallery unexpectedly and trying to catch her out, which was exhausting.

After tonight, Maud still had two weeks of the school term to get through, but they'd decided to bring the opening forward a week as the press interest was crazy around the mystery artist now and they felt sure someone would discover who it was, or one of them would slip up under the pressure, if they didn't act soon. Either that or the media would get bored with the story, as this had been going on for months.

Dot looked around her gallery with such pride. It was full to bursting and she was glad she was standing on the podium, because as soon as the guests had arrived and seen who the work was by, it had been like a feeding frenzy in a piranha bath. She sent up a prayer that Maud would be able to cope with the attention once they found out it was her. Camille and Cosmo had grabbed her into a warm hug and told her how clever she was to have found the artist first. They also demanded to know who designed the divine jewellery collection that sat beside each artwork. The delicate belt buckles were designed to compliment the habitat of the animal staring out from each painting. The two works were bound together, with sculpted glass display cases for the buckles, pushing them up from the floor and towards the artworks. Dot had had them created specifically for their show and the scene was breathtaking.

She looked around and sighed with relief when she saw Nate standing towards the back, with a brooding, dark look on his face. She leaned her head to one side to indicate a shivering Maud, who was pushed towards the far wall, just before the roped-off areas of the art installations. Nate looked to where she was indicating and he immediately dropped all of his own issues to protect Maud. Dot smiled in satisfaction and wished she'd had a minute to sort out her own love life with Elliott.

All eyes were on Dot and she cleared her throat. She was glad she had decided to wear a moss green fitted dress with a deep V at the front, which was daring for her new style. Clinching her waist was one of her favourite belts with ivy and brambles tangling together, and tiny blackberries hanging like jewels from the interlinked vines. Her mother had gasped in delight and asked her to get her one, which had made Dot's heart soar to heights it had never known before. She'd hugged her mum, who had looked confused by the tears in her eyes, and then pushed through the crowd to the podium.

There were serious-looking bouncers everywhere tonight, to protect the guests and the art. Looking at the smiling, excited faces, she tried to steel her nerves. Maybe she could do with some of her old clothes to hide behind, but she squared her shoulders and decided that tonight the real Dot and Maud were stepping forward. She felt a momentary pang that Maud's parents were not invited, but maybe it was for the best, as it was about to get even crazier here.

Music had been playing when everyone arrived. It was the sound of rustling in the trees and birds singing with the utmost joy, and then scents of the forest were filtered into the room and people gasped in awe as the scene was set for a forest gathering of animals and nature. Dot spoke as the music faded and everyone stopped chatting so that the room was almost silent.

Usually she liked to be the centre of attention, but Dot gulped, as sweat formed between her breasts. She began to explain how she had discovered an article about a new artist and fallen in love with their work, and then set out on a mission to find them. There were murmurs of approval from her guests and Dot started to relax. This was her arena and she would command it.

She spoke clearly and looked around the room, seeing the faces of her family and friends and hoping they supported her new work. 'While I was searching for this artist, I began to experiment with a new medium, wire and precious metals, inspired by the works I'd seen.' A hush fell on the room and people were looking confused, and then from the work to Dot in astonishment. She grinned as she bet that they were wondering what the hell was going on. Was the artist Dot? Had she done this as a publicity stunt?

Dot laughed at finally making them all shut up. 'Funnily enough, the mystery artist everyone is looking for had already walked into this gallery, and I'd met her.' A buzz of excitement rose again and flashbulbs popped in her face. Dot laughed and threw back her head, letting the tension drain away. She was in her element and she loved it.

'The artist and I discovered a mutual love of art. We became friends and started working together. She had been unsure of her abilities, as had I,' she gave a stern look to her family and friends who all looked at their feet, blushed and grabbed a glass or raised a drink to her and shamelessly cheered, 'but in each other we found inspiration and mutual support. We decided to join my sculptural jewellery designs with her beautiful paintings, to form our first public art show,' she continued once the revelry had died down.

'Without further waffling or tantalising, I'd like to introduce you to our new exhibition, 'If you love me, I'm yours,' and, although we will not be leaving any more of my collaborator's work on park benches, we are glad that the people who received these valuable works enjoy them and cherish them for the masterpieces they are.' Everyone started shouting and asking who the artist was, but Dot held a hand up to ask for quiet. She could literally hear everyone hold their breath in anticipation. 'Maud, would you come and take a bow?'

As Maud stepped up, wearing a simple hip-skimming dress in smoky grey with an off-the-shoulder, bust-hugging neckline and a beautiful skirt that swished around her knees as she moved, she looked as though her heart might literally burst from fear. At her waist was the original belt that Dot had given her, and the flashbulbs exploded and people cheered as she held onto Dot for support, and smiled shyly at everyone.

Dot imagined Maud's heart must be hammering in her chest, as she was scanning the room as if she wanted to run, but Nate had put a gentle hand into her back as she'd turned and pushed her towards the podium, so she'd had no choice but to move forward. Dot looked on and felt some of the tension leave her body. Nate was behaving and all was almost well with the world. He'd ignored both her and Maud all week, so she'd been surprised, nervous and delighted, to see him here. Dot sighed as he placed a soft kiss on Maud's exposed shoulder, as everyone else was facing forward, and then set her on her way, making her flush and then anxiously accept her fate as she moved towards Dot, who hugged her fiercely.

After a short speech and more rowdy cheering, Maud and Dot spent an hour talking to press contacts until they were both dead on their feet. They supported each other as they walked about the gallery, arms around each other's waists, as people stopped them to congratulate them on such profound work. Camille and Cosmo rushed over and flung their arms around them both, dramatically telling everyone in earshot how proud they were of Maud and their very own darling girl.

Maud and Dot had told their story over and over now, and they were both sure everyone must be bored with it. They had drunk champagne and watched as red dots had appeared on every single piece, to show they were all reserved and sold.

As the women chatted happily to the guests and tried to take in the enormity of what had just happened and how their lives might change, Dot noticed Nate leaning against a wall, one ear listening to what the people he was with were saying, while his eyes followed Maud's every move.

Even though he was annoyed with them, he had come to support them both. He'd kissed Maud's shoulder and it had given her the strength to go up onto that stage with Dot. Her lips twitched upwards and she looked at him and tried to convey how sorry she was. He smiled back and winked at them, making her heart swell and Maud's cheeks flush.

Dot had drunk a little too much and was feeling excited and giddy. Maud had originally asked Tom to be here tonight, but they'd moved the date forward so that he was still away. Probably sweet-talking his pregnant dinner lady, Dot thought with disgust. She would deal with him on Monday if Maud didn't. For now, she was going to enjoy being the centre of these people's world for a few hours, and celebrate their achievement.

Chapter Forty-Three

Maud had not expected this. It had only been just over a week after the show and it was still happening. She'd had the previous week off work, but now she'd have to go in and apologise for the chaos she'd caused. She'd thought that the art section of a few papers might mention Dot's new show, as she was famous after all, but it was Maud's face which was plastered across practically every paper locally. Each stated how a suburban schoolteacher was living a double life, and was actually the incredible new artistic talent everyone had been searching for. Then followed the tale Dot had spun in their shiny new press release. Maud had assumed no one would want to know more, once they found out it was boring old her and not someone famous, but she couldn't have been more wrong. If she'd realised this might happen, she would have never left the very first picture in the park.

Dot had woven a magical story of a girl who loved to paint, but was unsure of her talent. She wanted to share her art, but was afraid of rejection, so she left the paintings for people to pick up if they wanted them, with the tag line, 'if you love me, I'm yours.' The media had gone wild, and Maud was scared. People loved Dot's story too, but she was already well known and from a famous family of talented artists, so they expected nothing less from her. Dot was ecstatic that she was finally part of her family's artistic dynasty on her own merit and not just as the manager, and she kept calling Maud and crying as she was so happy.

Maud's phone rang off the hook from 5am and she'd had to creep into school three hours later in the rather muddy van of the school gardener, John, as the front gates were surrounded by local press. He'd smiled jovially, told her well done, and patted her hand in a fatherly way. It bought a tear to her eye as she still hadn't managed to speak to her own parents, who were just back from their holiday. She wasn't sure they would be quite as understanding as John was. His wife had found one of the paintings and now they knew it was worth a fortune, they were so excited. He'd never sell it, though, he'd told her with pride. He thought she was a lovely young lady and the children were lucky to have her there, plus the little artwork was now his wife's most treasured possession, even before she'd known its value. Maud had felt tears fill her eyes. It was so good to hear she had made someone happy in all this mess. John said his wife, Marjorie, had found the painting on a day she'd been told a friend had died and it had seemed like a message from the angels which had got her through. Now she knew it was from Maud, it meant even more. Maud got out of the car and squeezed John's arm in thanks for his kind words, taking a deep breath and ducking quickly into one of the side doors of the school building before anyone saw her.

As soon as Maud walked past the office, she noticed Daisy was in early too. Maud was pleased to see that she was looking healthier and Daisy glanced shyly her way and waved her into the reception. Maud headed in with trepidation, as she wasn't comfortable around her old friend yet.

'It's mad out there,' Daisy whispered urgently. 'I came in early in case you needed me. How did you get in?'

Maud's heart melted a little at the fact that Daisy was here for her and she tried to give her a super-quick hug, to show her she appreciated the gesture, but wasn't ready to resume their friendship yet. 'I sneaked in with John. Did you know his wife picked up one of the first paintings I left in a park?' When Daisy smiled but didn't let her go, she gently pulled away, but kept holding her friend's hand. Daisy held her breath and waited, and Maud knew she had so much to say, now Maud seemed ready to listen.

Before Daisy could speak, Maud looked around her to check they were alone and tried to find the courage to face Daisy. It was still so early that hardly anyone else was there yet. 'I know you're not a bad person, Daisy, and Tom must have literally made you drunk out of your mind. I believe you love Ryan and would never go out of your way to hurt him. It will take some effort, but I miss you in my life and it's all so crazy out there...' she gestured towards the main gates. 'I need all the friends I can get at the moment.' Daisy let out a big squeal and hugged Maud until all the breath was squashed out of her and she was whimpering slightly. Daisy quickly let go and sloppily kissed her cheek.

'Thank you for giving me a chance,' said Daisy, avoiding Maud's eyes. 'Ryan and I came to your show last week.'

'You did? I didn't see you.' Maud had been half-hoping Daisy would be there to support her and was astonished at how upset she had felt when she couldn't spot her.

'We got an invite from a very reluctant Dot, but we wanted to support you. We hid in the crowds. I'm so proud of you, Maud.'

Maud smiled and tried to control more tears that threatened to pour. 'So you and Ryan have sorted things out?'

Daisy sighed and rubbed her tired eyes. 'We're taking it slowly. Neither of us can believe this has happened. I'll have to make it up to him for the rest of my life, but he loves me and he's willing to let me try.'

'Well, thank goodness for that.' Maud was so happy for Daisy. She knew how much this relationship meant to her and that she'd learnt from this mistake. She wouldn't do it again. The pain wasn't worth it.

They turned as the headmistress walked in and asked if Maud could come into her office. Maud's stomach plummeted. This couldn't be good. She grimaced at Daisy, who was so happy now that she missed the look. She beamed at Maud and sent her on her way with a jaunty pat on her bottom, as she unmuted the phones and they immediately started ringing off the hook.

The headmistress, Mrs Ganty, called Maud into her office. For some reason Maud always felt nervous coming into this inner sanctum, even though she was a grown up. It must be a throwback from her childhood, when a call to the head teacher's office rarely meant anything good. Mrs Ganty spoke in a warm tone, but her smile didn't quite meet her eyes. 'I'd like to congratulate you, Maud, on your success as an artist.' Maud was about to speak, and hadn't been asked to sit down, but Mrs Ganty kept talking.

'I think it may be difficult for you to continue working here. The press has been camped out all night and no one can enter the school. We have managed to get rid of some of the reporters as we said you weren't here today, but a few are still hanging round. You understand that this isn't an ideal situation with children in the school?'

'Of course,' said Maud in shock. She hadn't expected to lose her job! She did understand they couldn't have people blocking the school gates or taking pictures of the families here, but she'd expected at least a little support for her predicament. She'd hoped they would be proud for her to be working there, but something was a bit off-kilter

She noticed that Mrs Ganty, who'd never let them be unprofessional and call each other by their first names, was twitchy and wouldn't meet her eye. 'Obviously we don't want to lose a good teacher, but I have a feeling you've found your real love... art.'

Oh bloody hell, thought Maud, realisation dawning. Not another one. She had wondered if it was possible to hate Tom more, but at this moment she did. Mrs Ganty had three children and a lovely husband. Couldn't Tom keep his penis in his pants for more than one second? No wonder she wanted Maud to leave. It would leave the path open for her. Maud wondered if she knew about Daisy... or the pregnant dinner lady? What a mess, with another stupid, stupid woman. No, scratch that, Maud would have felt sorry for her – if she hadn't been trying to oust her from her job.

Maud wasn't even sure she wanted the job any more, but her parents would kill her. Losing her job for being arty. What a nightmare. Then she remembered she'd sold all her paintings and nearly fainted, as she thought about the price tags Dot had put on them all. Maud could happily live off that one show for a year. Could she take a chance and follow her heart? She narrowed her eyes and looked at her employer. 'Shall we get through today and we can decide how to move forward?' She had steel in her voice now and Mrs Ganty had the good grace to realise that Maud knew what was going on here, and looked at her feet. Maud stalked from the room without a word, she was so fed up with being told what to do by people who didn't deserve her respect.

As the school bell rang for break, Daisy opened the door to the staffroom and found Maud slumped in a chair. She was wearing a fitted top with tiny stars sewn all over it and black trousers that hugged her hips and skimmed her now-svelte legs. She had cute black ankle boots on, with textured buttons on each side.

'You look amazing,' said Daisy in awe, as if she hadn't just seen her a while ago, although Maud admitted to herself that Daisy had predominantly been avoiding eye contact as she hadn't been sure what reception she would get. 'Your hair is a bit wild, where you've been running your fingers through it, but you are gorgeous nonetheless.' Yep, there was her usual Daisy, thought Maud. She had a constant foot-in-mouth problem.

Daisy walked over to Maud, who beckoned her to sit, and they talked quietly, before Daisy sprang up angrily and paced the room. No one else was around, they had all surrounded Maud and hugged her and high-fived her in excitement when they had seen her in reception earlier. The children had rushed in too, and she'd had so many questions fired at her that she could barely keep up. It had been decided by Mrs Ganty that she should do filing in the staffroom all day, so that the rest of the school could function with some semblance of normality.

Tom swung the door open and rushed in, excitement shining in his eyes. 'I drove back from my brother's late last night after you texted me the news. I'm so sorry I missed your show, Maud. I would have come back sooner if I'd known it was your work. You are so good at surprises,' he said, pulling Maud into his arms and trying to kiss her, before realising Daisy was there too and flushing bright red. Maud pushed out of his arms and stood up.

He looked slightly panicked but recovered quickly. 'Now you're a famous artist, Maud, you'll need a good manager. We need to plan our future so that you have peace and space to work without interruption, my darling.' He grabbed her hand and glared at Daisy to leave this private moment, but she stood firm.

Maud smiled at him and he sighed in relief. She put her hand into the bright purple squashy bag next to her, a present from Dot. Maud suspected that it was part of Dot's old wardrobe that she didn't want any more, but Maud wasn't complaining, it had lots of pockets and room for a small sketchbook, which she now carried everywhere. Locating her phone, she tapped the screen. She held it out to him and showed him her brand new social media page. It already had tens of thousands of followers, shocking to her, but quite normal as far as Dot was concerned, now that people knew who Maud was.

'Wow!' said Tom. 'That's great.' He kissed her cheek and hugged her to him. She stepped away as Mrs Ganty came in to make herself a coffee. Maud had counted on the headmistress not wanting Maud to be alone with Tom for long, so she'd sent her a text to tell her that he would be back at break time to visit the school and then waited for them both to arrive. They looked a bit worried when they realised they were all in one room together, and that Daisy was there too, and might hear something she shouldn't.

'I was just showing Tom my new social media page,' she smiled to the headmistress, beckoning her over.

Mrs Ganty looked confused. 'Why is there a picture of Tom on it?

'Because I'm her boyfriend,' said Tom pompously, as Daisy made a sick sound. He frowned at her, sending her a warning look and then the same to Mrs Ganty, who looked annoyed.

'You're not my boyfriend, Tom,' Maud stated clearly, making his mouth drop open in shock and his forehead crease in confusion. 'You are someone I was dating, during which time you slept with my best friend and my boss.'

Mrs Ganty's cheeks flamed as she looked at Daisy, and was

horrified when she realised the part she'd played in this mess. She tried to rally, but almost choked on her words as she said, 'Maud, obviously you will always have a teaching job here for as long as you like. Earlier I was just thinking of you, and the stress of managing two careers.' Maud could see pictures of lawsuits flying through the other woman's mind, and enjoyed the mental picture for a moment, before putting Mrs Ganty out of her misery. The woman had suffered enough by having to sleep with a loathsome creep like Tom.

'I don't want to work here any more,' she decided, holding up a hand to stop anyone talking until she was finished. 'But I do want a glowing reference as I'm a great teacher.' The other woman nodded mutely.

'Tom,' she turned to face him. 'If you treat anyone else in the disgusting way you've treated all of us, I will hit send, and everyone will know what you've done and who you are. I will be happy to make you pay for what you've done for the rest of your life.'

Tom's face was flushed and there was fire in his eyes now, but he had a parting shot. 'You were too frigid to sleep with me anyway. Why do you think I had to look elsewhere?' he pointed rudely to Mrs Ganty, who blanched and looked sick. 'Why would I sleep with her, either?' he jabbed his finger towards Daisy and snarled at her.

Maud was aghast and quickly got in the way as Daisy was about to floor him with her right hook. 'You told her you'd slept with her. She was drunk. You took advantage of a drunken woman.'

'No I didn't,' he shouted back, glancing around in agitation to make sure no one else was coming in or could hear them. 'She was too drunk to know what she was doing. I kissed her but then she passed out. I'm not a bloody monster! I like women, but I'm a good guy. I wouldn't do something like that.'

Daisy screamed over Maud's restraining shoulder. 'You told me we'd slept together and to keep quiet or you'd tell Maud... my best friend.'

Tom had the grace to look ashamed for a minute, but

brushed her comment aside. 'You turned me down and I wanted to pay you back. No one turns me down. I didn't say we'd slept together, you just assumed it. Women love me. I have never had a woman fall asleep on me before. It was humiliating.'

'So you lied to her, ruined her relationship by telling her she'd cheated and then destroyed our friendship,' Maud spat out, now ready to strike him too, for all of the suffering he'd caused.

Tom stopped for a second, as if he hadn't even given this a moment's thought, and he looked wildly around for a way out, but Mrs Ganty was now blocking the door.

Maud's eyes flamed and she just about restrained herself from scratching his eyes out for the devastation he had dished out, without even realising what he'd done. He'd literally been sulking and had wanted to pay Daisy back for rejecting him. 'You disgusting excuse for a human being.'

Mrs Ganty moved to the side of the door and pointed to Tom, then to it. 'Get out.'

Chapter Forty-Four

Nate was leaning against the wall next to the huge floor-to-ceiling window in his flat, and looking out at the street below. He was still upset about Dot and Maud's lies and felt that they'd made a fool of him and the rest of the family. Everyone else was still celebrating and he knew that Dot thought he was jealous of her new artistic ability, but he'd always known she was creative and wonderful. She managed all of them beautifully, handled clients and every minute detail of a gallery show with flair and sophistication. He'd never questioned Dot's place in the family business, she had only doubted herself. He understood she had been frustrated that she hadn't found the right medium to work with until now, but the jewellery she made was exquisite and the ability she had was astounding. He was so proud of her... but then he'd always been proud to call her his sister. She exasperated him and misunderstood him, but she was funny and lively, bonkers and sweet too.

He hadn't been able to speak to Maud since the show. He'd tried to congratulate her that evening, but she had been surrounded by people all night and he hadn't been able to get close enough to her. It had been so frustrating and he'd growled at a few people, especially Elliott, who knew why he was grumpy and ignored him as usual. El was shocked when he realised that Dot had made the exquisite jewellery showcased in the sculptural glass domes, but as he loved anything she did, his chest puffed out in pride and he beamed at her. She'd rushed over and thrown her arms around him for a hug and poor old El hadn't been able to stop grinning all night.

Nate was just about to reach for the phone, when it rang and made him jump. Before he could speak, Dot started berating him for being such a jealous freak and told him to stop avoiding her and Maud. Suitably told off, he smiled into the phone. He was actually glad she'd called, even though she was shouting at him for no reason. He'd decided he couldn't be bothered to be cross with them any more, as he missed them both too much. Dot was still talking and he began listening to her again, only to go quiet when the blood in his veins started to boil at her words and he started walking to the door with his mobile phone still in his hand, as Dot explained what an awful day Maud was having. His fists bunched around his car keys. They dug into his hand as he headed for the stairs and slammed the door behind him. He didn't need to say anything as he cut off the call. Dot had explained what Tom had done and Nate was appalled at the months of torture he had put these women through. If he was still at the school when Nate arrived, he would wish he'd never been born.

Nate looked at his watch, then pulled out from his parking space. It was getting towards the end of the school day now, so he'd have to step on the gas to get there before Maud tried to go home. What was Dot thinking of, letting her return to the school before giving her some sort of press training, or at the bare minimum giving her a heads-up that this was her life now? Dot should have known that the press would besiege the school, and ought to have had a steel-clad plan in place for Maud to take more time off, while she decided which direction she wanted to take her career in. He would have to find Dot later and wring her neck.

He got stuck in a little traffic as he got nearer the school, then he started to grow impatient. There seemed to be so many people outside. Dot had said everyone had left, thinking Maud wasn't there, but they'd obviously found out she was and had come back. Parents were being let through the school gates by two men wearing bright yellow tabards, who looked shell-shocked, but serious about protecting one of their own. Nate sighed and swung his car into a driveway opposite the school, which had a car already on the drive and a small bike lying on the ground beside it. He quickly turned away from the rabble on the opposite side of the road and knocked on the door, hoping a school parent lived here if the bike was anything to go by. The door was swiftly opened by a woman with blonde hair tied back in a jaunty ponytail, who looked to be in her early thirties. She was surprised to see such a handsome man on her doorstep and absently brushed her fingers through her hair, but then glanced across the road and cringed. 'I'm so sorry to bother you,' he laid on his best charm and gave her a winning smile. 'Do you have children at this school?'

The woman's face immediately clouded and she tried to shut the door. 'I'm not talking to the press about Miss Silverton, I've already told your friends,' she tilted her head towards the people on the pavement with cameras.

Nate put his hand on the door, but tried not to alarm her. 'I'm a friend of Maud's, but I can't get my car into the grounds of the school to get her out of there,' he explained.

The woman stopped trying to close the door and looked at him again, more closely this time. 'Nate Ridgemore?' she gasped, blushing and spluttering slightly.

He nodded and spoke quickly. 'Can I leave my car on your drive while I try and find a way to get Maud out?'

'Of course! Take as long as you like. I've got to go across and collect my son soon, but I was leaving it until the last minute, it's a madhouse. Do you want to walk across with me? I can get you in.'

Nate had no doubt he could get in, as he was so determined to get to Maud, but he realised, as this was a school, the children's safety would come first. Maud might have to wait until nightfall to go home. 'That would be great. Thanks,' he said, waiting for her to collect her bag and shut the door behind her. She was grinning and began chatting to him, asking how he had met Maud, but he was trying to keep his head down. No one would expect him to be here, so he hoped they'd think he was just another school parent coming for his child.

He had literally set one foot onto the pavement in front of the school bouncers, when flashbulbs went off in his face and people started to call out his name. He smiled apologetically at his new friend, but it seemed she was the one who had whispered his name to her friend just inside the gate, and then all hell had broken loose. She shouted to the security guards and they pulled them through the gates and then shut them, before using their bodies to block further entrance. The woman appeared delighted at the drama, but Nate just fretted at making Maud's day even harder. He'd been so set on seeing her and holding her after the day she'd had, he hadn't thought things through clearly. He said a quick hello to the people standing staring at him just inside the gate, thanked the woman he had walked across the road with through gritted teeth, and followed the signs for the school's reception area. He needed to get Maud out of here so that the press would leave and the children could get home safely.

Seeing Daisy come out of reception, he called to her and she ran into his arms and began crying noisily. He didn't really know what to do, as he'd come here for Maud, but Daisy had been treated appallingly too. He hugged her and asked her where Maud was. Daisy sniffed into his arm and then led him to the headmistress's office. He opened the door to find Maud, looking tiny and sitting with her shoulders slumped, staring at the floor. No one else was in there, so he approached her and hunched down in front of her face. She looked up with watery eyes. He pulled up a chair and sat down next to her, pulling her onto his lap where she curled into a ball and cried. He stroked her soft hair and whispered soothing noises while she calmed down, then kissed her gently on the nose and wiped her tears away.

He pulled her up to standing and looked deeply into her troubled eyes. 'He's not worth your tears...'

Maud's head shot up in surprise. 'Oh, I'm not crying about that detestable waste of space! I've lost my job and time with my best friend because of that man. I hate him. I told him that if he ever comes near me or my friends again, I'll plaster his face all over social media and tell everyone what a repugnant sleazeball he is. If he didn't have a pregnant girlfriend...' she said, glancing at Nate's shocked expression for a moment before continuing, 'I would have sent out the social media picture anyway. She's welcome to him.'

'Then why are you crying?' he asked, his heart lifting at the fact that Tom was no longer his problem.

'Because my parents are going to hate me for losing my job, and I can't tell them about it because I'm stuck here. I don't think they know yet. They've been on holiday and refuse to read the papers until they get home. They got back today, and now they will hate me, on top of everything else that's happened today.'

'Do you really want this job anymore? Haven't you got an exciting new career before you now?' he asked carefully, not wanting her to stamp on his foot for being a presumptuous ass.

She pressed her face into his chest and snuffled a bit, mumbling that her parents were not like other people and she always disappointed them. He couldn't imagine anyone being disappointed with such a sweetheart as Maud, but families could be tricky. He just had to look at his own tribe to know how messed up they could be. 'So let's go to visit them and explain what has happened,' he said simply.

Maud looked up in surprise. 'We?'

'Yep,' he grinned. 'How bad can it be?'

Maud giggled then and he gave her another quick kiss on her forehead, before pulling her out of the room. She grabbed her bag in a daze. 'How do we get out?'

Lots of children and parents were sitting in the main hall, and the headmistress was explaining that their departure would be delayed. Nate walked into the room and a hush fell as people started to recognise him and saw him holding Maud's hand. Some of the children began giggling and Maud smiled shyly and waved at one or two. Nate took charge and explained to the harassed parents what was happening. He was well versed in these situations and knew what to do.

He explained that Maud hadn't expected her work to be quite so popular. He waited while people laughed and then ploughed on. Both he and Maud would be donating a painting each to the school, to be auctioned at the gallery, and the money would go towards facilities or equipment the school needed to apologise for any inconvenience that day. Mrs

Ganty gasped in shock and some of the parents began clapping and cheering, as the school was in dire need of new sports equipment.

Nate explained that Maud would be taking time away from the school to give this furore time to die down, then she would decide on her future after discussion with the school and parents. Maud looked a bit shell-shocked at this, but he squeezed her hand to tell her to keep quiet for now and trust him. It was their only way out.

'Maud and I will go and speak to the press now,' he felt Maud shake with fear beside him. 'I have asked Maud's agent to arrange a press interview for tomorrow, so they will leave the premises when we do. It will then be safe for you all to return home.' Everyone started jumping around and clapping and they all got up and cheered Maud. She blushed and thanked everyone for being so supportive, turning away before she burst into tears.

Nate tried valiantly not to stare at the headmistress. He'd learnt from Dot when she'd called him earlier in a panic, that Mrs Ganty was one of Tom's women too. Dot had explained that the headmistress was the one who had let Maud down by sleeping with her boyfriend, not Daisy. He led Maud to the school gates. The parents and children were still in the hall, so they were on their own. 'You ok?' he turned and asked her. 'I'm sorry for taking over, but we have to speak to the media. Dot's organised a meeting for you both tomorrow. She's so excited, while you're trembling.' He rubbed his hands up and down her arms. 'You can do this.'

Maud didn't say anything other than to nod her consent. She hoisted her bag further up her shoulder and gritted her teeth. 'Let's go.'

Chapter Forty-Five

Maud breathed a sigh of relief as they got into Nate's car and drove towards her parents' house. She wasn't that terrified to see them after what she'd just been through with the press, she was just tired to her core. The journalists had been wonderful and had wanted to find out more about her story and her new work. She was very flattered, and not as frightened as she'd thought she'd be, as Nate had told them all about the meeting Dot had set up for the following day. He'd handed out Dot's business cards, reminding them they all needed to contact Dot for an interview with Maud, or to get an invite to the media launch. They had happily stood for a few photos outside the school, then by Nate's car, and had been left alone to drive away with minimal fuss. Maud had called Daisy from the car and told them the press were leaving and the children could go home. She also asked her to tell the parents and children they could all come to her next exhibition as her guests. She'd heard Nate splutter and then laugh heartily next to her, as he no doubt pictured Dot's angry face at all the extra work. Well, it served her right for dumping this mess on her doorstep in the first place.

She directed Nate to park in her parents' driveway and held her breath while she tried to calm her nerves, which suddenly flared up again. He got out, came round to her side of the car and opened the door. 'You're going to have to get out of my car at some point, Maud,' he joked, reaching for her hand.

She took it gratefully and tried to be braver. She peeked down at her clothes and sighed at how rumpled they looked now. Her mum would hate her top, and probably never talk to her again for being chucked out of her job.

'You'll be fine,' soothed Nate, wrapping her into a warm

hug as the door opened and her parents stood in the hall, staring mutely at the big man with his arms around their daughter, standing next to a shiny top-of-the-range sports car.

'Maud?' her mother looked about to say more, but her dad just coughed and beckoned them inside the house, when he saw their neighbours' curtains twitching at the sight of such an expensive car.

Maud kept hold of Nate's hand as they walked inside, which made him beam a wide grin at her parents, who grimaced back. Maud tried to stem the jitters, but her heart felt broken at the look in their eyes. They all sat down in the lounge after brief introductions and her mother busied herself making tea and putting biscuits on a china plate, before returning and sitting next to Maud's dad without a word.

Maud decided this was too painful. 'You've read the papers, then?'

'Why didn't you tell us it was you, Maud?' her dad asked, hurt obvious for all to see. She felt Nate stiffen by her side. He knew exactly how they felt.

'I didn't tell anyone,' she said simply. 'My friend, Nate's sister, is an artist's agent and she began searching for me after seeing the original articles in the paper. I got scared that I would lose my job, so I didn't tell a soul.' She omitted to mention Daisy had been in on it the whole time, as she had suffered enough lately, and Maud's mother would give her a stern talking-to for lying to her.

She sighed and went over to hug both her parents, which made them soften a little and they begrudgingly hugged her back. Her mum actually had tears in her eyes and was being remarkably quiet, whilst Maud had expected her to scold her at the very least.

'Does it matter if you lose your job?' her dad asked seriously now, patting his wife's knee. 'It says in the paper that your art is worth a fortune and you've sold every piece?'

Maud blushed and looked at Nate for guidance. 'Maud did sell every piece, but that doesn't mean she will every time,' Nate said, seeing her mum registering shock at his brutal honesty. He laughed and apologised. 'I'm an artist too, so I

219

know that art is subjective and a piece you love might be hanging on a gallery wall for a long time. Maud is new to this, so she's not very confident in her work, which is why she didn't tell any of us.' By including himself in that statement, he instantly formed a bond with her parents and he saw her mother's smile of sympathy that he'd been treated as poorly as they had. He could obviously see the sudden mutiny on Maud's face, as she was about to point out they had always thought her art was appalling, so why would she tell them anything? But he squeezed her knee and she clamped her mouth shut on the words she so badly wanted to speak aloud. Maud's parents were nodding at Nate with understanding and her mother sent her a stare to tell her she'd been very naughty. It was like being five again.

'Maud may well sell every painting she creates, but she's worried she needs a back up plan. She doesn't.' Nate said with confidence.

'We've heard of you and your work, Nate. So we realise you know an awful lot about art and can help Maud,' said Maud's dad, carefully. 'This has all been a bit of a shock, as you can understand. But we've spoken about this at length, haven't we, Rosemary?' he said, looking at his wife and holding her hand, 'and we realised that maybe we had been holding Maud back, and that was why she didn't tell us?'

Maud nearly passed out in shock. She sprang up to cuddle them both, as her dad asked Nate if he'd like to look around the house and garden, and the doorbell rang so Rosemary went to answer it, visibly annoyed at the interruption of her famous daughter and handsome new suitor. She quickly whispered to Maud that she was coming round to the idea of this art malarkey and had decided it was very chic to be a 'proper' artist, not one of these abstract or impressionist imposters. Maud just smiled and shook her head. Her mum would never change, but she was too happy at this moment in time to care.

Her parents' neighbours, Marcy and Don, rushed into the lounge in a flurry of excitement. Marcy's eyes lit on Maud and she pulled her into a fast hug and squealed in delight. 'Why didn't you tell us when we were last here that it was you,

Maud?'

Before Maud could speak, Nate wandered in from the garden where her dad had been showing him his neat shed, and both neighbours just stood in mute awe. Rosemary smiled brightly and introduced Maud's suitor, Nate, which made Maud want to die of embarrassment on the spot. 'Nate's a friend, Mum,' she said in a high-pitched voice, as her cheeks flamed and she got the urge to run and jump out of the nearest ground floor window, even if it was closed.

'Don't be so coy, Maud,' said Nate, coming and wrapping his arms around her waist, making every part of her flush red. He kissed the top of her head and introduced himself to her neighbours as Maud's boyfriend. Maud nearly fainted on the spot. Was that what he had become? She rapidly decided she quite liked the idea and leaned against him for support.

Marcy and Don looked as if they couldn't believe their luck, as Maud realised they would finally have some gossip of their own to share with their reporter friend and he could stop boasting that he knew everything. 'How on earth did you keep this a secret from us?' They turned towards Maud's parents, with enquiring eyes. 'You must be so proud of Maud. We certainly are. We know two famous artists now.' They looked at Nate and Maud and went over to congratulate them both again.

Maud's dad had the grace to look embarrassed and was about to speak, but her mum butted in. 'Oh, we knew how important it was to Maud to keep this a secret until her gallery opening, so we couldn't tell a soul,' she giggled coquettishly, as Maud's mouth hung open at the bare-faced cheek of the woman, but also admiring how quickly she rallied from an upset. Nate looked like he was thoroughly enjoying himself, and her dad brought out a bottle of good red wine he'd been saving and offered everyone a glass.

'Did you know, she sold every single piece of work at her first show? We're so proud of her,' Rosemary said, making Maud almost choke on her wine. 'Luckily, we have lots of her work stored here for safe keeping.' Seeing the neighbours' eyes almost bug out as they mentally worked out the net value of a house full of valuable art, Maud panicked slightly.

'Mum...' said Maud hastily, not wanting word to spread that her parents had valuables in the house, in case it caught the attention of thieves. Especially as she'd cleared out every single piece when she'd visited earlier in the year. She gave her mum a warning stare, which told her to stop her babbling and for once her mum frowned, and then listened. 'Remember I took those paintings to my studio as they were taking up too much storage room here...?' Her mum looked mortified, and then like she'd been sucking lemons, which Maud rather enjoyed. She'd told Nate that she'd stolen the paintings away during dinner one evening and he'd found the story hilarious, so he was quietly trying to stop himself laughing, but his shoulders were bobbing up and down slightly, which gave the game away. Maud was actually glad her mum was embarrassed. She should be, for the years of not supporting her daughter's dream and pretending it made her ill.

'But we do have the gorgeous one in the kitchen,' her mum remembered with mutiny in her eye. She rushed to collect the painting of the house, which they obviously hadn't seen before, even though they were regular visitors here now. They all oohed and aahed over the detail and skill of Maud's work. Maud sighed and was suddenly very tired. Nate seemed to notice the change in her and led her to the couch to sit down and put her empty glass on the side table.

'Looks like our Maud will be having a career change and leaving teaching to spread her artistic wings,' said her dad, beaming down at her with pride.

Rosemary smiled at her too, as she stood next to her husband. 'Of course it helped that we nurtured Maud's talent and let her express herself as a child. You should have seen the way she marked the walls with her fingers and then started painting all her clothes with pictures of our cat.' Maud laughed manically and began to feel a bit like this was an out-of-body experience.

Marcy came and sat next to Maud, so that she had to budge up and was practically sitting on Nate's lap, which he didn't seem to mind at all. 'What about the studio at your house? It said in the paper that you paint from home. I bet that's amazing too? How exciting having your own studio at home, although you could probably afford a huge place now, Maud. What's it like, Rosemary?'

Rosemary quickly sipped her wine and was, for the first time in her life, lost for words. Maud spoke for her. 'Mum and Dad love the little studio at the bottom of my garden, they positively hang out there, don't you, guys?' she laughed to soften her reproving words.

Nate lifted her from his lap and got up, then put out a hand for her too. Her dad smiled at his chivalry and Marcy winked behind his back and made a thumbs-up sign, which made her face flame again.

'I think Maud's had a long day and needs to get some rest. She had to give a press interview today, as her launch was so successful and photographers traced her to the school where she works. I was hoping to take her out to dinner before she falls asleep on her feet. It's been a pleasure to meet you all.' After lots of congratulations about her interview, everyone said their goodbyes with promises of getting together again soon. Nate shook her dad's hand and got a pat on the back in return, which made him puff out his chest in pride, as if it was so important to have their blessing on his feelings for their daughter.

As they said farewell and her dad walked them to the door, Maud heard her mum brag about how thrilled she was that Maud had finally found a suitable young man. It was a good job she'd been too busy to tell them about Tom, as they'd be horrified to find out what kind of man he was.

Chapter Forty-Six

Nate was becoming agitated. Things had been going so well. He'd taken Maud out to dinner after meeting her parents and he'd finally stayed over and spent the evening sleeping with her in his arms, naked skin to naked skin. It had taken all of his self-control not to ravish her then, but she'd been so battered by her emotions that she'd stripped off, almost making him have a heart attack, then asked him to stay the night and got into bed. He hadn't taken much persuading and had thrown his clothes off in haste, not giving her a chance to change her mind after all this time. But when he'd kissed her, she'd sighed dreamily and fallen into a deep sleep.

He had lain next to her for hours, hoping she'd wake up after a short rest, but it hadn't happened and instead she'd curled herself into him and he'd wrapped his arms around her as she slept. He'd been rock hard and suffering all night until he'd finally fallen into an exhausted sleep himself. He'd had dreams of sexy black shoes with red roses painted all over them, that had suddenly come alive and started entwining themselves along her silky legs and then around them both as they writhed in ecstasy.

He woke up and groaned, as it had seemed so real, then realised that Maud was now wide awake and was kissing her way up his throat and pressing her bountiful breasts against his slick skin. He'd growled and rolled her onto her back, which had made her laugh and her skin flushed at her brazen seduction, although she was suddenly shy now that he was fully awake.

He'd pinned her arms over her head so that he could finally look at the body he'd been dreaming of since the first time he'd seen her. He knew she was self conscious, but her shape was perfect to him. She still had soft curves and he couldn't wait to bite into them and make her cry out with pleasure. He had stared into her eyes and she'd wriggled a little, making him even harder. He'd released her arms and began kissing his way down her body until they joined together and she screamed his name.

Remembering how he'd carried her into the shower afterwards, he'd soaped every inch of her tender flesh as she'd come apart in his arms. The water had washed away the last few months, as he licked her mouth. She responded by darting out her tongue and he drew her into another passionate kiss. He just couldn't get enough of her. Eventually she'd giggled and told him the water was getting cold, so he'd towelled her dry and carried her back to the still-warm sheets while he prepared breakfast in bed for them both.

The problem was that reality crept back in as soon as she discovered he'd turned both of their phones to silent mode the night before, and taken the main line off the hook. When she slid the buttons across to activate the phones, about a thousand messages appeared. They'd spent the next two hours answering them and then he'd had to get back to the gallery while she rushed to get ready for her press conference with Dot. He'd reluctantly left and had promised to be back that night, but work had got in the way for both of them, and it had suddenly been a week since he'd seen her. They'd spoken every night and she was alive with excitement about being able to paint every day. He knew the feeling well, so he didn't intrude, but felt miserable without her.

Eventually he decided that the only way he could see her was if she joined him at his parents' house that weekend. The media had called him incessantly to ask about Maud, as Marcy and Don, whom he'd met at her parents' house, had told the world that they were seeing each other. Tom had apparently sent her a nasty text saying she was a slut and had been seeing Nate all along, which she told Nate she hadn't bothered to reply to. Nate had wanted to ask her to block Tom's number for her own safety, but didn't want to come across as a jealous boyfriend. That was the part that was making him so grumpy.

He'd announced to Maud and her parents that he was her boyfriend. What had he been thinking? He'd been so full of testosterone that he'd blurted it out. Maud hadn't disagreed, but he knew she'd been shocked. They'd never discussed it, and hadn't since. Maud was probably terrified about having another psycho boyfriend and he felt sick, letting someone into his life this way. He'd not had a proper girlfriend since Lena. He'd kept everyone as casual dates, and suddenly he was declaring to the world she was his girlfriend. It was his own fault that he was now having to hide at his parents' house, as his flat and studio space were surrounded by press, waiting for a comment on his relationship with Maud.

Maud had texted him a cute little message to apologise for her parents' neighbours' behaviour. He'd brushed it off, saying it didn't matter, but he was feeling increasingly claustrophobic being back at home and having to live with his own parents' antics once again. Maud said hers were still a bit angry with her, although they were also secretly enjoying the attention they were getting from their bridge club members. They'd even been offered their own interview in the local papers. They'd shyly called Maud and asked her permission. Welcome to his world!

He was watching to see her car arrive at the house from the upstairs window, fed up with listening to his parents harping on about how Dot had got the art gene from them, and wanting him to listen for hours to their crazy ideas for her birthday party. Dot had told him she was looking forward to it this year, so that was one good thing to come out of all of the planning meetings. Everyone always got so drunk that a table of food and an open bar would be enough anyway. He couldn't work out what all the fuss and a year of planning was about.

Seeing Maud's car pull up and her sexy legs stretching out after she'd opened the door, he decided that he'd had enough of being grouchy and single and it was about time he stopped pussy-footing around and claimed his girl. Taking the stairs two at a time, he was out of the house and had swept her up into his arms before she closed the car door.

Chapter Forty-Seven

Maud looked into the mirror and ran her hands down the dress she was wearing. She'd been eating properly again and her figure had settled back into womanly curves. She decided she preferred this version of herself. The waif look that suited Dot just didn't work for her. Nate seemed to enjoy her body whatever her size, and he showed her at every opportunity. It was getting embarrassing. She grinned at herself and saw how smug she looked. It felt good to be desired so much by a man like Nate. Sure, he could be grumpy and bossy, but so could she when she was trying to finish a work of art.

She'd had to move into a new studio, as Nate had said she'd need somewhere safer to store her art and keep people away from her home. She thought it was because they had a free studio next to him and then she was there for sex on tap, but who was she to complain? The man was red hot.

She looked for her black shoes with the roses painted on them and frowned. She was sure they'd been around earlier. She sighed and grabbed a spare pair she'd thrown into her suitcase this morning and slicked on some soft pink lipstick. Her dress was sewn in tones of dusky pink to deep plum. It had a fitted skirt and the bustier was cut across her breasts with several straps of ribbon going from the centre of her bust to wide on her shoulders. It was feminine and exotic, and she loved it.

Today was Dot's big birthday party. She'd already spent a few hours with Maud discussing their latest projects together, and chatting excitedly about her party. She looked amazing in a long gold dress that shimmered as she walked. Only Dot could pull it off, the dress was cut so low at the back you could almost see her bum cheeks as she moved... almost. She looked stunning. Maud had given her a beautifully-wrapped present earlier and Dot had cried. It was a painting of Dot, Maud and Daisy, surrounded by woodland creatures and their habitats. All three women were smiling and hugging. Maud didn't usually paint people, but this one had taken ages and she was thrilled with the result.

Daisy had apparently run home from school as soon as the press left that day, and was waiting on her Ryan's doorstep when he got home. He'd raged when she'd told him what had really happened and driven to Tom's to confront him. Luckily, Tom had jumped on a bus to his real home. They'd found out he was actually living with the pregnant dinner lady now. Ryan had held Daisy as she'd cried and cried, but they had both been so relieved that she hadn't cheated, and he'd said he was so sorry for doubting her. He hadn't had much choice in deciding if it was true, as she'd confessed. Daisy had said they'd not let each other out of their sight since. They couldn't come tonight as Ryan had a gig, and Daisy had gone with him, but Daisy had bought Dot a CD of whale music, so that she could relax while she was working. They still hadn't quite sorted out their differences, but were united over what a nasty specimen Tom was. Little did Daisy know that Dot already had a weird sculpture her old school friend had sent her that made strange whale-like noises, and hated the sound! She'd appreciated the sentiment nonetheless.

Taking a deep breath, Maud left the room and descended the main stairs. Camille and Cosmo had welcomed her into the family, even though she still wasn't sure of her exact status in this madcap group. Nate had called her his girlfriend in front of her parents, which had shocked her, and he'd tried to talk to her about it days ago, but then his parents had descended on him and hadn't left them alone since. She felt so jumpy around Nate that her nerves were wrung out. He'd tried to entice her into his room as soon as she'd arrived here, but it felt disrespectful to his parents. He reminded her about their naked day in bed and she made a sick sound as he'd grabbed her for kisses, until she had to come up for air and admit that she'd been in heaven that day.

Since the art exhibition with Dot, she'd been inundated with commission offers and she'd made the mistake of accepting a few before Dot had shouted at her very loudly and stamped her pretty little feet until she'd directed them to her agent, with apologies for her inexperience. Whoops. She'd been so busy she'd had barely any time to see or speak to Nate, as Dot was still very demanding.

She couldn't wait any longer to be in his arms again, though, and might have to break her own rule tonight, about respecting his family home with no sexy shenanigans. The party was already in full swing and rooms were flowing with music, laughter and brightly-dressed waiting staff weaving expertly between the guests and topping up the already brimming glasses. She immediately spotted Nate, leaning against an ornate pillar woven with ivy and fresh flowers, with twinkling lights sparkling in between. There were several of these all over the house and the balconies were draped with hanging greenery and flowers. It looked like a nymph's paradise. Nate was near the stairs, which suggested he might be waiting for her, but when she saw he was surrounded by beautiful women, who all had faces tilted up to listen to his every word, breasts heaving and hands fluttering on his arm, her heart sank and she felt ridiculous for even thinking she could compete. They had been cocooned in their own little bubble for so long now, with Nate always there to solve her problems and soothe worries away, she'd forgotten that it wasn't real life and she'd have to step back into reality soon. Supposing she turned out like Lena. Supposing she got so jealous that he was all she could see?

The thought terrified her, after what she'd been through with Tom. She would never harm Nate or herself, but she was starting to have strong feelings for him and she craved him all the time. It was different to anything she'd ever felt and she was confused and frustrated. She waited until a group of people came down the stairs and blended in with them, a false smile on her lips. She needed a drink. She walked in the opposite direction to Nate, but saw him glance up the stairs while one of the women was speaking.

Maud wandered round in wonder. She spoke to some people she'd met at the gallery and then Dot grabbed her and began introducing her to all sorts of interesting and completely zany guests. Maud enjoyed every minute of it and forgot her worries, throwing her head back and laughing at something Elliott said, before gasping as a hand snaked possessively round her waist and Nate ran his warm fingers down her spine.

'I've had enough of watching you be entertained by the other men in the room.' he growled and he began nibbling her ear, which made her skin light up and flame. She'd tried so hard to keep away from him, but it was too much for a regular girl like her to manage. He kept touching her when no one could see and whispering what he'd like to do to her, until he swept her into a secluded corner of the terrace and ravaged her mouth. She pressed her body into him and groaned. He had far too many clothes on and she raked her fingers through his hair. Hearing people approach the garden she reluctantly pulled away and stared with glazed eyes into his.

Nate smiled and put his arm around her shoulders, to shield her slightly dishevelled appearance from the interlopers. 'Don't try and hide from me again. I'll just find you.'

Maud smiled and hugged him. 'I wasn't hiding from you.'

'Yes, you were. Why?' he asked with interest.

'I'm scared,' she said simply.

'Me too.' He held out his hand for her, kissed her on her nose and led her back inside as he could hear his mother calling his name. He had confided in Maud that he was forever sorting out one drama or another with his parents, so it didn't faze him, but this time he was taking backup and he pulled Maud after him, stroking his hand over her backside as he stood back to let her enter the room before him. She slapped his hand playfully away and he grinned wolfishly, telling her clearly that she was coming to him later and they would sort all of this out, one way or another.

Nate was using every opportunity to brush past Maud, touch her skin when no one was looking and grab her in dark corners of the party when she least expected it, to devour her mouth leaving her flushed and wanting. Then, as soon as they re-joined the party, flustered and giggling, he would be dragged away by another party-goer and then return half an hour later and draw her into a corner again. There were so many glamorous people here, they were wearing anything from designer cocktail dresses to pyjamas, and Maud loved it. This was her element now and she felt welcome and relaxed. She'd had a few glasses of wine and was flushed with arousal from Nate's continuing efforts to make her stay with him that night. She could have told him that she'd changed her mind about not staying in his room, but it was so much fun playing cat and mouse with him all night. He was one determined man and no matter how many women threw themselves at him, he managed to shake them off and make a beeline for her.

The party was soon in full swing and there was a DJ in one room and a full band in another, at the furthest point of the grand house. In between were all sorts of acrobatic performers and everything was sparkling with little lights, which were strung everywhere. It looked like something out of a fairy tale and she felt like a princess, even though it wasn't her party.

Elliott was being hilarious too. He was so drunk and kept draping his arms across Maud's shoulders and telling her how much he adored Dot. Maud had told him she already knew that countless times, but he still wanted to tell her again. Dot had stood up when called and was about to make her birthday speech, so El drew Maud closer to hear above the revelry, but gradually everyone had gone quiet as Dot began to speak. Just as she opened her mouth, Camille stepped in and took the microphone. She gaily told everyone, as she twirled to include them all, that she was super-proud of her talented daughter and her delightful artisan work. Camille pointed to her waist where she was wearing one of Dot's pieces from the first show. Cosmo had bought it for her, before he even knew that Dot made them, and Dot had burst into happy tears when she found out. Everyone cheered and saluted Dot when Camille took a bow.

'I think we should let her off giving a speech this year,' said Cosmo, joining his wife and taking the microphone.

Someone shouted from the back, 'As long as she doesn't sing!' to which everyone roared with laughter and Dot saluted them all good-naturedly, not quite knowing what they meant.

Maud saw that Dot was a bit teary-eyed from her parents' speech and sent her a kiss, but then noticed that she was staring at Elliott next to her and frowning at the brunette that had just draped herself all over him. Dot suddenly looked angry and headed their way, and Maud wondered if she'd finally worked out her feelings for him, so she moved forward to cut her off as she looked as if she'd like to do someone some damage.

'Dot!' said Maud, grabbing her arm and leading her to the side of the room, whilst smiling at everyone that stopped them briefly to kiss Dot and congratulate her. 'You ok?' she asked.

'For some reason, that girl who's practically horizontal on El is winding me up. I may have toned down my look, but I'm not dead yet. He's my friend and she's all over him.'

Maud looked his way and he was happily chatting to the said brunette and swaying slightly, glass in hand. 'He seems happy enough about it to me,' she said, testing the water for Dot's response.

Dot looked confused and then her eyes narrowed at Maud. 'Is she his girlfriend?' It didn't look like Dot was too happy about that idea.

'I don't know,' said Maud honestly, 'but he's spent the last half hour telling me how much he loves you.' Dot's mouth hung agape and her eyes flew open. She leaned on the wall for support and threw off her shoes, as if they'd been killing her feet for the last two hours.

'He what?'

'Dot,' said Maud gently. 'Elliott has been in love with you for years. He only dates other people because you don't notice him. He's human. He hurts.'

Dot frowned, and then flushed as her eyes darted back and forth. Maud watched her trawl through her memory banks for possibilities that what she'd said was true. Maud waited for her to see it as clearly as everyone else did and, when that moment dawned, a smile lit up Dot's face and she hugged

Maud excitedly, almost knocking them both to the floor.

Nate found them sitting on the decked area outside on the veranda with their bare legs hanging over the side, resting on the cool grass. He walked over as Maud and Dot turned, and Dot jumped up and hugged the woman with him, who was sitting on a mobility scooter. She looked curiously familiar, wearing a headband with a parrot at a jaunty angle on her long grey hair. She was dressed in a patterned wide-strapped top, with a bright blue cardigan over the top and a ruffled skirt that exploded like a cloud around her legs as they approached.

Nate was laughing and carrying her drink, which seemed to be a humungous glass of Baileys, as the fragrance of chocolate and whiskey wafted around them. Nate offered Maud a hand and pulled her up too. 'Nan came in and declared the party officially open, even though everyone's been there for hours,' he told them, making them both giggle, eyes sparkling.

He smiled at Maud, keeping hold of her hand now he'd found her again. 'Have you met our nan, Elize Ridgemoor?'

Maud smiled politely at the woman, holding out her hand to say hello, while whispering to Nate that she could see where Dot got her original look from.

'I heard that, young lady,' chided Elize with a twinkle in her eye as she regarded her grandson and the flushed woman by his side. Maud saw that she'd noticed his hand cupping her waist and the way she leaned into him. Maud moved her body away from Nate's slightly, aghast that she might have offended Dot's nan, but Elize just cackled with laughter and drove further towards them, almost knocking them onto the grass. 'Go and get me an iced Martini,' she told Nate, 'while I interrogate this lovely lady of yours.'

Nate looked at the huge glass he'd just got for her at the bar and sighed as he put it down on an intricately-carved iron table beside an overflowing planter. 'Go easy on her, Nan.'

Chapter Forty-Eight

Nate's nan had been a hard taskmaster. She'd asked Maud to walk alongside her and had made her sit on a low wall with lavender bushes at its base. It smelt heavenly, but Maud had suddenly sobered up and been a nervous wreck about talking to the matriarch of the family. Maud knew from the long telephone conversations she'd had with Nate, sometimes into the early hours of the morning, that his nan was a very famous artist herself and Maud was in awe of her work, so she was a bit tongue-tied.

Elize had looked at her thoughtfully for a while, while Maud sat feeling terrified, then she had leaned across and taken her hand, making Maud feel instantly more at ease. Elize had asked her about her relationship with Nate and they had talked for an hour about Lena whilst Maud learnt more about the man she was falling in love with. Nate returned with the drink, but Elize had brushed him away and said they both now needed coffee as it was getting cold outside. Nate had grabbed some soft blankets from a hamper beside one of the double windows which led onto the terrace, draped them across the shoulders of his two favourite women and then sighed as he went in search of coffee.

It had been a magical night and her life had been a whirlwind since. She'd had invites to so many parties and events that she could barely keep up. Dot had hired them both an assistant and Maud was trying to manage the new pace of her life. It was madness. Dot insisted that it would calm down, but for now they would have to sleep less and do more.

Nate had crept into her bungalow a few times over the past couple of weeks and they were growing more comfortable together, but they still hadn't had time to talk about what was happening with them. He had been so busy with his new exhibition that she knew she'd been a bit distant with him lately. He'd had to meet the gallery deadline, so he had put her off on the last few nights she had suggested. She was terrified that he was bored with her now and didn't know how to tell her.

Both Dot and Maud had been at work in Dot's studio the day before Nate's next launch, with the door wide open as it was a stuffy day and they'd needed some air. A man in a smart suit had casually walked in and handed them a note to say a hotel suite had been booked for them on the following night for Nate Ridgemoor's private gallery viewing, as an extra birthday present from Nate to his gorgeous little sister and her best friend. Both girls had been surprised and excited when they'd read the handwritten invitations, which were exquisitely made with black card and gold writing with filigree edges.

Dot and Maud were relaxing the following night in a sumptuous hotel suite with textural grey furniture, crisp white linen and vases overflowing with fresh flowers. Modern art hung on the walls of the interconnecting lounge area and there were two bedrooms for them to get changed privately, even though they had squealed and danced around in delight when they'd seen the place and both jumped up and down on Dot's bed. After having showers and discovering the complimentary champagne, they sat with fluffy white towels wound around their wet hair and snuggled into the softest pale grey dressing gowns, which had been folded on the beds.

Maud sighed in pleasure and stretched out her newly-painted toes. 'Surely I shouldn't be using your present too? I haven't heard from Nate much lately.' Her voice faltered slightly, but she held back the wobble she knew she could so easily succumb to. This was Dot's day and she was here to support Nate, even if he hadn't phoned to ask her personally and had just sent the invite with Dot's. Maud felt he was distancing himself from her, so maybe he was another player, who had just wanted to get into her pants and then move on to find new prey. Dot had warned her often enough. Maybe she should have listened? Perhaps he was trying to let her down gently, but it was too late, she already felt devastated. She was smiling over-brightly for Dot, but inside she felt like she needed to be sick. The champagne was softening the edges, but a lone tear escaped from her eye. She brushed it away and leaned back onto the pillows of the bed, trying to make herself chill out and enjoy the moment. If this was one of the last times she was with Nate, then she might as well savour it. They'd have to bump into each other occasionally, as he was Dot's brother and Dot was the agent for both of them, plus their studios were next to each other. It had seemed like a great way to be near him at the time, but now Maud had visions of running upstairs to her studio and peeking round doors to avoid him. Just looking at him would break her heart. She'd have to move and Dot would have to understand. Dot knew they'd been seeing each other and hadn't commented on it, which was unlike her, so Maud wondered if she was scared Maud would end up causing him emotional problems like Lena had, when he was just starting to move on from his past.

Dot shrugged in answer to her question, as if she'd almost forgotten what Maud had asked. 'My mind is racing,' she apologised, 'of course you should be here. It's much nicer with a friend, and I'm really nervous about Nate's new show. It's different from his other ones and he's like a bear with a sore head. He keeps shouting at everyone in the gallery. They are all getting fed up and I had to tell him to back off yesterday.'

Maud's heart sank. If Nate was angry with everyone, then maybe he was worrying about breaking up with her and it was affecting his work. She held her breath for a moment, 'How is it different?'

Dot pulled a face. 'He hasn't let anyone but me see his latest work. The pictures are so beautiful, but not what his current clientele will expect. This work is really something else. They've been hidden in his studio for months and he won't even let Mum and Dad see them. He's banned everyone. You'll have to wait like everyone else to see what they're like. He's sworn me to secrecy.'

Maud felt sad that Nate hadn't trusted her with his work and finally understood how he must have felt when he'd found out about her own art. She'd evaded him for months and not trusted him. Now he was returning the favour and sending a very clear message to her. She felt tears spring from her eyes and she sniffed. Dot looked at her in confusion as someone knocked sharply on the hotel door and, without having time to ask if Maud was ok, she jumped up to answer, making sure her dressing gown was secured tightly at her waist and peeking outside.

A liveried doorman addressed her by name, so Dot stood aside and let him come into the room. In his arms were two big black and gold boxes, tied with blood-red ribbon. He walked over to the coffee table in the centre of the lounge between the bedrooms and placed them reverently down with a smile. Behind him were two women and a man who had been instructed to do the ladies' hair and make up.

Maud walked into the room from her position by the doorway to find out what was going on, as Dot was suddenly rushing around in excitement. Maud was led to her room where one of the women set about styling her hair while the man pulled a tall make-up trolley into the room and began putting colours next to Maud's face and scrutinising her skin. She tried to protest, but he told her it was part of Dot's present and handed her some more champagne, so she accepted her fate and tried her best to enjoy the experience, even though her heart was breaking in two.

An hour later, Maud realised that it was fun to be pampered this way and the three glasses of champagne had helped to ease her pain. Dot walked in with her hair pinned up with tiny diamonds dotted everywhere and silky blonde tendrils escaping down her neck. Maud gasped, as she looked like an angel. Her make-up complemented her blue eyes and made them stand out so that you couldn't take your eyes off her. 'You look so beautiful, Dot,' she got up from her chair and twirled Dot around so she could take a closer look. Dot was still in her dressing gown, but laughed happily as she turned around.

'You look great too, Maud,' she said, reaching out with a look of awe to touch the soft waves that Maud's hair had been set into. 'It isn't as dramatic as my look,' said Dot candidly, 'but with your smoky grey make-up and dark kohled eyes, you looked like a seductress. No man will be safe with you around looking like this!'

Maud blushed, but had to admit she did feel good. The girls hugged each other and then went into the lounge to say thank you and then goodbye to the stylists. Giddy with excitement now, they pounced on the boxes as soon as the door closed. They had been told they had to wait to open them until after hair and make-up, which had been torture for Dot, who was so impatient and hated surprises. Maud knew the boxes were for Dot, so she wasn't as bothered, but was happy for her friend and curious to see what Nate had bought.

Dot took the first box and handed the second to Maud. 'It's for you, silly!' laughed Dot. 'We have one each.' Before Maud could speak, Dot had thrown open the lid of her gift and delved into the layers of gold tissue inside. She reverently pulled out a shimmering silver dress. She dropped her dressing gown immediately and Maud tried not to blush. She was getting used to Dot's open personality, but she was still such a prude inside.

Dot's dress skimmed her slim hips and fell in waves to the floor. It fitted her waist and had a subtle pattern that you could only see when she moved. Maud could tell that she loved it. Inside the big box was a smaller one and Dot pulled out one of her own belts and some silver shoes. She quickly clasped the belt around her waist and ran to look in the floor-length mirror in her bedroom. Maud followed her and felt elated by her friend's happiness. Nate had gone to so much trouble for her that it made Maud sniffle again.

'No more tears,' said Dot, scolding her, whilst twirling this way and that to admire her reflection. 'Why were you crying earlier?' she asked over her shoulder.

'I was just happy for you,' lied Maud, which seemed to appease Dot.

'Have you seen Nate lately?' asked Dot, obviously

remembering Maud's earlier comments all of a sudden.

'Um... No. Why?'

Dot shook her head at her brother's stupidity. Another one bites the dust, she thought. Bloody Nate! Then she remembered the second dress box for Maud and rushed back into the lounge, grabbing Maud's hand and dragging her along. Standing Maud in front of the parcel, she pointed to it. 'Open it.'

Maud leaned down and opened the box. Inside the same gold tissue paper, but the smaller box was on the top. She opened that first and then frowned as she pulled out her own black high heels with the roses painted on them. Dot looked equally confused.

Maud set the shoes aside, hating the disappointment she felt, and reached inside the bigger box, expecting to see one of her own dresses neatly pressed and ready to wear. Nate must have stolen her shoes when she visited his parents that time. No wonder she thought she'd lost them. Maybe he'd taken a dress too, so that she could enjoy playing dress-up with Dot and her expensive clothes? Her lip wobbled and she wanted to sit down, but Dot was standing next to her and put a hand on her arm in sympathy, so she refused to be that girl. She didn't want Dot's pity. She just wanted to get out of here.

Dot nudged her to pick up the dress, neither of them saying anything. Maud reached in and pulled out the dress, without opening her eyes. Dot nudged her again, this time more urgently, and she sighed, before looking down and gasping in surprise. She was holding a fitted dress with a wide neckline and delicate cap sleeves. It was completely different to Dot's dress, as every inch of the fabric had been hand-embroidered with little climbing roses that wound their way around the dress and reached up from the hem.

'It's beautiful,' she whispered reverently as Dot rushed to help her try it on. Modesty forgotten, she dropped her dressing gown and stepped into the dress, which fitted as if it had been made for her – which it had!

The dress stopped at her knees and she bent to put on her shoes. The look was incredibly sexy and daring as the front of

239

the dress was boned, meaning she didn't need a bra, and the back was pretty non-existent. She felt wild and euphoric, but didn't really understand what was happening.

Dot was staring at her strangely and hadn't said a word while Maud was getting dressed. She seemed to be quietly digesting what she was seeing. The dress had been designed to match Maud's hand-painted shoes and to reflect her incredible art. Suddenly Dot leaned forward and hugged her fiercely, almost cracking a rib, until Maud laughed and gently pushed her away. They looked at the time and decided to have another quick glass of champagne to celebrate looking so fabulous, giggling all the way to the lounge.

Chapter Forty-Nine

Nate was driving Elliot mad with his constant pacing of the gallery. It would soon be full to bursting with people, but he didn't understand why Nate was so nervous that he'd almost changed his mind and cancelled the whole damn thing. He was always grouchy before a show and this one had been set up in record time, but he was behaving like a caged tiger and Elliott wasn't feeling much calmer. He'd confided to Nate that he'd finally told Dot how much he cared for her and she hadn't run a mile. In fact, she'd kissed him. That was too much information for an older brother to hear, though, and Nate had sent him a pained look before beginning to pace again.

Elliott realised that Dot had been a bit drunk at her party, but they'd almost ended up in bed. He'd tried to resist her as she was tipsy, but she'd been so alluring and he'd waited for so long for her to want him too. He'd come to his senses at the last minute and tucked her in alone, but she hadn't spoken to him since. By this point Nate had his fingers in his ears and had been singing loudly, 'la la la la.' He didn't want to hear it. He'd explained that he knew El had listened to him moaning about women enough over the years, and had given him advice on how to confide in Maud about his past, but Dot, well – she was his sister.

Now Elliott was confused. He didn't know if Dot wished the kisses hadn't happened or if she thought he'd led her on and let her down. It was such a mess. Nate's own love life wasn't much better. He'd purposely kept Maud at arm's length, as he'd been so busy with this exhibition. It had probably stirred up many emotions he hadn't wanted to burden her with, while he dealt with them. Elliott wondered if she was as confused as he was by Nate's behaviour. She must be worried that she hadn't seen Nate as much while he worked night and day to finish this exhibition. Elliot knew that he also needed time to put his past behind him and make room to start afresh. Elliott decided it was time he disappeared and left his friend alone in his misery to wait it out for another hour until everyone arrived and he could move on with his life. Hopefully Nate would be more relaxed after the show was over, but for once, Elliott put his own life first and let Nate work his emotions out alone.

Elliott knocked at the hotel suite door and waited for someone to answer it. He could hear Maud call to Dot that she could see Elliott through the spy hole in the door, but before she could open the door he started banging on it again and demanding to see Dot. Maud quickly let him in and jumped back from the shuddering door, before gesturing towards Dot, who was looking stunned. He strode over to her and took her into his arms, surprising everyone including himself, and making Maud scurry to her room to give them some privacy.

Dot announced that he must be slightly drunk, but he then told her that she was now his girlfriend whether she liked it or not. To his amazement, Dot seemed surprised and then thrilled, as she told him she loved this more forward side of him and was relieved he'd turned up. She leaned her head into his neck and explained quietly that she'd been mortified about seeing him, after the last time they'd met, when he'd spurned her amorous advances at her birthday party. It seemed she had been secretly fretting about it ever since.

Dot pulled him over to sit on the side of the soft couch with her and sighed heavily. His stomach rose up and he dreaded what she was going to say next, but it was just that she hadn't told Maud about their almost-night together, as she seemed to be having enough trouble with Nate. Elliott reached out and kissed Dot again, savouring the feeling of having her in his arms, as if she had always been meant to be there. He wasn't about to let her go, whatever problems her friend was having with his best mate.

'I feel awful about how often I've been mean to Nate and

all of the times when he'd tried to help us get together, even though we're his best friend and sister.' She looped her arms around Elliott's waist and pressed her cheek to his chest, listening to his rapidly-beating heart as he kissed her shoulder. 'I shouldn't have kept Nate and Maud apart early in their relationship by telling Maud he was a womaniser.' Elliott's eyebrows shot up at this. Nate liked women, but after being so badly burnt emotionally and physically, he didn't mess them around. He was so honest it was brutal sometimes. It wasn't Nate's fault that women regularly threw themselves at him.

Dot was still thinking out loud. 'Now maybe Maud is holding back in case he treats her the way Tom did?' She reluctantly let go of Elliott and he stood back and whistled at her gown. He hadn't noticed it earlier, but now he had, he wanted to kiss every inch of her beautiful body.

'Maud's just told me she's not sure she should go to the exhibition,' she said quietly, so Maud wouldn't hear, even though the bedroom door was shut. 'She's got to go.'

Elliott was confused now. 'You shouldn't make her go if she doesn't want to. Nate is really grumpy and pacing around. If they've argued, then it's better she stays away until later, as he's just said that this is his most important exhibition to date. He's worked like a demon for the last couple of weeks and Maud can't ruin it for him.'

Dot looked at him as if he was mad, and called Maud into the room. As the door opened and Elliott saw what she was wearing he went quiet and just stared, open-mouthed, until Dot gently pushed his jaw shut and gave him a knowing smile.

Maud's brow was creased and she started playing with her hair. She looked confused and asked them what the hell was going on. 'What is it with everyone today and this dress?' She absently ran her hands down the fabric and stood looking very uncomfortable all of a sudden.

'You are going to the exhibition,' said Elliott in a voice that had a finality in it, 'even if it is the last thing I ever do and I have to carry you there myself. You're going.'

Chapter Fifty

Dot, Maud and Elliott stood just by the main door and peeked inside. The gallery was buzzing and they could already hear people commenting that the paintings were the pinnacle of Nate's career, even though they couldn't see them from where they were hiding. Nate looked like he was getting agitated and, although he was thanking people for their kind words and nodding along with their conversation, he didn't appear to be concentrating and the colour of his face suggested that his blood was boiling with anger. He grabbed his phone and rapped a text out before sliding his finger across the screen and sending it on its way.

Elliott's phone bleeped in his pocket and he drew it out for them all to see. Where are you? the message demanded from the screen. Maud guessed that Nate would have spent the last hour pacing in his flat above the gallery before making himself brush the nerves off and go downstairs. She started shaking at the thought of seeing him, but knew she would have to soon, as Nate obviously needed Elliott's support tonight more than ever, for some reason. He was wearing a black pressed shirt and trousers and, although he outwardly appeared calm, Maud could feel the tension emanating from him from her place by the door. His hair was slicked back from running his hands through it in agitation so many times, and he really needed to calm down or have a drink.

As if sensing her thoughts, he grabbed a glass of champagne from a passing waiter and stopped to speak to his parents, who were in a loud conversation about one of his artworks with a customer. They were in deep discussion about the meaning of the paintings and turned with glowing smiles, to ask Nate if they had been right.

Elliott had evidently seen and heard enough, as he grabbed Dot's hand and pushed Maud into the gallery ahead of them and a weird hush spread around like wildfire as soon as people began to notice their arrival. 'What a way to make an entrance!' joked Dot in Maud's ear, as flash bulbs went off and she almost tripped over in surprise. Elliott steadied her, but Maud didn't understand what was happening. Why would anyone take pictures of her at Nate's show? They all knew they had been seeing each other. She understood the press were interested in her latest work, but she was far from properly famous yet, maybe a little notorious in her hometown, that was all.

She slowly turned and stood frozen still for a moment. She couldn't breathe and she felt like her heart might burst from her chest. Her head whirled around, taking in the scene before her in confusion. She drank in the sight of the art. Every piece was a masterpiece! They were so sensual to look at that you almost felt you could see inside the artist's beating heart. Her own pulse began to race and she looked around in a blind panic for Dot, who had blended into the background and left her standing alone, like an idiot. She peered down at her dress with a frown and back up into Nate's stormy eyes. He looked unsure for the first time in his life, but he was standing right before her.

No one else had uttered a word and suddenly conversation began buzzing around again, but all she could do was stay rooted to the spot and stare at the art. There were landscapes of rambling shores and broken buildings, some had fire and some had water, but all had layers of under-painting. Each scene was dark and reached through the surface layers. There were red roses climbing everywhere you looked, they curled under the main images and swirled around every surface until you could look at nothing else. They were extraordinarily beautiful and full of passion, as if forces of nature were taking over and commanding the land, the way she had taken over his life and now commanded him, he seemed to be telling her.

There was a sudden hush again and people turned as Nate stood before her and they waited to see what she would say.

He held out his hand to her and she was astounded to see his black shirt was rolled up at the sleeves and his arms, scars and all, were there for anyone to see. He wasn't hiding any more. She felt hot tears spring to her eyes and he leaned forward to gently brush them away with his thumb. He handed her a little black box, which she took and opened with the utmost care. She gasped as she picked up a sparkling diamond ring with a handwritten brown tag attached to it, in his distinctive slanted handwriting. On it, she read: 'if you love me, I'm yours.'

Everyone present practically climbed over each other and craned their necks to see what the woman who had enslaved such a famous artist would do. She looked into his eyes as tears fell from hers and she took his hand, drew him to her and everyone cheered as she slipped the ring onto her finger, leaned in and kissed him.

'I love you,' was all she needed to say as the room erupted into applause. Maud clasped the little brown tag to her heart, looked into the eyes of the man she loved, and whispered into his ear as she fell into his arms, 'I'm yours.'

THE END

Fantastic Books
Great Authors

CROOKED
CAT

Meet our authors and discover
our exciting range:

- Gripping Thrillers
- Cosy Mysteries
- Romantic Chick-Lit
- Fascinating Historicals
- Exciting Fantasy
- Young Adult and Children's
  Adventures
- Non-Fiction

Visit us at:
www.crookedcatbooks.com

Join us on facebook:
www.facebook.com/crookedcatbooks

Printed in Poland
by Amazon Fulfillment
Poland Sp. z o.o., Wrocław